Miss Billings Treads the Boards

Miss Billings Treads the Boards

Carla Kelly

Seattle, WA

Camel Press
PO Box 70515
Seattle, WA 98127

For more information go to: www.camelpress.com
www.carlakellyauthor.com

Cover design by Sabrina Sun

Miss Billings Treads the Boards

First published by Signet, an imprint of Dutton Signet,
a division of Penguin Books USA Inc. in 1993

ISBN: 978-1-60381-915-2 (Trade Paper)
ISBN: 978-1-60381-916-9 (eBook)

Library of Congress Control Number: 2013949700
Printed in the United States of America

To Gail McDaniel,

My dear friend

Books by Carla Kelly

Fiction

Daughter of Fortune
Summer Campaign
Miss Chartley's Guided Tour
Marian's Christmas Wish
Mrs. McVinnie's London Season
Libby's London Merchant
Miss Grimsley's Oxford Career
Miss Billings Treads the Boards
Mrs. Drew Plays Her Hand
Reforming Lord Ragsdale
Miss Whittier Makes a List
The Lady's Companion
With This Ring
Miss Milton Speaks Her Mind
One Good Turn
The Wedding Journey
Here's to the Ladies: Stories of the Frontier Army
Beau Crusoe
Marrying the Captain
The Surgeon's Lady
Marrying the Royal Marine
The Admiral's Penniless Bride
Borrowed Light
Enduring Light
Coming Home for Christmas: The Holiday Stories
Marriage of Mercy
My Loving Vigil Keeping
Her Hesitant Heart
Safe Passage
The Double Cross (Book 1, The Spanish Brand Series)-NEW

Non-Fiction

On the Upper Missouri: The Journal of Rudolph Friedrich Kurz (editor)
Louis Dace Letellier: Adventures on the Upper Missouri (editor)
Fort Buford: Sentinel at the Confluence
Stop Me If You've Read This One

HARDCASTLE: I tell you, she don't dislike you; and as I am sure you like her—
MARLOW: Dear sir—I protest, sir—
HARDCASTLE: I see no reason why you should not be joined as fast as the parson can tie you.

She Stoops to Conquer (Act 5)
Oliver Goldsmith

1

THE PROSPECT OF A holiday in Yorkshire, far removed from the probability of social exertion in London, should have thrilled Henry Tewksbury-Hampton, Fifth Marquess of Grayson, right down to the marrow, but it did not. He had received Pinky D'Urst's letter with a sigh. Ordinarily the thought of a month at D'Urst Hall and its trout streams would have delighted him, but another suspicion reined him in. Pinky had a sister, a sister somewhat long in the tooth, who was probably not relishing the idea of impending old maidenhead.

"Oh, I know how it is, Pinky," Henry had thought to himself as he sat in his dressing room, waiting for his valet to finish the patient arrangement of each strand of thinning hair. "You will casually enumerate all of your sister's sterling qualities, and before I know it, I will be trapped in yet another engagement not to my liking. Well, I'll go to Yorkshire, but not for your sister!"

"Patience, my lord," murmured the valet. "We must do it, mustn't we? We don't wish to appear lacking in the essentials, do we?"

Dash and bother, now he was thinking out loud, and within

earshot of a silly prig of a valet with enough hair on his head for both of them. And was that a smirk from Wilding?

Henry turned his head carefully, so as not to bother the careful arrangement of his neckcloth. "Don't toy with me, Wilding," he said. He tried to use a firm tone, a dangerous tone, but even to his own ears, it sounded querulous. As Wilding stared at him with that irritating, affected way of his, Henry felt his spirits sink within him. And now I am talking out loud and unable to tyrannize even a valet, he thought. If I were to tell some stranger that I had once captured an entire brigade of Frogs at Cuenca, he would probably smirk and simper like my valet.

Henry shook his head, and the valet sighed. "My lord, now I must begin again," he chided.

Henry grabbed the comb from his valet's hand and dragged it through what remained of his hair, noting how thin it felt through the comb. He eyed the valet in the mirror. "Wilding, I am going bald. Let us not split hairs about this anymore." He stared at himself ruthlessly in the mirror, less than pleased at the man who glowered back. He turned sideways. "And I certainly seem to have picked up an extra stone or two since my return from Spain, even discounting what I should have regained after cooling my heels in that damned prison."

Wilding giggled and then sobered immediately when his master narrowed his eyes. He took the comb back. "My lord, you have excellent bones."

"Wilding, go away, will you?" It was said quietly, but the valet seemed to understand when enough was enough. With the dignity peculiar to those who serve, the valet set down the comb and swept from the room. He paused in the doorway for a final shot across the bow. "When we feel more like it, we need only tug on the bellpull, my lord," he suggested.

"Oh, cut line, Wilding," said Lord Grayson wearily. He threw himself into a chair by the window and propped his stockinged feet on the ledge, undoing the top button of his breeches and sighing with relief. "Bone structure, my left eyeball," he said. "I am over my weight, and beginning to bald, and no one loves me except my tailor." He reconsidered. Even his tailor was in some doubt, particularly after yesterday's argument about roomier coats. "But my lord, a creaseless fit is essential," the man had protested, shaking his head at my lord's objections until the chalk holder behind his ear flew out. "But all I want is to be comfortable," was Lord Grayson's heartfelt plea. "Doesn't anyone understand comfort anymore?"

Henry chuckled, despite his misery. Comfort was standing barefoot and ankle-deep in summer mud on an Andalucian road, with one's breeches ventilated with holes and shirttails hanging out. It was commanding Spanish Irregulars who cared not how elegant his coat, but only how deep the fight in him.

But those days were long over. He sighed again. The fight in him had gone out. It was true; no one needed him.

It was a lowering thought, and one that didn't bear thinking on, but in the bright light of that June morning he kept thinking. His estates were well-managed, his houses in order. And only last night, as he sat at table with his friends, he actually found himself voicing some conservative thoughts on government that he had heard once from the mouth of his long-dead, still-lamented father, something he swore he would never do.

The occasion had given him a real start. This morning he could only admit that he was becoming stodgy. It was a matter of time before gout took over and he discarded all his Whiggish principles. He winced at the thought and turned around in his chair to gaze again upon his well-stuffed image in the full-length mirror. "Henry Tewksbury-Hampton," he murmured, unable to keep the edge from his voice, "if you were to see yourself on a road in Spain, pistol in hand, four stone lighter, and with that spark in your eye, you would not recognize yourself."

He sat back again and closed his eyes. And you have become that which, as a young man, you despised: a flutter-by with no ideals, scarce ambition, and less enthusiasm; a man lazy beyond excuse.

Wilding came back into the room, his arms full of folded laundry. He stopped and eyed his master as he would a pouting child. "What, are we still just sitting there?" he asked in tones reminiscent of the nursery. "We should have had our shoes on ages ago."

Henry stood up his full height in his stockinged feet, which was a considerable reach. "If we do not quit addressing us as a schoolroom boy, we will find ourselves at the Registry Office, looking for a new pigeon to pluck," he said.

Wilding closed his mouth in tight-lipped disapproval and remained silent as he helped his employer into a waistcoat and coat for a visit to his solicitor. Ordinarily Henry would have repented and engaged him in some pleasantry sufficient to smooth over any ruffled feelings, but today he felt no such inclination. He kept his own counsel as Wilding helped him on with his shoes, straightened his neckcloth yet again, and pronounced him fit to inflict upon London.

On his progress to the front door Henry glanced at the early-morning cache of letters already resting on a table. None appeared to be of any serious interest. The Season had burned itself right down to the socket, and invitations now were few, indeed. Besides, yet another season spent in card rooms at whist tables and not circulating around ballrooms at waltz tempo had made him less than a favorite of anxious mothers. He was too old for the young girls in their white muslins, and not old enough for their sisters past first prayers.

He gladly shut the door on his valet's twitterings and fidgets. No, thank you, he would walk to his solicitors. It was a healthy walk across St. James's Park, but the day was beautiful and he was not otherwise engaged. It would be a pleasure to dispense with any conversation and proceed at a leisurely pace.

His luck held out for a mere three blocks when he was accosted by his nephew and heir, Algernon Mannerly, Viscount

Minden. "Uncle!" cried the young man with all the delight of a relative who had not seen him in years, even though it was only last night at White's. "Uncle! What a distinct pleasure!"

It was far from a pleasure for either party, Henry observed wryly as his nephew, all watch fobs, too tight pantaloons, and extravagant waistcoat minced forward. But there was no escaping Algernon down some heaven-sent alley. The row of houses he was passing were all connected and admitted no such relief. He would have to face his nephew. Ordinarily he bore the ordeal with a bland stoicism that would have gained the approval of a whole regiment of Spartans. But somehow today was different.

"How well you look this morning!" chirped his nephew, preparing to mount up to the stratosphere with a whole list of compliments.

Henry held up his hand. "Stop, Algie," he said, his voice calm, but full of command. The effect pleased him. "Stop," he said again, relishing the look of bewilderment on his nephew's somewhat vacuous countenance. "Tell me, Algie. Do you like me?"

Algie thought a moment, and Henry felt the urge to suppress a laugh. "This is a not a hard question," he added gently when Algie appeared unable to express himself.

"Of course I like you, Uncle," Algie managed at last. He struck his man-about-town pose, but his assurance was betrayed by the way he began to whirl his monocle on its long riband around his gloved finger.

Henry watched the rotation a moment, then put out his hand to stop it. "Why?" he asked.

Algie frowned. His brow creased as he hastily pocketed his monocle. The effort of thinking caused his feet to turn inward, and he stood there, pigeon-toed, skinny-legged, and bereft of idea. Henry coughed delicately, wondering at the mean streak in himself that he was peeling back at Algernon's sorry expense, but doing nothing to alleviate the younger man's discomfort.

"Why?" he asked again. "Come, come, Algie."

The mild reproof brought a wild look into Algernon Mannerly's eyes. "Be … because you always pay my quarterly allowance on time, Uncle!" he admitted in a rush and then let out a sigh of relief at his provision of an answer, any answer. He resumed his sophisticated pose. "Which reminds me, Uncle, could you advance a little toward the next quarter? My tailor is devilish expensive and demanding something against that time …" He paused then, only just in time, but Henry took up the sentence.

"... 'gainst that time when your well-loved uncle sticks his spoon in the wall and you inherit all?" he finished.

Algernon tittered, and the monocle began to rotate again. "Uncle, how you carry on!"

Henry did not smile. "I advanced you quite generously last quarter, if memory serves me right. Why should I do it again?"

"One of us must cut a dash in London, Uncle dear," was Algernon's lame riposte. "We Graysons owe it to our set."

Henry considered this. He walked around his nephew, observing the effects of fashion as the monocle twirled faster. "Buckram wadding in your shoulders, eh, Nevvy?" he asked. "And have you really padded your calves?" He stopped in front of his nephew. "I am not so sure that you have succeeded in the attempt, Algie."

"Well, neither have you," Algernon burst out, goaded into response.

"Ah, true, but I make no such pretense. And I am so rich that women do not care particularly how I look." He stopped the whirling monocle again. "And I think I will not advance you a single groat. In fact, Algernon, since you do not like me so well, I think I will direct my solicitor to cut your allowance. Leech off your mother, my dear sister, for a while. Good day, Algie." He tipped his hat to his nephew, who stood, toes inward again, his mouth open.

"But, Uncle!" he protested.

"I have no intention of cocking up my toes anytime soon, just to oblige you, Nephew. Perhaps when you can practice some economy, I might reconsider any further reduction beyond the one I am making this morning. Good day," he said again, his voice serene, as he continued his walk.

"And that is my intention," he said a half hour later as he sat in his solicitor's office, a glass of Madeira at his elbow. "Abner, don't look so dismayed! Algernon is a worthless young chub."

Abner Sheffield, of Sheffield and Johnston, settled back in his chair, regarding his client. "I wouldn't advise it, my lord," he said at last. "Worthless chub that he is, he will only plague his mother, and she will plague you with tears and endless recriminations and calls to duty."

Henry rested his chin on his hand. "I fear you are right. But by God, it stung me when he said that the only thing he liked about me was my prompt payment of quarterly allowances! Am I such an ogre?"

Abner only smiled. "If you will permit an observation from a family retainer of long standing …"

Henry waved his hand irritably. "Go ahead, Abner, go ahead. It can't be anything worse than what I have been chastising myself with this morning."

The solicitor picked his words carefully. "You used to be quite a charming gentleman and—"

"And I am not anymore?" Henry interrupted, in spite of his guarantee.

The solicitor smiled again. "No, you're not. You are frivolous, and moody, and turning into a lazy fellow, something I thought I would never see." He paused and watched the effect of his words on Lord Grayson's reddening countenance. "But, unlike your nephew, I really do like you. I always have. The young man who went away to war—what is it, nearly ten years ago now?—is still there somewhere. And I have hopes to see him again sometime. You've changed, Lord Grayson, but you can change again." He leaned forward. "And when you do, you won't feel the necessity to ask your nephew such a question."

Henry's hot words retreated back into his mind. He picked up the Madeira glass and looked into its amber loveliness. "My sister says I should hurry up and marry. She says that will solve my problems."

The solicitor shook his head and proffered a refill, which Lord Grayson refused. "I shouldn't think that marriage ever solved anyone's problems." He laughed. "It usually makes them worse." He leaned back again. "Since we are not pulling any hairs this morning, I have something I have wondered about for eight years, my friend."

"Well, speak away, Abner," said Henry gruffly. "I don't appear to have any secrets from you, who knows my character so well!"

"Now, don't be testy. I do this only out of my regard for you, which seems to have weathered well. My question is this, Lord Grayson. When you and some of your men were languishing in that Spanish prison …"

Henry started to smile. His smile grew into a large grin that showed all his teeth. He leaned back in his chair, too, and laughed. "Go ahead, Abner," he insisted. "I can't wait to hear how you're going to phrase this. Don't keep me in suspense." Abner joined in the laughter. "I think you answered my question already, but let me ask it anyway. Did you—could you—have escaped when your men did, one at a time?"

"Of course, my dear solicitor, who loves me well. Say on, sir."

"You waited until your fiancée gave up, broke off that engagement, and married someone else, before you escaped, didn't you?"

Henry leaned forward and planted his elbows on the solicitor's desk. "Does anyone else suspect?"

The solicitor laughed again and shook his head. "It was only a suspicion of mine. Maybe it was something in one of those letters of yours that we received occasionally. You were always so anxious to know her state of mind. And when I finally wrote you what I thought was the sad news, you escaped, swam out to a blockader, and made your way to England."

"Well, you have me now, Abner. Is it to be blackmail?" he teased.

"I was merely curious, my lord. You know, I do believe that you could find, somewhere in the wide world, some woman who actually loves you."

"And not my money?"

Abner nodded. "My daughters are fond of you, but they are only twelve and thirteen. Take a look around this summer, my lord. Marry someone, breed, and I guarantee that your nephew will only become a bad memory. You may discover there are many people who love you."

Henry shook his head. "That, sir, is highly unlikely, but I do like your receipt. I have been summoned to Pinky D'Urst's in Yorkshire."

"A great deal can happen between here and Yorkshire, my lord," said the solicitor. "And I suppose you wish me to procure some money for the journey?"

"That was my intention, Abner, in accosting you here," Henry agreed. "You have further entertained me, and, I confess, convinced me not to change my worthless nevvy's allowance. But do me a favor, sir, of scaring him when he comes bolting in here." Henry took out his watch. "Oh, probably ten or fifteen minutes after I have left. It may be that I mean to improve my faulty character, but he is fair game."

"Done, sir," the solicitor concurred. He wrote in his ledger a moment and with the bellpull summoned a clerk. He held out his ledger to the shirt-sleeved clerk. "Lord Grayson would like this sum. Prepare it for him, please."

The man left. Abner Sheffield rose and held out his hand. Henry grasped it, smiling at the older man. "I shall see how much of your advice I can stomach this summer, old friend."

"Admirable, my lord," said the solicitor, coming around the desk to walk his client to the door. He stopped, his hand on the marquess's shoulder. "Do you know, my lord, you could do me a favor."

Henry raised his eyebrows. "What, sir? You would ask a favor of a lazy fub who runs from matrimonial entanglements and is not beloved of his nephew?"

The solicitor went back to his desk and rummaged in one of the drawers. "A small matter. It will require a little exertion on your part, but only a very little."

"We have already agreed that I need a little exertion, Abner. What is your errand and how can I help you? Only name it, and I will tell you if it is out of the question, or merely dashed inconvenient."

Abner smiled. "It is only a small matter. I have another client name of Katherine Billings. Last week I was settling her father's estate for her." He sighed and sat down again. "He was a sad case."

Henry perched himself on the edge of the desk. "How so?"

"Oh, Reverend Mr. Billings was a raging eccentric who had a small fortune that he spent on sketches of the Italian masters, too many of them forged, I might add. He and his daughter spent years in Italy, even though he had a vicarage and a living in Dorset. Seems he got in over his head and spent beyond his means. When he died last month, it was necessary to sell everything he owned to squeak through with his creditors."

"It seems a strange occupation for a vicar," said Henry, interested in spite himself.

"I always considered him one of England's finest eccentrics. From a good family, though, the Billings of Motlow. Loved the plays of Shakespeare, Sheridan, and Congreve, too, if I am not mistaken." The solicitor laughed. "His daughter tells me that his sermons—when he got around to them—were interlaced with the most colorful literary allusions. Quite unlike the usual liturgical fare, wouldn't you agree?"

Henry nodded. "He had the one daughter?"

"Yes, poor little thing. He dragged her here and there, and she went without a murmur."

"Spineless?" Henry asked. The conversation was beginning to bore him.

"Lord, no," said Abner emphatically. "She was merely a woman of no means. Tell me if such a one has an opportunity for free expression."

"I neither know nor care, sir," Henry replied, examining his fingernails.

"Well, the fact of the matter is this. He had one remaining sketch. The daughter had hoped to turn it into a bit of cash for herself, quite naturally, but my initial report said that it was a forgery and therefore worthless."

"And now you find out this is not the case?"

"Quite so. I have other clients seeking to verify the value of paintings and the like, and I gave her information intended for someone else. The sketch is worth a tidy sum—one that might allow her, if she manages carefully, to set up housekeeping and avoid her present duty."

"Which is?" Henry prompted.

"She is taking up a post as governess." The solicitor made a face. "So you see, with these tidings, you will be rather a knight in glittering array to this damsel in distress."

Abner took out a sheet of paper and wrote on it. "The little sketch is by some bloke named Giotto, and it is of a couple of chunky angels flying about. I only hope she didn't discard it at my bad news. Deuced if I know how such fubsy angels could remain airborne, but you know those Italians."

Henry allowed as he did. "And the damsel's name and direction?"

The solicitor wrote. "Katherine Billings, and she is going to Leavitt Hall. Leavitt is not far from the Great North Road, near to Wakefield." He handed the paper to Henry.

Henry looked at the name and folded the paper into his pocket. "Well, Abner, a description?"

"I told you they were chunky angels."

"No, no. I mean Miss Billings. I don't want to blurt out this information to just *any* Katherine Billings I chance to meet at Leavitt Hall," he joked.

"Oh, a typical young female." Abner thought a moment more. "No, that's not all. In fact, far from it." He chuckled. "You won't have any trouble making sure you have the right female. She has a head of black hair gorgeous enough to make a man get ideas. She's twenty-six, I believe. At any rate, past the age when I would ever dare ask. She also has a most magnificent figure, a trim ankle, and beyond that, I didn't notice."

Henry grinned. "Thank goodness for that! I'll do your good deed, Abner, as long as it promises to be only a little exertion. I'll improve my faulty character gradually, thank you."

"I doubt she'll relieve your boredom, Lord Grayson, but Kate Billings is certainly worth a glance as you breeze in and out of her life." The solicitor walked his client to the door, where the clerk waited with his money for the journey. "It won't be but an hour or two out of your way."

"You promise I won't feel the strain?" Henry teased and shook hands with his solicitor. "Then I accept your commission. How hard can it be to help a damsel in distress?"

2

IT WAS NOTHING A lady should think, but as the miles lumbered by, Miss Katherine Billings began to realize how much she was enjoying travel on the mail coach.

She had begun her journey in London, prepared to endure the misfortune of boorish company all the way to Wakefield in Yorkshire. As she took her seat, she vowed she would keep her own counsel, read the improving books she had brought along, and otherwise let the inmates of the mail coach know that she was not One of Them. But then Goodwife Winkle and her little daughter Jane climbed aboard at Shelly, and Jane would have dark curls that cried out to be combed around one's finger, patted, and rearranged. Of course the only place to do all that was from Katherine's lap. As the coach became more and more crowded, this did somewhat relieve Mrs. Winkle, who, from the look of her lap, would very soon present Farmer Winkle with another olive branch.

That should have been sufficient condescension among the lower classes, if only that pensioned third mate of the old *Agamemnon* hadn't stumped on board, wooden leg and all, at Cross Corners. He insisted on regaling them with his adventures at distant Trafalgar, bringing it down through the years until it seemed only yesterday since the French lords and Spanish dons had come out to play in what became England's bathtub. The old sailor's language was a bit salty, and at times Katherine had to clap her hands over Jane's ears, but he kept them wide-eyed and open-mouthed all the way to Baskin. Even Mrs. Winkle, who had every right to complain, could only regret his leaving, even though it did allow them a breathing space on the mail coach.

" 'Tis an education you can get on the coach," she commented to Katherine as the coachman cracked his whip and the journey continued.

Katherine smiled and tucked Jane more tightly into her lap as they rocketed along at ten miles an hour, maybe more. "I had not expected it, but you are right, Mrs. Winkle."

A schoolboy, returning home, had joined them at Baskin, along with a tonsured priest, and a young person, who, from the looks of her muscled arms and faint odor of sour cream, was probably a milkmaid.

Mrs. Winkle looked at Katherine expectantly. In another minute she understood. Dear lady, you want to know more about me, don't you? she thought, as Jane began to slumber, but you are too polite to ask a question of Quality. She looked out the window then, a frown between her eyes. But I am no more Quality. She took a deep breath and turned again toward the farmer's wife, who regarded her.

"I do not suppose the education I am getting today will be of use to my new employer, Mrs. Winkle," she said, and in the saying realized that she had stepped over a wide gulf from which there was no retreating. "I am to be a governess at Leavitt Hall. Do you know it?"

"Who doesn't, Miss … Miss …"

"Billings. Katherine Billings," Katherine responded, matching Mrs. Winkle's wary look with one of her own. "What can you tell me of the place?"

She hesitated a moment, then her words came out in a rush. "They say Squire Leavitt is a noted lecher, Miss Billings."

The milkmaid nodded vigorously. "I work for the old loose fish, ma'am," she offered. "And don't he come around to try out the new milkmaids?"

"My dear!" admonished Mrs. Winkle.

"Heavens!" said Katherine, her voice faint. "I have met only his wife. She appears to be somewhat sickly." She remembered well the interview in the office of Sheffield and Johnston, her late father's solicitors. Mrs. Leavitt had seemed on the verge of collapse throughout her interrogation of Katherine's background and skills.

Her eyes on the schoolboy, who appeared to be sleeping, and the priest, who was deep in his Breviary, the milkmaid leaned toward the other two women. "And don't I always say that the woman who stays healthy has a husband who knows where his own sheets begin and end?" She cast a significant look at Mrs. Winkle's bulging middle as Katherine blushed.

"True enough," Mrs. Winkle murmured. "My Edward knows his own pasture." She looked at Katherine with real concern. "Do you think this is such a good idea, Miss Billings? I mean if you was forty-five and with snaggle teeth, it might be a different go-round. I don't know, miss. I think I would worry for you."

"Oh, I am sure that I can take care of myself."

Take care of myself. As the milkmaid and farmer's wife continued speaking to each other in low tones, Katherine sighed and looked out the window again, her enjoyment in the day wiped away. She was twenty-six and on her own, to make her way in a world that seemed to grow more unkind after Papa's death.

He had died suddenly, hit by a drunken carter as he crossed a rain-swept London street. When a neighbor summoned her into the street from their rented rooms, she found Papa gasping his life away and still clutching the oilskin packet purchased from the art dealer, which was to have been her twenty-sixth birthday present.

"It's Giotto, my dear. Happy birthday," had been his final words to her as she cradled his ruined head in her lap.

Even now tears came to her eyes and escaped to her cheek. She tried to brush at it, but Jane was a heavy weight in her arms, and she could not. Another tear followed, and another, and then Mrs. Winkle was wiping her eyes for her. "Dearie, maybe it won't be as grim as we fear," she crooned as she would to her own child. "But I say it is too bad that women are at the mercy of men. Too bad."

Katherine shook her head. "I wasn't thinking of Mr. Leavitt, not really. I …" She paused, wondering what she was doing, confessing her own grief to these women so obviously inferior. But her own heart was breaking, and she took another step away from her upbringing. "Papa died two weeks ago, and I am alone in the world."

The words came out of her in a rush, and it was done. She accepted a handkerchief that smelled strongly of incense from the priest, who had put away his Breviary and was also listening intently now. "Tell us," he said, and his eyes were kind.

With only the slightest hesitation, she told them of Papa, who was much better at spending money on art than he was at being a vicar. "He lived for old paintings," she said as the tears flowed freely. She dabbed at her eyes and blew her nose. "We even spent three years in Rome." She gave her listeners a watery smile. "He was supposed to have been studying homiletics and the writings of Paul, but he spent most of his time in art galleries."

The coach rolled on through the greening countryside, awakening to summer, as she told of Papa's good birth and comfortable circumstances, squandered on art he could not afford. She did not tell them of his passion for Shakespeare and the Restoration dramatists, figuring that too much of that would convince them that Papa was a flibbertigibbet. And what if he was, she thought to herself as she blew her nose again, and the priest provided another handkerchief. What if he was? She had not regretted a minute of their eccentric life together, not really, except that it ended so ignominiously on a rainy London back street.

"But all those paintings?" asked the ever practical Mrs. Winkle. "Surely they were worth something? Do you have to be a governess?"

"Most of them were forgeries," Katherine said. "Papa loved art, but I fear he was too easily gulled. My solicitor was able to sell the occasional sketch or charcoal drawing, but the rest of it …" Her voice trailed off. Papa's accumulated fakes and forgeries had made a most excellent bonfire. By selling his library and the few good paintings, Abner Sheffield, Papa's solicitor, had seen to it that she was debt-free, but broke in the bargain.

She almost told them of the Giotto Papa had clutched even in death. It was a penciled cartoon of two angels, probably intended as a pattern for a fresco. Rolled up and lovingly wrapped in oilskin, it rested in the bottom of her trunk. Sheffield had assured her of its worthlessness and advised her to consign it to the fire, but she could not. It had been Papa's last gift to her, and she would not part with it, no matter its little value. But she did not tell them of the Giotto. It was a matter too close to her heart, and she could not bring herself to cry again.

"And so I have to work," she concluded as the coachman blew on his yard of tin and the coach began to slow down. "It won't be so onerous."

Mrs. Winkle patted Katherine's knee. "Dearie, I hope you are right. If some other situation should present itself, I would consider it, if I were you."

"Maybe you'll marry," suggested the milkmaid.

"With what?" Katherine asked. "Most men look for at least some dowry." And I have nothing but a worthless, rolled-up sketch of two fat angels bumbling through an Italian sky. A man would have to be crazy …

The milkmaid uttered an expletive of her own that made the priest jump and dive back into his Breviary again. "Why must it always come back to men, I ask!" she declared indignantly.

That appeared to be the unanswerable question. As the coach lumbered and creaked to a halt, Mrs. Winkle straightened her dress and looked out the window, blowing a kiss to the sturdy, sandy-haired member of the agricultural fraternity who waited impatiently for the coachman to drop the step. When the door opened, he grinned at his wife and retrieved his sleeping daughter from Katherine's lap.

Mrs. Winkle left the coach first, helped by the priest. "Miss Billings, I know I am dreadful forward, but if you ever need help, our farm is ten miles south of Heanor. Everyone knows it."

Touched beyond words, Katherine could only smile and blow a kiss of her own. Still Mrs. Winkle hesitated. With an effort she leaned close to Katherine's ear. "And I hope to heaven you can tell good men from bad ones, miss."

"I do, too," agreed Katherine, "oh, I do, too."

The schoolboy and milkmaid remained on the coach, and it filled to overflowing with clergymen of the Scots persuasion, frugal with words, space, and interest in others' business. They crowded close together, but no one spoke. It had begun to rain, and the parsons smelled of wet wool and oatmeal.

As the miles rolled away, the rain worsened. As Wakefield neared, Katherine felt her stomach begin to tangle into troublesome knots. Mrs. Leavitt, in that breathless, tired voice of hers, had warned Katherine to be watching for Wakefield. "I will send a boy with a gig for you there. You can wait in the taproom of the Queen Anne until he arrives." Well, thought Katherine, a taproom will be another new experience. I only hope the boy with the gig isn't tardy.

"Wickfield," bawled the coachman finally. It was raining

harder now, and his voice was indistinct through the curtain of water.

Katherine wrapped her cloak tighter about her. When the coach stopped, she helped herself down while the coachman hurriedly unroped her trunk from the top and carried it in great splashing steps to the tavern. Katherine squinted through the rain at the sign that swung back and forth. It was the Hare and Hound, not the Queen Anne. She started to protest, but the coachman was already back in his place, whistling to his horses.

The ostler's boy had already taken her trunk into the taproom, and she followed him. "This is Wakefield?" she asked, hoping to make herself heard over the rain that drummed down. Mrs. Leavitt had certainly not mentioned the Hare and Hound, and there didn't appear to be another tavern in the village, or not one that Katherine could see in the pounding rain.

The boy nodded and held out his hand. Katherine begrudged him a penny of her dwindling supply, and he tugged his forelock at her. He left her in the room that was empty, except for a barmaid polishing glasses behind the tall counter. Katherine settled herself on a bench by the door, hopeful of rescue, and soon.

Time passed and the rain thundered down. She made herself small in the corner when several men came in for ale and conversation. She examined the coins in her reticule again, hoping that there in the dark with the drawstrings closed they might have multiplied into enough coins to see her back to London. But what would there be in London? The thought was depressing in the extreme, but her mind kept worrying around to it, no matter what else she thought: she had nowhere to go except to Leavitt Hall.

The rain let up as the long June afternoon dwindled. After the men drained the last of their ale and left, Katherine went to the doorway and peered out, scanning the road for Mrs. Leavitt's promised boy and gig. As she watched, anxious to get her future underway, a gig came tooling down the road toward the Hart and Hound. She looked closer. It was no boy at the reins, but a man.

As he came nearer, the fear that it was Squire Leavitt himself dissolved. It was a young man, dressed casually in leather breeches and open-necked shirt, with the sleeves rolled up. He held the reins in one hand, perfectly at ease with himself and the horse. He was handsome, too, with hair as dark as her own, but curly, and worn rather longer than fashion dictated. He had drawn it back with a ribbon, reminiscent of her father's era. He was somewhat thin-lipped, but he had a generous mouth, with prominent laugh lines. Katherine let out her breath and loosened her grip on the doorsill.

He pulled the gig to a neat stop directly in front of her and leaped from the gig with all the ease of a true athlete. He walked gracefully toward her, holding out his hand. Surprised, she took it and stood blinking at him as he made a great flourish and kissed the back of her hand.

"Gerald Broussard," he exclaimed. His voice was melodious and rich, and there was just the faintest hint of the French in the pleasant way he swallowed his *r's*.

"Katherine Billings," she said faintly, quite taken with his casual perfection.

His smile widened across his generous mouth. He winked at her, and before she could protest such flippant manners, he bowed again.

" 'Good morrow, Kate, for that's your name, I hear,' " he quoted, still grasping her hand.

In spite of her sudden shyness around such an overpowering man, she laughed and tugged at her memory.

" 'Well have you heard, but something hard of hearing; they call me Katherine, that do talk of me.' " She wriggled out of his hold. "And besides, Mr. Broussard, it is afternoon, and not morning."

But Broussard was not to be sidestepped by her practicality.

" 'You lie, in faith,' " he continued, " 'for you are call'd plain Kate, and bonny Kate, and sometimes Kate the curst.' " He paused, winking his dark eye at her again, and Katherine, charmed, could not help but notice his improbably long eyelashes. "And so on and so on," he concluded. "You've come not a moment too soon, Miss Billings; may I truly call you Kate? Now, where is your luggage?"

"You may call me Miss Billings," she said firmly and pointed to her roped trunk inside the door of the tavern.

"Very well," he agreed. "Whatever you wish." He put the trunk in the back of the gig and handed her up to the seat. He joined her there, spoke to the horse in French, and they started off at a spanking pace.

"How far is it?" she asked when they were on the road.

"Not far," he offered. "We're between Wickfield and Pontefract."

"Don't you mean Wakefield?"

He shook his head, and she wondered all over again if she had misunderstood Mrs. Leavitt last week in London. She glanced at Broussard's elegant profile. Oh, surely not. Obviously the gregarious Mr. Broussard had been sent to collect her.

He laughed then and slapped a lazy rein on the horse's back. "Master Malcolm is positively salivating to see you," he said with a grin in her direction.

Katherine sucked in her breath and felt her face glow hot and cold by turns. "Whatever do you mean?" she asked faintly, clutching the seat and resisting the urge to leap from the gig. She should have listened to the milkmaid.

"Oh, he'll rant and rave, but you'll soon be happy to dance to his tune."

Katherine gulped. "Maybe you had better turn this gig around, Mr. Broussard."

"Gerald, *s'il vous plaît*. Don't get stage fright yet! He may have some rackety ways, but we all perform our best under Master Malcolm."

"You, too?" she exclaimed, half starting up in the seat. "Good God!"

"Yes, of course! Do sit down, Miss Billings, before you frighten Talleyrand." He looked at her more carefully. "I suppose you are concerned because of your age, but I am sure you will do, Miss Billings. I must admit that Master Malcolm usually likes his females older and with some experience. He says he does not like to teach them everything."

Katherine shuddered. She grasped the reins that Broussard held so loosely and stopped the horse in the road. "Take me back or I shall scream," she commanded.

Broussard stared at her and reclaimed the reins. "Surely you have sufficient experience to know that this will not be a painful event, Miss Billings. Where is your *esprit de corps*?"

Katherine slapped Broussard across his generous mouth and took back the reins. "You must be out of your mind to think that I would ever agree to any such thing from Master Malcolm Leavitt!" she exclaimed as she tried to turn the horse around.

Broussard stared at her, his hand to his mouth. As she watched in amazement, he started to laugh. With an exclamation learned from long years of travel abroad, Katherine leaped from the gig and tugged at her trunk.

Broussard was beside her in a moment. He started to put a hand on her shoulder, but the look she gave him stopped him in midmotion.

"Miss Billings, I fear I have made a mistake."

"So has Mr. Leavitt, if he thinks I am a … a straw damsel, sir!"

Broussard leaned against the gig as she struggled with her trunk. "And who is this Monsieur Leavitt you keep speaking of?"

"Why, your employer, sir," she sputtered.

Broussard held up his hand. "*Mais non*! Perhaps you and I should introduce ourselves again, and we will see where we have gone wrong." He held out his hand again, which she refused to touch. "I am Gerald Broussard, third actor of Malcolm Bladesworth's Traveling Company. And you are the actress he engaged from Bath?"

Katherine's eyes opened wider. "I am no such thing! I am a governess from London, engaged by the Leavitt family of Leavitt Hall near Wakefield."

"But that is yet another thirty miles. This is Wickfield. Oh, dear. I think I see our *contretemps*."

Katherine let go of her trunk. "But I thought … I asked if it was Wakefield … but of course the rain was coming down so hard I could not perfectly hear. Oh, dear, indeed, Mr. Broussard."

Broussard's mouth was swollen at one corner and bleeding slightly, so he merely twinkled his eyes at her. "And when you and I traded those lines from *Taming of the Shrew*, well, I was certain you were the one I was set to fetch. Tell me, was there not another woman on the mail coach?"

Katherine shook her head. "No, sir. At least, not an actress. Oh, dear," she said again and started to laugh. "I have been informed by a woman who got off earlier that Mr. Leavitt was a noted … well, she called him a lecher."

Broussard slapped his forehead. "… who likes his females to have some experience. Ah, this is rich! I shall have to use this in a play someday! My most sincere apologies, Miss Billings. Do forgive me for frightening you. I meant no harm."

It was easy to be charitable to Gerald Broussard. She smiled at him. "Forgiven, of course, sir. This was a mistake." She leaned against the gig, too. "I suppose I should ask you to take me back to Wickfield. Perhaps I can continue on to Wakefield." She hated herself for sounding so doubtful. There wasn't any point in eliciting the sympathy of this kind person who could not help her.

He crossed his arms and looked sideways at her. "But surely you do not wish to go to Leavitt Hall, not after what you have told me."

"No, I do not," she agreed, "but I do not have any choice, really."

"Alone in the world?" he asked gently, after a moment of silence.

She nodded.

"I, too." He was silent another moment. He cleared his throat and without looking at her said, "We still need an actress, Miss Billings."

"Oh, I could not!"

"You'd rather go to Wakefield?"

It was a quiet question that brought tears to her eyes. She would not look at Broussard. "Of course not, sir," she said just as quietly.

Again he was silent for a moment. Then quietly, "Miss Billings, I fear you are at what we call *point non plus*. And let me assure that you Malcolm Bladesworth may be a tyrant, but he is not a bad man. Far from it. What will it be, Miss Billings?"

Katherine thought a moment more. "I seem to have no choice, do I?" she murmured.

"Not today, at least." He was standing in front of her then, his hands on her shoulders. "Come with me! We have a performance of *Taming of the Shrew* tonight that needs a 'lusty widow.' Perhaps things will look different in the morning. Please, Miss Billings."

She couldn't look him in the eyes. "That's a small part, isn't it?" she said after a moment's reflection.

"Yes. You'll be on stage for several scenes though, hanging about Hortensio, and that last scene is important." He took his hands off her shoulders. "But you know the lines, I think."

She nodded. "I know the play well. But Mr. Broussard, I am a clergyman's daughter! Whatever will people think?"

He looked around him at the deserted road. "What, are you well-known in Wickfield?"

Katherine laughed, in spite of her misery. "I know no one here, you scoundrel! And yes, I will do it. But only for this night."

3

HENRY TEWKSBURY-HAMPTON STROLLED BACK to his house on Half Moon Street with a meditative air. The day was warming, and he appreciated the little breeze that carried summer winds. It was a welcome change from the damp and chill of winter, especially that chill that had been gathering around his heart for so many years. How odd, he thought to himself. My solicitor engages in plain speaking, and I am immeasurably reassured. He laughed to himself. "Perhaps I will take your advice, Abner, and marry and breed. Heaven knows I ought to, and it might be fun."

The thought was pleasantly erotic. He strolled a little farther and sat down on a bench by a stream that crossed the bridle path, slightly out of breath by then, and irritated with himself. "It is only, sir, that I want my wife and the mother of my children to be *my* idea, and not what my family thinks proper. I suppose I am stubborn."

So I am, he thought. I only hope that I know my own mind when I see that special face—he looked down ruefully at his plentiful girth—and that she will look beyond my currently excessive avoirdupois. That can change, too, even as my faulty character. He laughed again. However, I cannot do much about my thinning hair. She'll have to love a balding man.

He ambled farther into the park at a sedate pace, observing the gardener setting out begonias, and children scampering about the bridle path, a trial to nursemaids who wanted to chat. Marry and breed, he thought to himself again—an excellent prescription for the megrims.

Still smiling to himself, he arrived at Half Moon Street to be met by his valet. The smile vanished. He handed his hat and cane to Wilding.

"My lord, did we forget our appointment with our sister, Lady Clingwell? She is pacing about in your sitting room, and none too pleased, I might add," Wilding chided, his scolding indulgent.

I can't face that worrywart, he thought. Putting his finger to his lips, he took the stairs two at a time, Wilding right behind him.

"But, my lord! 'Tis your own sister!"

"If my mother can be trusted. I have had my doubts for years," said Lord Grayson serenely as he took his old campaigning saddlebags from the dressing room. He dusted them off with his bedspread while Wilding squeaked and wrung his hands.

"My lord, whatever are we doing?"

"*I* am going to Yorkshire as planned, Wilding," he replied, taking two of his well-pressed shirts from the bureau and cramming them in the saddlebags, along with a handful of neckcloths he wadded as Wilding squeaked again, sat down on the bed, and fanned himself. His smallclothes and toilet articles went in the other bag. While his valet took everything out and tried to refold it more neatly, Henry changed into his riding clothes, pausing only to let Wilding help him with his boots.

"Surely we cannot mean to ride all the way to D'Urst Hall!" Wilding exclaimed, his voice weaker now, more subdued.

"I, Wilding, not we," Lord Grayson said firmly as he settled his hat on his head. "I will eventually get there to Pinky's, but I am not putting a schedule on myself. Besides, I have a small errand for my solicitor."

"I am to follow with the rest of your baggage?" Wilding asked.

"You may pack me some clothes, Wilding, if you please. The usual." He was silent a moment, as if considering the matter. He put his gloved hand on his valet's shoulder and gave it a gentle shake. "Let that be your last official duty in this household."

"Wh … what?" quavered the valet, reduced by this sudden turn of events to blancmange. His knees smote together almost audibly.

"I have left a tidy severance for you with Abner Sheffield, plus a glowing recommendation, Wilding," he explained, looking his valet in the eye and feeling not a twinge of regret. "I think it is time we took ourselves off to the Registry Office, after all."

Wilding stared at his master. "After all these years, my lord?"

"Yes, after all these interminable years. You will have no trouble engaging another position, I am sure, Wilding. I left you a character reference that should take care of that. Good day to you." Lord Grayson slung the saddlebags over his broad shoulder, took another look around his room, then closed the door quietly behind him. He took the backstair to the main floor to avoid any danger of his sister. Keene, his butler, waited below.

"Keene, I am off to Pinky D'Urst's Yorkshire estate. You may direct my mail there. I should arrive in two weeks."

Keene did not even blink an eye. "My lord, Yorkshire is not in the polar reaches. Two weeks?"

"Yes. I intend to take my time."

"Very well, sir. You intend to travel on horseback such a distance?" Again, not a muscle twitched in Keene's face.

"Yes." Lord Grayson laughed, but not loud enough for his sister's hearing. "I expect I will be eating my dinner off several mantelpieces. But this is my intention. Keene, you may now remove that mulish look from your face and take my knocker from the front door."

Keene struggled to maintain his composure. "And what am I to tell Lady Clingwell?"

"Only that you are in entire ignorance of my whereabouts. I doubt anyone else will be curious." He held out his hand, and the butler shook it. "Put the staff on holiday pay, Keene. And Keene, I recommend Brighton to you. It will put some color back in your cheeks. Good day to you."

Lord Grayson strolled to the stables, engaged his favorite mount, and was soon riding out of London.

He did not travel far that first day, just far enough into the country to put London well behind him. At the inn he passed up what looked like a feast from the *Satyricon* and dined on chicken breast, bread with no butter, and water. He was awake half the night, staring at the ceiling and resolving never again to keep the irregular habits of London, with late rising, endless evenings in clubs, and bedtime when the sun was coming out. "I will regulate my habits until I go to bed at dark with the barnyard fowl and rise with the larks," he resolved, even as his stomach rumbled.

The next day was more of a trial. By noon his ample backside was on fire, and the muscles inside his thighs hurt as they had not in years. Not since that first week of hard riding in Spain had his nether regions endured such punishment. See here, Henry, you are not leaping over hedges or cramming yourself against the pommel to escape the Frenchies, he thought as he gritted his teeth and posted sedately onward. Lord, am I this out of shape?

By the third evening, after his virtuous dinner of chicken and bread eaten standing up, he had no trouble falling to sleep as soon as he settled his long frame into the comfortable bed. His dreams were of beautiful women, and he woke refreshed finally.

Riding was still a purgatory, but he rode slowly, enjoying

the beauty of the English countryside in early summer. His thoughts naturally traveled to Spain, which he had left eight years ago, sliding down a rope from a prison wall and into a week of gut-wrenching fear that finally ended with a plunge into the sea and a long swim to a British man-o-war looking for him across the bar on a high tide. He thought of his former comrades, living and dead, and was grateful, despite his current pain and empty stomach, to be alive.

The end of the week found him close to Wakefield and much too near the end of his journey. "Bolt, it is not that I do not like Pinky D'Urst," he told his horse as they meandered along. "Indeed, I love him like a brother, but he will be too solicitous, and his wife keeps much too good a table. Pinky can wait another week."

And there was Pinky's sister to consider. Florence D'Urst was not a bad-looking woman, if one discounted a rather sharp nose and chin that threatened to meet someday, and eyes set too close together. He knew, even though no one had told him, that the D'Ursts and the Graysons were anxious for him to marry Florence. "No," he told Bolt, who only tossed his head. "I won't do it. Why should I have to wake up every morning of the world to find that face sharing my pillow? Why should I be forced to make love with my eyes closed?"

He thought then about the woman he was looking for. "She must know her own mind and not agree to everything I say, even if I am a marquess and too rich for my own good. After all, since when did a title and a fortune qualify one to be omniscient? I would like her to be pretty, of course, but that is not a prerequisite." He smiled to himself, thinking of Spanish women he had bedded to his great enjoyment and theirs, too. "She should love me ferociously. That would be sufficient."

He idled along in pleasant reflection, close to whistling. After another sparse luncheon, he traveled sleepily into a warm afternoon. It would be a simple matter to find a tree to rest under for a few minutes, and if the minutes stretched into hours, what did it matter?

He was about to decide to look in earnest for a shady spot when he opened his half-closed eyes to see a man standing on the empty road in front of him. He peered more closely, more wide awake now. The man, caped and masked, appeared to be pointing a pistol at him. How bizarre, he thought, as sleep still crowded his brain. It appears I am to be assaulted. He reined in Bolt and rested his leg across the pommel of the saddle, surprisingly at charity with the road agent.

The man came closer. "Stand and deliver," he said gruffly, waving the pistol about.

The voice sounded vaguely familiar to Henry, but he could think of no road agents among his acquaintance. He watched, frowning as the man thrust his pistol closer. The pistol wagged about as though the hand that held it shook.

"Sir, is this your first robbery?" Henry asked pleasantly. "I would be most obliged if you would not wave that pistol about in such a fashion. Those things have a habit of going off, you know."

The words were scarcely out of his mouth when the man fired. In rapid sequence Henry saw the flash, smelled the acrid odor of powder, and felt a slap on the side of his head. With a groan he slid to the ground, the reins falling from his hands. He struggled to remain conscious, watching as his riding coat turned red.

He opened his half-closed eyes as the highwayman threw down the pistol with a shriek. "Oh, I did not mean to do that, my lord!" he exclaimed and then ran down the road, in perfect imitation of Bolt, who had already bolted.

"How bizarre," Lord Grayson murmured again. His mouth was filling up with blood from his head wound. He settled himself on the soft earth so it would drain out. "Wilding, you are a better valet than a road agent." His eyes closed.

When he opened them again, it was still afternoon, and the

birds still chirped overhead. He was cradled on the somewhat bony legs of his nephew and heir, Algernon Mannerly, who was weeping and sniffling. "Really, Algie, have some countenance," he said, his voice sounding dreamy and far away in his own ears, which seemed miles apart from each other. Algernon blubbered on.

"Algie, that is most unattractive, especially from my point of view," Henry murmured. He wanted to go back to sleep, but his nephew's noisy tears were a distraction.

Algernon cried harder, hugging his uncle to him. "Have a care, Algie," Lord Grayson admonished. "My head appears to be splitting in two."

With a gasp Algernon leaped to his feet, dropping his uncle back in the roadway. Henry groaned and struggled to remain conscious.

"I … I … I didn't mean this to happen," Algie stuttered, backing away.

"I am sure you did not," Henry reassured him as he lay in the road, damp in his own blood. "Pray explain yourself, Nevvy. Am I such an ogre?"

Algernon came no closer. He took out a handkerchief and began to dab at his bloody breeches. "I was supposed to rescue you from the highwayman, and you would be so grateful that you would increase my quarterly allowance again." He started to wail louder as he dug at the blood. "Now he has killed you, and my breeches are ruined!"

Henry raised his eyebrows at Algie's artless declaration and groaned with the effort. "And I suppose you will tell me that the highwayman was my own dear Wilding?"

Algernon made an effort and was rewarded with hiccups instead of tears. "We met at Sheffield and Johnston's. It seemed like such a good idea over a bottle of your brandy."

"My bran ... Good God, Algie. You plotted my death in my own house? How unmannerly of you," Henry said. He struggled to raise himself onto one elbow. "I must tell Sheffield not to be so convincing in the future."

Algernon wrung his hands. "Not your death, Uncle! I was supposed to rescue you! I wish you would pay attention. We didn't think you would mind if we borrowed your matched pistols."

Henry lowered himself to the ground again and groaned louder. "You numbskull. They have hair triggers. Lord, Algie, I can't believe you are my heir. I fear for the family."

He couldn't say anything more. His mouth was getting numb and his eyes insisted upon closing. "At least go get a doctor."

Algie stopped dabbing at his pants. "Yes! Yes! Capital idea! Why didn't I think of that?" He started down the road. "Don't go anywhere, Uncle. I'll save you yet!" He was gone.

Henry turned himself onto his back. He had always enjoyed looking at the sky through a screen of leaves, but the view left much to be desired this time. His head drummed like a call to arms. To think that he had gotten through all those years in Spain with scarcely a scratch, and here he was, lying on a deserted road—and by the looks of it little used—shot by his former valet and to be "rescued" by his worthless nephew. "What were you two thinking?" he murmured, then closed his eyes.

When he opened them again, the blood was drying on his riding coat and the sun was going down. Not wanting to, but unable to resist, he put his hand to his head, just above his ear, where the drum still beat the loudest. He expected to find a crater, but there was only a neat furrow. He gingerly traced the shallow route of the ball, noting that the blood had dried there, too.

"Where in hell are you, Algernon?" he growled, rising up on both elbows this time. The last thing he remembered was seeing his nephew sprinting down the road, still dabbing at his pants as he ran. He considered the matter. Algernon Mannerly was a citified dandy who probably could not find this little back lane again if he looked from now to the end of the century. Besides that, he thought sourly, Algie is probably wild with grief over the ruination of his precious pantaloons. And Wilding? He was probably still running.

I shall have to rescue myself, Henry thought. He lay back down again, finding a more comfortable position for thinking things through. His eyes closed again, and he drifted away.

When he came to himself again, it was nearly dark. See here, Henry, he thought, you are getting no closer to rescue, and someone probably should take a look at your head. He struggled into a sitting position, gasping at the pain, but glad at the same time that he was not beyond help. He crawled to the road's edge and hauled himself to his feet, clinging to a tree until the fog in his eyes cleared. With an effort he looked in both directions on the road. Bolt was nowhere to be seen. "Remind me to sell you to a knacker man, should we chance to meet again," he said out loud. "Useless horse, worthless valet, and dreadful nephew. Was ever a man so blessed?"

The trees were close together along the road. He willed himself to keep moving as he helped himself along from tree to tree, leaning to rest often, but not sitting down, where the temptation to remain there would probably prove too great. Somewhere along the road he shucked himself of his coat. The smell of blood was worse almost than the pain in his head. There was only a sprinkling of blood around his collar, and he could move easier now.

When he thought he could not walk any farther without pitching over, he came to the outskirts of a village. The one street appeared deserted, but some discretion, probably left over from his more cautious days in Spain, compelled him to stay in the shadows. He rested against a rain barrel and considered his situation. If he staggered up to some householder's door and threw himself into their sitting room, he would probably be whisked at his command to D'Urst Hall, which couldn't be more than a few hours away. Pinky and his wife would see to his comfort.

Somehow, even in his extremity, the idea did not appeal to Lord Grayson. "You would probably have to suffer the tender ministrations of Pinky's sister, and then there would be an obligation … Thank you, no," he said to himself. Gingerly he patted his pocket, wincing at the pain and wondering why it was that every part of him was hurting now. Of course, he had fallen off a rather tall horse. Everything ached. He had to lie down, and soon. He patted his pocket again and grunted in satisfaction. His wallet was still there. "Wilding, you will never do as a highwayman," he said. "Although I fear that I must leave you a less-than-glowing recommendation when next we meet."

But if it was not to be Pinky D'Urst's, what? He was too tired to think. He squinted in the twilight, wondering why even that tiny gesture pained him. There appeared to be a barn ahead of him, with saddled horses around it, and some farmer's carts, but again, no people. He heard a roar of laughter from inside the barn. "Perhaps it is a cockfight," he told himself. "I will just find a wagon and lie down in it until I feel better."

None of the farmer's carts appeared too promising, most of them smelling of cow or sheep dung. His head spinning, he staggered to a wagon closest to the barn's back door. With some effort he crawled inside and found himself staring at a skeleton. It was seated with its legs crossed and wore a crown. "Bizarre, indeed," he murmured when the fear left him. There were swords on the wagon bed around him, as if flung there by a harried assassin. He touched one. It was wooden. As his eyes grew accustomed to the dark interior, he saw robes and ornate chairs and wigs on their stands. He thought he could see a Roman fasces, an eagle standard with SPQR written in gilt painting, leaning up against a stuffed owl.

"I must have lost more blood than I thought," he decided and curled up on a pile of capes that appeared to be made of velvet, but on closer inspection were really threadbare corduroy. His hands shaking with exhaustion, he covered himself with another cape and fell into unconsciousness.

4

"I AM ALREADY FULL of stage fright, Mr. Broussard," said Katherine Billings as they neared the village just beyond Wickfield. "You are so sure that I can do this?"

"*Mais oui*!" exclaimed Gerald Broussard with a Gallic kiss of his fingers in her direction. "Tonight I am Lucentio, and I will see that Hortensio steers you around the stage and cues you, should you become confused." He looked at her as they bowled along. "But somehow I do not think you will become confused, Miss Billings."

"Call me Kate," said the proper Miss Billings in a resigned voice. "Whatever will Mr. Bladesworth say?"

"Leave Master Malcom to me, Kate," said Gerald. "And here we are!"

"But … but that's a barn!" Kate exclaimed as they rolled to a stop before a ramshackle-looking structure.

"Actors cannot be choosers," Broussard said as he helped her down from the gig. "Tonight it is the Globe Theatre, my dear Miss Kate Billings. Shall we go inside?" he asked, offering his arm as if they were entering the Theatre Royal off Drury Lane.

"Lead on, sir," she said. "I must be out of my mind."

Globe Theatre it may have been for the night, but to Kate it still smelled like a barn and looked like one. True, it had been swept out, and benches placed in rows, but even the pungent odor of tallow candles could not compete with the fragrance of cows and horses. Kate looked around with interest. The stage was a platform raised upon wooden barrels and was perfectly bare, except for a rank of short candles on its edge, still unlit.

She looked at Broussard, who was smiling at her. He touched her arm. "To make the magic work, Miss Billings, I beg you to look at it through an actor's eyes. Tonight we perform Shakespeare."

"And we do not insult the Bard with Cibber's profanations, but use the words of the master," boomed a hearty voice behind her.

Kate whirled around to see a massive figure dressed in Elizabethan garb, bearing down on her. "Beg … beg pardon?" she stammered, her eyes wide. Before she could move, the man had grabbed her in a strong embrace, lifting her off her feet. "Welcome to the Bladesworth's Traveling Company!" he shouted and kissed her on both cheeks.

Before she could say anything, Gerald Broussard intervened. "Mr. Bladesworth, let me introduce Katherine Billings to you."

Malcolm Bladesworth set her on her feet suddenly and stepped back a pace. "My dear Monsieur Broussard, I do not believe that I asked for a Katherine Billings." He rubbed his whiskered chin and twinkled his eyes at Kate. "Correct me if I am wrong, but weren't you to pick up one Penelope Cranville?" While Katherine looked at him in amazement, he stalked around her. "This, I know, is not Miss Cranville, who is quite fifty and much less bounteously endowed. My eyes must have been momentarily blinded by her magnificent bosom."

"Really, sir," Kate protested.

"Yes, really!" He looked at Broussard, who was trying to hide his own smile. "Not that I am disappointed, mind you, provided the lady can act."

Gerald took Kate by the arm. "This is Katherine Billings," he said again, "and I have … how do you say it? … made a muddle."

With scarce effort Bladesworth picked up Kate and set her on the stage, leaving her legs to dangle over the edge. He sat beside her. "Explain yourself, Gerald, and be quick. We go on in half an hour."

As Katherine Billings listened in growing amusement, Broussard explained himself. While his command of English was excellent, the task of explaining his muddle became such an exertion that it reduced itself finally to sentences half-French and half-English, and a multitude of gestures, all delivered under the glare of Malcolm Bladesworth.

"And that, sir, was my mistake," he finished in a rush. "But she knows the lines and said she would help us tonight."

Bladesworth was silent a moment, rubbing his fingers over the faded corduroy of his cape. He glanced at Katherine. "Cibber's or Shakespeare's lines?" he rumbled.

"Oh, Shakespeare's, sir," she responded quickly. "My father did not care for Cibber's changes in the text."

Bladesworth took her hand in his meaty one. "Then will you be Hortensio's 'lusty widow' tonight? If you know the words and look sufficiently saucy, we can steer you around the stage."

"I know the words," she replied. Good manners told her that she should withdraw her hand, but she did not want to. It was nice to have her hand held by someone who seemed genuinely interested in her.

He kissed her hand with a loud smack that seemed to ricochet off the back wall. "Done then, madame!" he shouted. "I suppose it would be too much to ask, but do you sing, as well?"

"Well, I do. At least a little."

Bladesworth got off the stage and helped her down. "The muses are smiling 'ponst us, my boy," he told Gerald. "Then

Kate, my dear, you can entertain the rustics between acts three and four."

"But—"

"Ivy!" he shouted suddenly. "Ivy, love of my life, my Adam's rib. I need you!"

There was a rustle offstage, and then a woman as small as Bladesworth was massive stepped out, also dressed in a shabby costume of the Elizabethan era. Ivy Bladesworth hurried forward and held out her arms to her husband, who gently helped her off the stage. He smiled at her fondly, even as she stood on tiptoe to put her finger to his lips.

"Hush, Malcolm. We already have people lining up outside." She nodded to Kate. "And who might you be, my dear?"

"Ivy, let me introduce Katherine Billings," Malcolm said in a stage whisper that still smote against the back wall. "Gerald has snatched up the wrong woman."

"Really, Gerald," Ivy scolded in her mild voice.

"She is a governess on her way to Leavitt Hall near Wakefield," explained Bladesworth. "Miss Billings, Mrs. Ivy Bladesworth."

Ivy took Katherine's hand in hers. "And now you find yourself among low company, Miss Billings. I suppose Malcolm will tell me that he has gently persuaded you to join our troupe?"

Kate smiled. "I have consented to remain for this evening's performance."

"And sing between the acts," Malcolm reminded her and then struck another pose. " 'Her voice was ever soft, gentle and low, an excellent thing in a woman.' *King Lear*, act five, scene three, my 'super-dainty Kate, for dainties are all cates.' "

Ivy laughed at Kate's expression. "He always quotes and quotes until I can't remember if it is Shakespeare or Malcolm! You are so kind to help us," she said, still clasping Kate's hand. "Tomorrow you will go on to your previous engagement?"

Kate withdrew her hand. "As to that, I do not know if I would be welcome now. After all, I was to be in Wakefield today and not tomorrow."

Mrs. Bladesworth rested the back of her hand on Kate's cheek in a gesture that was a distant memory of her own mother, dead these many years. "La, my dear! You need not fear. A pretty face is always a welcome sight, even if it is a day late."

Tears sprang to Kate's eyes. "That may be the problem, Mrs. Bladesworth," she said in a rush of words and then stopped herself. "But you cannot be interested in my problems. You don't even know me."

"Dear Miss Billings, don't you know that all women are related?" Mrs. Bladesworth grasped her hand and pulled her along. "Now we need to find a dress that fits a lusty widow. Ah, you come along too, Maria and Phoebe."

The woman, with her own daughters in tow, hurried Kate along to a cow stall with a tarpaulin thrown over part of it, calling out orders as she removed Kate's bonnet and told her to unbutton her pelisse. "I should have introduced my daughters. Maria is the one looking through the trunk."

A blond girl, all dimples and china blue eyes, peered around the trunk and dipped a quick curtsy. She pointed with her chin as she shook out a dress. "And that is my sister, Phoebe, making calf s eyes at Gerald."

"Maria!" declared Phoebe, stamping her foot and speaking in a voice as carrying as her father's.

Unperturbed, Maria stuck out her tongue. "Ninnyhammer!"

Mrs. Bladesworth placed Kate's bonnet on a mound of hay. "Girls! Let us at least pretend that you have manners!" She faced Kate, her hands spread out in age-old appeal. "My dear, you will think us dreadfully ramshackle."

Kate hid a smile as she draped her pelisse next to the bonnet and obligingly turned for Mrs. Bladesworth to unbutton her traveling dress. I don't know what I should be imagining, she thought. Whatever trepidation she had felt was fast being replaced by a warmth she had not experienced before, not in years. I wonder if this is what a family feels like, she thought, as she raised her arms and Mrs. Bladesworth removed her dress.

"Now, my dear, you will be wanted in act three, scene three as a wedding guest. Hang about Hortensio. Hortensio!"

Kate grabbed the dress that Mrs. Bladesworth held, clutching it to her as a tall youth hurried to the stall and draped his arms over the railing. He nodded to Kate amiably, unmindful of her discomfort, and held out a handful of stiff-looking bristles to his mother.

"This is my son, David. This is Miss Billings. She will be your lusty widow tonight."

He dipped his head in Kate's direction as she clutched the dress higher, and then dangled the bristles at his mother. "Mama, I cannot get these to stay on my face!" He glanced at Kate. "Miss Billings, can you manage these? I cannot."

Mystified Kate shook her head. Mrs. Bladesworth took the whiskers from her son and hurried from the stall, speaking over her shoulder to her daughter, who still rummaged in the trunk. "Marie, find the corset—you know the one—and help Miss Billings. Come, David, and let us age you fifty years in the next ten minutes!"

"Ah!" Maria pulled a wicked-looking contraption from the trunk. "Hurry, Miss Billings!"

Kate peered around cautiously and put down the dress. "Oh, surely I don't need that!" she exclaimed.

"You must," Maria insisted. "It will push up your bosoms wondrously!"

Kate sucked in her breath. "I will not!" she declared. "They are already high enough!"

"But you must be a lusty widow," Maria insisted. "And besides, didn't I hear you tell Papa that it would be only for tonight?"

Kate grumbled and allowed Maria to lace her into the corset. She raised her chin and kept her eyes resolutely forward, refusing to look down at her own creamy expanse of bosom that seemed to grow greater with every lace Maria tightened.

"Perfect!" Maria exclaimed at last.

Kate looked down and gasped. "Is all that *mine*?" she managed as Maria neatly dropped the dress over her head and buttoned her into it.

"Yes. I told you it was a wondrous corset." Maria looked down at her own slim frame. "I begged and begged Mama to let me use it, but what does she do but declare that you cannot get Great Danes out of Pekinese."

Kate laughed in spite of her embarrassment. "Well, I never thought of nature's bounty as a Great Dane before. Surely I can wear a shawl with this?"

"What? And cover up such a magnificent asset?" boomed a now-familiar voice behind her. "My dear Miss Billings, on she whom nature smiles, let no man frown! Turn around now, and let me see if you pass muster."

Her face on fire, Kate turned around. Malcolm Bladesworth nodded and rubbed his chin, a gesture she was already becoming familiar with. "Magnificent. You will be our lustiest widow yet. And when you sing your song between the acts, be sure to bow deeply. The rustics will love it."

"Mr. Bladesworth! My father was a clergyman!" Kate burst out.

Malcolm threw back his head and laughed. "So was mine, m'dear, but I still seem to recall him glancing at the occasional bosom!" He gave her one last admiring stare. "Now if only you can act, too, perhaps you might consider a life on the wicked stage."

"Never," Kate declared firmly, rendering her word less emphatic by adding, "I would die of pneumonia in such a state of undress, or at the very least suffer a putrid sore throat."

Bladesworth laughed. " 'Come, come, you wasp; i'faith, you are too angry.' Act two, scene one, my dear Miss Billings." He took her by the hands and pulled her from the cow stall. "And now it is time to tread the boards. Chin up, and remember your lines."

"But …" Kate began as Malcolm swirled his shabby cape around him and headed for the stage area. He turned around and bowed to her.

"My dear, one piece of advice: don't stand too near to Petruchio. He does love to pinch."

"Oh!" exclaimed Miss Billings, as though Petruchio had already done his duty.

She found herself a quiet corner out of the way of the actors, who stood at the edge of the much-darned curtain. Someone had thrust a well-worn copy of *Taming of the Shrew* into her hands, and she read again the part of Hortensio's widow. She leaned back against the wall of the barn and closed her eyes. Only this morning I was a respectable young woman on her way to a job in Wakefield. But you don't want to be in Wakefield, she reminded herself, thinking again of Squire Leavitt and the milkmaid's warning. Kate sighed and looked around. Do you wish to be here? She had no answer for herself.

Before she could worry the thoughts around in her head anymore, Gerald, dressed now as Lucentio, and another young actor in servant's clothes who must be Tranio, pulled back the shabby curtain that hung on a rope stretching from one edge of the loft to the other. The stage was bare. As she watched, interested in spite of her worries, Gerald and the other actors bowed to the audience, took their places on the plank stage, and became wealthy young student and servant, intent upon Padua and its famed university. She smiled at the familiar lines, read to her first by her father, and settled back.

She did not know what she expected. Perhaps because she had become so worn down with worry, the sharp-tongued comedy grabbed her and shook the misery right out of her. Here soon was Maria, playing the gentle Bianca, and here was Hortensio, her whiskers now in place and walking, stooped, with a cane. The Bladesworths' other daughter—was her name Phoebe?—must be Katharina, the shrew.

If Kate Billings was prepared to be mildly entertained,

Katharina's entrance ended all complacency. With stentorian tones as penetrating as her father's, Phoebe Bladesworth commanded the stage, casting all in the shadow and using it like an instrument. Kate sat up to watch. She had attended plays in Covent Garden and Drury Lane; even seeing the immortal Sarah Siddons before her retirement, but Phoebe Bladesworth glowed with a fire all her own. She ranted, she raved, she teased, she pouted. She was Katharina the shrew.

"Whatever is she doing here?" Kate whispered out loud. The younger Bladesworth daughter belonged on a London stage, not in a barn, dressed in a costume that should have been relegated to the dustbin years ago, performing for farm folk.

"Miss Billings! Hurry now!"

Kate leaped to her feet, dropping the playbook, as Hortensio gestured to her from the edge of the stage and then tugged her on with him as Petruchio, in his jape's costume, made a bow to the actors and spoke his lines.

"You're a lusty widow now, ma'am," reminded Hortensio as he put his arm around her waist and leered at her. His beard was starting to come off, and he didn't look a day over fifteen to her, but as Kate leered back and giggled loudly when he patted her rump, the audience laughed and whistled. Summoning her courage, and secure in the knowledge that she didn't know anyone in or near Wickfield, Kate patted him right back. The audience howled and Petruchio glared at her. Kate only raised her bosom higher and sniffed.

Hortensio tugged her back beside him, and the action continued onstage. Soon Petruchio hoisted the shrieking shrew over his shoulder and exited, and Malcolm, performing the role of father, led the actors in to the bridal feast as the playgoers stamped their feet and clapped for more.

The curtain closed, and Malcolm took her hand. "Well done, lusty wench," he exclaimed, beaming his approval. He gave her a little push toward the closed curtains. "Go out there and sing for us before act four."

"Oh, but sir," she protested, her fear returning.

"You must know a bawdy song or two," Malcolm said as he prepared to draw back the dusty curtain.

Kate stared at him. "I told you, I was a clergyman's daughter!"

He only twinkled his eyes at her and shoved her out in front of the curtain. Holding her skirts well away from the candles on the stage's edge, she looked at the audience. All the stamping had stirred up the dust and dried manure from the barn floor. And there in the loft pigeons fluttered and cooed.

Kate held up her hands, hoping they would not shake. "Hush, now," she began. "How can I sing?"

To her surprise they quieted down and looked at her expectantly, their faces upturned and eager. This was not a time for Italian art songs or Wesley hymns. "I shall sing 'Robin Is to the Greenwood Gone,' " she stated.

Papa had always declared she had a pleasant voice. Kate clasped her hands in front of her and sang to the farmers of Wickfield. The simple Elizabethan melody was perfectly suited to her voice, which soared until even the pigeons were silent. When she finished, the audience was still. To her surprise and real gratification the applause first began backstage, and then the farmers took it up. Kate smiled in genuine delight and remembered to bow deeply to her audience before retreating behind the curtain.

"Magnificent!" Malcolm declared as he grabbed her in a bear hug. "I was sure you could not be so beautiful for nothing! My dear, you have a prodigious voice!"

He hurried her offstage as the curtain drew back on act four and Petruchio's country home. He led her to the back door, where Maria and Gerald stood, breathing in the clean evening air. "Go through your lines in act five. Magnificent! Magnificent!" he chortled. "I must go find Ivy."

"That was nice," Maria said. She handed Kate the playbook she had dropped earlier. "Now, let us trade lines. Gerald?"

But Gerald was standing in the doorway, looking at the stage, his eyes wistful. Maria sighed and turned back to the book. "I do not know why he bothers," she grumbled. "Papa has already declared that Phoebe is much too young, and besides, Gerald is poor." She giggled, her good humor restored. "But so are we all! Come, Miss Billings."

"Please call me Kate," she replied and took up the book. She glanced shyly at Maria. "Did I … did I really sing well?"

"Oh, Miss B … Kate, you have a lovely voice! I cannot understand why you have never thought of the stage before."

Kate regarded Maria. "My dear, it is not usually the first choice of anyone." She paused, embarrassed. "That is, most people don't … well …"

Maria touched her hand. "I know," she replied softly. "Actors are low company."

"Oh, I didn't mean …" Kate stammered in confusion.

Maria shook her head. "We know what you are thinking. And I must say, you are generous to help us out tonight. Shall we go over the lines?"

Their heads together over the book, they read the lines back and forth to each other until Maria was satisfied. "That will do," said Maria at last. "And now I must go on," she said as Gerald hurried to the door again and beckoned to her. She laughed. "Lucentio and Bianca must marry in haste, so he can repent at leisure!"

She stopped at the door. "You still have some time, Kate. We'll be packing up as soon as we are done. If you wish, you could take those candlesticks from act three and put them in the prop wagon." She gestured toward the wagon that was backed up close to the door.

"Certainly." Kate picked up the candlesticks, noting with amusement how the heavy sticks could look so rich and golden from the audience, which could not see the paint flaking off. Tawdry illusion, she thought first and then laughed to herself. And how it took me in, too. It was pleasant, at least for a moment, not to think about tomorrow, and the Leavitts, and her fate as a governess if she dared arrive a day late with no satisfactory explanation. She hiked up her skirts and climbed the small folding ladder that led into the prop wagon. I shall merely tell them I had a prior engagement as a lusty widow in *Taming of the Shrew*. The absurdity of that answer made her shake her head.

The prop wagon was dark, but she waited until her eyes became accustomed to the gloom. She looked around her, jumping a little in fright at the skeleton sitting with its bony legs crossed. "I suppose you are Hamlet's father's ghost," she said out loud, "or perhaps the rest of 'poor Yorick.' " She looked at the swords, touching the wooden blades carefully and then chuckled. "I don't think anyone will perish from these weapons, unless they are susceptible to splinters."

She straightened the swords and set down the candlesticks. Perhaps if I wrap them in some of this old fabric, they won't chip so much, she thought. Kate tugged at what looked like a moth-eaten cape on top of a nearby pile. It wouldn't give; she pulled harder. She gasped as a man materialized from the pile of old costumes. He struggled upright as she stood, her mouth open, too surprised to scream.

He sat there, as if unsure of his surroundings. He shook his head to clear it and groaned. Kate shrieked and grabbed up one of the candlesticks at her feet. She brandished it over her head. "Don't you come any closer!" she exclaimed to the man who sat still, his hand to his head.

"See here, miss," he began, his voice faint. He reached out his hand toward her. Kate leaped back and stumbled against the skeleton. Without a word she slammed down the candlestick on the man's neck. He pitched forward among the swords, unconscious.

Kate dropped the candlestick and threw herself on her knees by the man. She tried to turn him over on his back, but he was too substantial to budge and the space awkward. She gasped and put her ear to his back. After a long moment in which her own heart seemed to stop thudding in her breast, she was rewarded with a slow, steady pounding. She sighed with relief at the comforting sound.

"Thank God I have not killed you," she breathed. She touched his neck, and her hand came away wet and sticky. "Oh, no!" Visions of standing before a magistrate to plead guilty to assault crossed her mind's eye, and she gulped and shook the man.

He was completely insensible to her urgings. Tears sprang into Kate's eyes. She pulled the cape over him, tucking a corner of it under his head and wiping her hands on it. With a sob she stumbled from the wagon.

Malcolm was gesturing to her from the back door. "Hurry, Kate, my dear governess. It is time for scene three!"

She ran to him, reaching for his hands. Malcolm stared at her and then laughed. "What, did the skeleton startle you?"

She shook her head and opened her mouth several times before the words tumbled out. "There was a man in the wagon! I … I hit him with a candlestick, but I do not think he is dead!"

Malcolm tugged at his false beard, stood a moment in indecision, then grasped her hand, pulling her toward the stage. "He'll have to keep until after the wedding feast. Now take a deep breath, Kate and compose yourself." He inclined his massive head toward her. "I am sure it is only a drunkard. He will likely be gone by the time we are through." And then he was pulling her onto the stage as the play went on.

5

WHEN LORD GRAYSON REGAINED consciousness, he found himself facedown on the wagon bed, staring at a pile of wooden swords next to bony, skeletal toes. He closed his eyes again, declaring to himself, "When I open them, I will be in bed at Half Moon Street."

He opened one eye and then the other, but the view was still swords and toes. He lay where he was, unable to summon the energy to roll over and constricted by the narrow space. His head throbbed like a species apart, pounding like a pile driver on the back of his neck. With some effort he worked his hand up to his head, feeling again the furrow caused by Wilding's bullet. The wound was crusted with dried blood.

His hand traveled to the back of his neck, where the pile driver was working the hardest, and came away wet with his blood. As he lay there contemplating this new ruin to his head, he remembered a woman with a remarkable bosom. Surely not, he thought. He remembered that she was small and could not possibly have had the strength to deliver the blow that was even now making him queasier by the minute. She must have struck me with something, he concluded. God, what a woman.

I hope I do not see her again until I feel better.

Grunting softly, Henry eased himself up. He sat absolutely still until the nausea went away and then leaned back carefully against the pile of old clothing. He thought at first that he would leave the wagon before anyone returned, but he could not. He ached everywhere, and even the tiniest shifting of position made the hairs rise on his back.

As he sat considering his situation, he heard a great wave of applause from the barn. What *is* going on in that place, he asked himself. It couldn't be a cockfight. People didn't applaud like that at cockfights, at least, not the ones he had attended. His hand went to the back of his neck again. And rarely did women with blunt objects and magnificent bosoms frequent such low business. He sighed and resigned himself to whatever fate awaited, sorry that he had taken off his riding coat, now that the night was cooler, and grateful that he still had his wallet in his pocket. Surely he could buy his way out of any trouble.

In a few moments he heard the sound of people leaving the barn. They talked among themselves in low tones, with an occasional burst of laughter. In another moment the light from a candle thrust in his face made him squint and try to cover his eyes.

"Ods bodkins," boomed out a hearty voice that made his head throb even harder. "Whatever did you catch here, Kate?"

"Oh, please talk softer," he begged. "My head is killing me.

A great rumble of laughter from the man holding the candle washed over him. "It's no wonder, m'boy. You've been crowned with a candlestick." The man sniffed Henry's shirt-front. "Well, you don't appear to have been drinking. Let me give you a hand up."

Before he could protest, the giant of a man lifted him to his feet. Henry's knees buckled under him, and he sagged to the floor. Helplessly he waved the man away. "Please just leave me alone and let me die in peace."

But the giant wouldn't leave him alone. The man whistled.

"Kate, there's blood all over his shirt." The man called to others. "Let this be a warning to anyone who tries to bother Miss Billings."

"Billings, did you say?" he managed.

"Yes, laddie, but don't trouble yourself. Gerald, Davy, give me a hand with this one."

In another moment he was lying on the grass outside the wagon, staring up at a circle of people, all dressed fantastically from another era. As he lay there puzzling it over, his eyelids drooping, the circle parted and the young woman with the remarkable bosom knelt beside him.

"Promise you will not hit me again," he said, attempting a feeble joke.

"I can but apologize, sir," she replied, her voice penitent, "but whatever were you doing in the wagon?"

"Yes, laddie, what *were* you doing in the wagon?" boomed the man.

He could have told the truth then, told them of Algie and his stupid blunder, and he would have, but he looked again at the young woman, and her eyes were so anxious. She seems genuinely concerned, he thought, even though she doesn't know my name or my title. Henry turned his head slowly to look again at the tall man, who was now kneeling on his other side.

"First tell me something." He made a feeble gesture with his hand that took in the group observing him. "What have I stumbled into?"

The man rested his hand gently on Henry's chest. "We are actors, laddie, and I am Malcolm Bladesworth, actor and manager of the Bladesworth Traveling Company."

Henry closed his eyes with a long sigh. To his surprise the young woman rested her head on his chest.

"Oh, please, do not stop breathing!" she implored.

He had no intention of dying. He opened his eyes as her hair tickled his face. The dark tresses smelled of lavender and of woman. His hand went to her hair, and she raised her head to look deep into his eyes. He had never seen such concern before on a woman's face, and it warmed him.

"I am not dying, but it was a close call." He paused for what he hoped was good dramatic effect. "I was set upon first by assassins and fled to your wagon."

Henry had not misjudged his audience. The women in the circle gasped, and Bladesworth gathered him into his arms.

"My God, man, did they shoot you, too?"

Henry nodded and groaned, not so much from the pain, but to keep the woman's hand on his arm. To his extreme gratification it tightened. "I was shot in the head."

In another moment the woman was running her hand gently over his head. Her fingers stopped above his left ear and gently traced the route of the ball.

"Oh, Mr. Bladesworth, he is not fooling! Assassins?" the woman asked. She looked about her, resting her hand on his head in an oddly protective gesture. "Sir, who are you that someone would wish to assassinate you?"

"I am Henry Tewksbury-Hampton, Marquess of Grayson. The assassin was my nephew and heir, Algernon Mannerly."

To his surprise Bladesworth chuckled and helped Henry into a sitting position. He looked over Henry's head to his wife. "Ivy, think how lucky we are to be so poor! None of our numerous offspring has ever been tempted to do us in."

Several of the young people standing about in the circle chuckled, and Henry wondered if the Bladesworths grew their own acting troupe. The young woman still kneeling beside him on the grass took his hand. Henry tightened his grip on her fingers. "Don't leave me here," he begged her. "Who knows but what Algernon will come back for another attempt?"

She returned the pressure of his fingers, leaning closer until he wanted to bury his face in her obvious charms. "I am sure Mr. Bladesworth would not consider such an uncharitable act, sir, my lord."

Call me Henry, you beautiful creature, and let me rest my head on your magnificent bosom, he wanted to say. He closed his eyes instead, thought a moment, and groaned again. " 'I have it, and soundly, too! Help me into some house, Benvolio, or I shall faint.' "

To his intense delight the people standing around burst into applause. What an odd gathering this is, he thought, as Malcolm Bladesworth helped him to his feet, with the beautiful young woman assisting from the other side. He allowed his head to loll against her creamy shoulder, which also smelled of lavender and woman.

"Well, sir, or laddie, or Lord Grayson-whoever-you-are, you know your Shakespeare, too," murmured Bladesworth. "Act three, scene one. Come, Ivy, let's put him into the coach." He directed his words back to Henry. "We have to travel, laddie, but you're coming with us. When you're feeling better, we can sort all this out."

"I am relieved to hear it," Henry said, noting from his viewpoint that the lovely woman had a mole right where her cleavage disappeared into her bodice.

They led him slowly to a shabby coach from another era, one that he had not seen the likes of in his own stables for many years. Painted elaborately on the side in peeling gilt letters were the words, THE BLADESWORTH TRAVELING COMPANY. Actors down on their luck, he thought, as someone opened the door.

Before he tried to figure how they were going to get him up the two steps and inside, the woman stopped. "Mr. Bladesworth, I must change first," she said.

Oh, no, Henry wanted to beg, but he sighed instead, and was rewarded with the touch of her gentle fingers on his face. "I won't be long," she whispered as Malcolm lowered him to the ground again.

He sighed again as she hurried away, and lay there in the grass by the coach, watching as the men loaded the prop wagon.

Everyone worked surely and swiftly, as if they had done this a hundred times before. Benches from the barn were lashed securely to the outside of the wagon, and the rear board raised and chained in place. Still dressed in Elizabethan costume, one of the young men of the company hitched the horses to the wagon traces, and another climbed onto the wagon seat, holding the reins.

After what seemed like half the night to him, the young woman returned to his side. Henry could barely suppress his disappointment. She was dressed sensibly in pelisse and traveling dress, with no sign of the beautiful bosom bared for his viewing pleasure. She knelt by his side and produced a damp cloth that she dabbed carefully around his ear, following the route of the ball.

"Well, my lord, I think you will have a rather lower part to your hair," she suggested finally, a smile in her words. Her voice was low and deep for a woman and sent a pleasurable tingle down his spine. She moved him onto his side and dabbed next at the back of his neck. "I am so sorry for my contribution to your misery," she said.

He touched her hand. "I am sure I will feel right as a trivet in a day or two," he said. "Don't trouble yourself with remorse."

"I should, you know," she said seriously. "It isn't every day that I brain a marquess with a candlestick." She sat back on the grass and smiled at him. "Of course this hasn't been what you would call a regular day."

"I heartily concur," he agreed. "Highly irregular."

Before he could explore any more channels of conversation with her, two of the younger Bladesworths helped him to his feet. The woman climbed into the coach and held out her arms as they laid him across her lap. He sighed with contentment, even as his head throbbed. In another moment the older woman Bladesworth had called Ivy and two other young girls sat down, Ivy sitting with her younger children. The floor was covered with boxes. The marquess was draped across Kate,

Phoebe, and Maria, and covered with a blanket.

"Dreadful awkward of me to put you all out," he said, even as his eyes closed. It was harder and harder to remain awake.

"My lord, we are used to inconvenience," Mrs. Bladesworth replied. "Indeed, I think that next to Shakespeare and Sheridan, it is our specialty. We'll find a bed for you in Leeds, our destination."

"Leeds?" he asked. "Leeds?" That was close to Pinky D'Urst's lair. He laughed softly to himself. I will be within hailing distance of my wardrobe, so carefully packed by Wilding, that ridiculous excuse for a valet, and even more inept highwayman.

The glorious female leaned over him. "Do you know someone there?" she asked, her voice so melodious to his sorely tried ears.

"Not a soul," he lied without a qualm and closed his eyes.

"We will make our fortune in Leeds," Maria confided. "Papa's business partner is to meet him there with the purchase price for a theatre."

"A theatre?" Kate asked.

Phoebe nodded. "It is a wonderful old building, but in much disrepair. We will repair it and perform great plays there." She sighed. "For the past two years we have traveled about between England, Ireland, and Scotland, and sent all our receipts to Papa's partner to invest for us."

"It has been a sacrifice," said Ivy, looking fondly at her daughters, "but none of my dears have complained. Soon we will be able to stay in one place."

"And Gerald will write wonderful lines for all of us," said Phoebe.

"For you, at least," quizzed Maria. "Especially parts where you have to kiss the handsome émigré Frenchman!"

"Mama, she is deliberately baiting me!" said Phoebe with great dignity, and ruined the effect by sticking out her tongue at her sister.

"So she is, my dear, but let me remind you that you opened that conversational line," Ivy replied.

The door closed, and they rumbled off. For all its antiquity, the coach was well-sprung. They rolled along sedately, and the motion was soothing, but not soothing enough to compel Lord Grayson to slumber. He wanted to open his eyes, but they were too heavy.

For several miles the younger children spoke quietly among themselves. Soon Henry heard their deep breathing as sleep won out over the discomfort of sitting upright and traveling country lanes. The beautiful woman did not sleep. In a gesture that must have been absentminded, her fingers caressed his hair, smoothing it down and then running her fingers back through it until he wanted to purr with contentment.

The older woman seated across from her spoke. "My dear Miss Billings, the actions of this day must surely be different from what you envisioned when you woke this morning!"

Miss Billings! His eyes fluttered, but he did not betray himself. Surely this could not be *the* Miss Billings Abner Sheffield had requested he find? But she was speaking.

"Indeed it is!" said Miss Billings. She hesitated, until Ivy Bladesworth assured her that the younger girls were asleep.

"Maria, Phoebe, and I can be trusted with your confidence," she said.

Kate touched Lord Grayson's hair, grateful that he slept. "I was sent to be governess at Leavitt Hall." Her voice hardened. "I discovered in the mail coach from one of the other passengers that Squire Leavitt is a well-known rake. And then Gerald Broussard made his mistake at Wickfield, and I have ended up with you, instead of the Leavitts."

As the coach rumbled through the sleeping countryside, she told the Bladesworths of Papa's death and her need to make her own way in the world. "I don't know what to do, Mrs. Bladesworth," she concluded. "My resources are so limited."

She sighed. "I have a worthless sketch by Giotto in my trunk and a few books."

"And a lovely singing voice," spoke up Phoebe suddenly. "I think you should stay with us."

Stay with them, Lord Grayson thought. Please, Miss Billings, stay with them, and I will find a way to stay, too, even if I have to perjure myself beyond redemption.

"Stay with you?" Kate asked softly. "I am no actress, Phoebe."

"You're a fine lusty widow," chimed in Ivy.

"And no one else can do justice to that corset," teased Maria.

Amen to that, thought the marquess, his eyes still closed.

The four women laughed companionably. Maria reached around her sister to touch Kate's arm. "I thought I would lose all countenance when you bowed so low after your song, and the farmer in the first row swallowed the snuff he was dipping!" She laughed again at the memory.

They were silent a moment, then Ivy spoke up, her voice filled with decision. "You say you are a governess?"

"Yes, ma'am, or so I had hoped to be. I know enough of history and poetry, and a little arithmetic to teach the young. And my Italian is conversable."

"Then teach my young ones," Ivy urged. She looked at her two younger daughters, asleep and jumbled beside her. "They know their Shakespeare, my dear—it's almost mother's milk—but they don't remain in one place long enough to have regular instruction."

"I don't know," hesitated Kate.

"Kate, it is a wonderful notion!" Phoebe agreed, warming to the idea. "You could play the small roles and sing between acts to please Papa, and be our governess, too!"

Ivy sighed. "I fear we could not afford to pay you, but it would be a situation this summer that might allow you time to think about your future and plan a bit." A crease appeared between her eyes and her voice was firm. "I, for one, could not willingly turn you over to the Leavitts. And neither would Malcolm, I'll be bound."

Kate was silent, her hand resting on the marquess's shoulder. "I have discovered that it is not safe to be alone in the world." She ran her hand lightly over the wound above Henry's ear. "You may have to keep the marquess, too, if his life is truly in danger," she mused out loud and then looked at Ivy. "Very well, I will do it."

Phoebe clapped her hands, and Maria, with a meaningful glance at the marquess, told her to hush.

"I will do it if Mr. Bladesworth agrees," Kate amended.

"He will," said Ivy. "Trust me."

Kate smiled and leaned back against the well-worn cushions. The marquess was heavy on her lap, but he was warm and proof against the chill of early summer. Her fingers went to his hair again.

"How sad it must be that Lord Grayson has no one he can trust."

Ivy's voice was stem again. "Imagine a nephew so venal that he would shoot his own flesh and blood."

Phoebe sighed. "I think it is romantic. Gerald should write a play about it."

"...and cast you as Kate Billings, beautiful governess who thumps him with a candlestick," teased Maria.

"It would be a good play," Phoebe insisted. She leaned over the marquess's blanketed legs to peer at Kate, whose face was growing rosy for no accountable reason. "And Kate would fall amazingly in love with him, and they would marry and create a houseful of little heirs who would not want to brain their papa!"

Kate giggled and then grew serious. "It would take a marvelous playwright to compose such a play. Is it a tragedy? A comedy? I hardly know yet." She smoothed down the marquess's hair again. "I wonder why he is not married already. He must be somewhere in his thirties, and I think he is handsome."

You dear girl, thought Henry. Keep speaking so, and soon my head won't ache at all.

"His hair—what there is of it—is a handsome chestnut shade," said Kate. She shrugged. "And if he is a bit over his weight, who cares?" She giggled, her hand to her mouth. "At least he won't be one of those men who is compelled to pad himself here and there to make an impression."

"Yes! Especially there." Maria laughed.

"Maria!" admonished her mother. "You are too vulgar by half!"

Maria turned the full force of her gaze upon her mother and opened her eyes wider. "Mama, *what* do you think I meant?" Ivy uttered an exclamation and resolutely shut her eyes, but she was smiling. In a few minutes Maria and Phoebe arranged themselves against each other with the practiced air of veterans of late-night coach travel. After a few more drowsy words passed between them, they slept as the coach rumbled through the moon-filled summer night.

It was then that she first noticed the even rhythm of Lord Grayson's breathing. Good God, she thought in panic, did he only just now go to sleep? Has he heard all this conversation? She watched him closely for a moment and then gradually relaxed again. Kate, you are entirely too suspicious, she scolded herself. Surely a marquess can be depended upon not to dissemble. She watched him sleep, her own tired eyes taking in the dried blood on his face and the disturbing reality of that bullet path above his ear.

"You are a lucky man, my lord," she whispered out loud. "Another inch …" She couldn't see the ugly lump on the back of his neck where she had struck him with the candlestick. "I hope you will forgive me."

She rested her hand on his shoulder again and closed her eyes.

Forgiven, my dear Miss Billings, he thought. When she was breathing evenly, he opened his eyes. From where his head rested in the crook of her arm, he could see the wonderful profile of her face at rest. Her nose was straight and matter-of-fact and exhibited no tendencies of curving downward to meet a rising chin, like Pinky D'Urst's unfortunate sister. Her lips were full and soft, and he wanted to kiss her, even though his head pounded and his body ached. He contented himself to be cradled in her arms, and tucked in such wondrous proximity to her fine bosom. How grateful I am that you feel such remorse, my dearest Miss Billings, he thought. I am feeling just unscrupulous enough right now to hope that it rebounds to my benefit.

He reflected on the vagaries of fate. If someone had told him that morning, as he mounted his horse and continued his journey toward Pinky and the other inmates at D'Urst Hall, that by nightfall he would be shot in a misguided prank by his former valet who was in league with his own nephew and heir, he would not have believed it. Even less would he have believed that he would promptly fall in love with a governess treading the boards with some shabby traveling troupe.In his mind, even disordered as it was by the events of the day, there was no question that he was in love. He had often wondered what love would feel like, and how he would know. Indeed, as he approached his middle thirties, he had begun to despair over the subject. Was there someone special for him? Other of his friends seem to have tiptoed their way through the delicate business of wooing and stayed on their feet. Why not him? Was he too particular? Had he never given the matter his full attention?

But here he was, looking up at the sleeping face of the woman he loved. It was so simple. He frowned. No, it was not simple; far from it, in fact. Somehow he had to remain with the troupe and woo this luscious woman at his leisure. He sighed. He would be a lucky man indeed if Abner Sheffield, once he got wind of Algie's foolishness, did not set a Bow Street Runner on his trail. He smiled and relaxed as much as he could without waking up his love. I hope I am skillful enough for this little tableau, he thought. And bless her heart, she seems even partial to overstuffed men.

He watched her in the moonlight until his own eyes began to droop. All pretense aside, I shall sleep now, he thought.

6

THEY ARRIVED IN LEEDS with the farmers' carts hauling produce and animals to the city's great open-air markets. Kate woke to the protest of chickens trussed upside down in a nearby cart and the rumbling of Lord Grayson's stomach. She looked down at the man still sprawled across her lap, and he looked up at her, a smile on his face.

"Beg pardon," he apologized. "Hearing all those chickens led me inevitably to eggs—which I prefer poached—and that led to the obligatory rasher of bacon, and then toast with marmalade, and a really fine oolong." His stomach sounded again. "Now, if an aubergine cart or turnip wagon should happen by, there will be no difficulty."

Kate laughed out loud and then looked quickly around her at the Bladesworths, who slumbered on, oblivious to the early morning racket of a market town. Lord Grayson's eyes followed her gaze.

"I think the Bladesworths have different sleeping habits than we do," the marquess whispered. "Not for them the dawn peeking through lace curtains, and the luxury of stretching one's toes and waiting for the maid to lay a morning fire."

Kate sighed. "That does sound wonderful. My legs have quite gone to sleep."

"I am certain that I could sit up," the marquess offered.

Kate held him where he was with a hand on his chest and shook her head. "You would wake up Phoebe and Maria. I can manage. How are you feeling?"

"My head aches," he admitted, but flashed what Kate could only call a winning smile. "It has hurt before and probably will again, but I hope I will not be dealt any more stunning blows by a lady rejoicing in the name of Miss Billings. May I ask, is it Katherine Billings?"

Kate looked at him for a long moment, as if considering her next statement. "You seem to know me," she began cautiously. "How is this?"

Before the marquess could answer her question, Malcolm Bladesworth, his eyes bleary and his hat askew, pounded on the side of the slowly moving carriage. "Rise and shine, everyone," he boomed in his best stage voice. "The Scylla and Charybdis await us."

"This I must see," murmured the marquess, "although my head already feels like clashing rocks. Help me up, my dear." He grasped the strap near Kate's ear, and with her hand under his back, hauled himself up to sit beside her. Phoebe and Maria squeezed closer together and sat rubbing their eyes and exclaiming over their papa's loud voice.

Kate looked at the marquess. He had closed his eyes and appeared a shade paler. "Are you all right?" she asked.

"I think so," he answered after a long pause. "I'll feel better when this coach quits spinning about. Dashed unpleasant." In another moment he opened his eyes one at a time and looked out the window. "So that's the Scylla and Charybdis," he murmured, his look of relaxed amusement at odds with the dried blood crusted on his neck and shirt.

Ivy Bladesworth was awake by now. She shook her little girls awake and prodded the boys sleeping on the coach floor. "Yes, it's an inn. We always stay here in Leeds, mainly, I suppose, because the innkeep is generous about lodging us. He has literary pretensions, as you can tell from the name, and he allows us to perform for him in his sitting room, as part of our keep." She brushed at the wrinkles in her traveling dress. "We will make this our headquarters, at least for now."

The coach followed the prop wagon into the innyard. Phoebe and Maria straightened each other's bonnets. "I hope Papa will let us go with him to the Banner Street Theatre," Phoebe said. "I will stand on the stage and imagine an audience of one thousand."

Kate shuddered. "That makes my blood run cold."

Phoebe patted her cheek. "And you can sing between acts."

"Never!" declared Kate firmly.

The coach rolled to a stop and the young Bladesworths, now wide awake, leaped down before the coachman, their older brother Davy, let down the step. Kate nodded to her Hortensio. "Can you help me with Lord Grayson?" she asked.

With Davy helping him on the outside, and Kate on the inside, and Maria providing encouraging sounds, they helped Lord Grayson from the carriage. The bracing air of early morning brought color rushing to his face. In a moment he could stand by himself, even if he did lean against the coach wheel.

"Much better," he said. "Uh oh—there on the starboard beam."

The innkeeper was bearing down on them, all smiles that turned to a frown when he saw the marquess's bloody shirt. "Think of a good fib," the marquess whispered to Kate as he approached. "My brain is quite gone still."

Kate stepped forward, both hands outstretched. She smiled at the innkeeper and grasped his hand. "I am so glad to see you, sir. We have need of your assistance."

The marquess leaned away from the wheel. "Name's Hal Hampton," he said and managed a self-conscious laugh.

The innkeeper came closer, the suspicion deepening in his eyes. "If this is foul play, lad, I don't want the likes of you in my inn!"

"Oh, la, no," said Kate, clinging to the innkeeper by now. "Some scenery fell on him at the last performance. He was quite insensible, but is much more himself now."

"He won't be requiring a surgeon, will he?" asked the innkeeper, patting Kate's hand and giving her a knowing wink. "There's a good barber just down the road."

Kate shook her head. "All he needs is a bed and a basin of warm water, sir, and if you have some soft cloths, that would be good." She detached herself from the innkeeper and took Hal's arm.

The innkeeper looked Hal over. "I suppose we can arrange that." He nodded to Ivy Bladesworth, who was getting down from the carriage. "You can't be too careful, Mrs. Bladesworth. And isn't everyone talking in Leeds about the foul murder on the Great North Road and the missing body!" Kate felt Hal stiffen under her grasp. "Murder?" he asked. The innkeeper took Hal by the other arm and led him toward the building. "Or something like. Seems a marquess was on his way to visit his friends." He looked around, as if the murderers were lurking among the chickens and geese in his inn yard. "They've found the horse and a bloody riding coat, but that's all. I don't wonder but the runners will be on the trail soon."

"Oh, Lord," said the marquess involuntarily. The innkeeper looked at him.

"How's that?" the man asked. "Say, are you *sure* that was just scenery?"

"Couldn't be more sure of anything," Hal said. He leaned heavily against the innkeeper, who was hard put to remain upright. "It's just that the pain comes and goes."

The innkeeper whistled and hurried faster until Kate had to skip to keep up on the other side of the marquess. The innkeeper led them into the inn, calling to his wife for hot water and towels, as he helped Hal up the narrow stairs. He opened a door at the top of the stairs and helped Hal to the bed.

"There, laddie. I'm sure you'd rather that Mrs. Hampton helped you off with that bloody shirt. My wife will be here in a moment." He looked around the room. "I'm sure you'll be comfortable enough here." He paused at the door then bounded back into the room to stand before Kate. "And what do you do, my dear?" he asked.

"Do, sir?" she asked in surprise. Whatever did the man mean?

"She sings between acts and performs small roles," said Hal from the bed, where he sat with his head in his hands.

"And you?" the innkeeper asked.

"My head hurts so bad at the moment that I cannot remember, my dear keep," Hal said. "Do excuse me while I lie down."

"Of course, laddie, of course. If you need anything, just send your wife to sing out. Sing out!" The innkeeper chortled at his own cleverness and closed the door behind him.

Her eyes wide, Kate sank down into a chair next to the bed. "He thinks we're married!" she exclaimed. "Oh, this is such a bungle!"

"It is, isn't it?" agreed the marquess with a serenity that tweaked her nerve endings. "I promise to be a most conformable husband."

Kate opened her mouth to speak, but the marquess wasn't through. "Let your first official act in that capacity be the removal of my boots."

"I think not," Kate said crisply, her hands on her hips. "I am beginning to suspect that you are a rascal."

The marquess grinned. "According to my own calculations I have not been a rascal in years. In fact I was getting a bit boring, even stodgy. Well, then, if you insist on being missish, send for Malcolm, dear wife, and ask if he has a nightshirt that might fit me. He seems the likely candidate."

Kate stormed to the door, turned back, jabbed her finger in the air at the marquess several times, and flounced from the room. Malcolm Bladesworth was coming up the stairs, baggage in hand, as she stood outside the door, wondering whether to laugh or to cry as she contemplated the ruins of her reputation slithering down about her ankles.

"The landlord thinks I am the marquess's wife," she whispered to Malcolm. "What am I to do?"

Malcolm threw back his head and roared with laughter. "Think of the absurdity, 'my super-dainty Kate.' You've gone from governess to marchioness in less than twenty-fours! I defy anyone to duplicate this feat among the peerage. I do hope Gerald is taking notes for the new play. This one could make our fortunes."

"Malcolm, you are not taking this very seriously!" she protested.

He chucked her under the chin. "My dear Miss Billings, you must learn to be a bit more flexible."

He continued up the stairs, laughing as he went, but turned back to her on the landing. "I have an extra nightshirt. Davy!" he called down the stairs. "Lord Gray … Now, what is he calling himself?"

"Hal Hampton," she offered, her voice frosty.

"My dear Kate, a man could hang icicles on your words," he said mildly and then looked at his son. "Hal Hampton needs a nightshirt and some assistance, Davy. Lively, now."

Davy bounded past her. Malcolm removed a nightshirt that looked as large as a jibsail from his baggage and tossed it to his son, who caught it on the fly, grinned at Kate, and went into the bedroom.

"The marquess is a big man, but I defy even him to fill that nightshirt," Malcolm said. He winked at Kate. "There'll be room in it for you, too, Lady Grayson!"

Kate gasped and blushed as Bladesworth continued down

the hall, laughing until he wheezed. In another moment the landlord was at her elbow with a basin of warm water and towels draped over his arm. "My wife has some powders somewhere for your husband's headache," he said, handing the bowl to her.

I could end this right now, she thought as she accepted the towels and basin. I could declare that the man within is a marquess—*the* marquess—who was supposedly assassinated, and urge him to summon the constable. Then I could set down this bowl, walk out of this inn, and end this charade. I could make my journey to Wakefield and throw myself on the Leavitt's mercy—and then what?

"Are you all right, Mrs. Hampton?"

Kate looked up into the landlord's face. After a long minute she smiled. "I am fine, sir, and my … my husband and I thank you for your kindness. Those headache powders will be much appreciated."

"Excellent!" the keep exclaimed. "And I will direct my wife to bring up some breakfast for you and a bowl of gruel for the invalid."

"Gruel, by all means," Kate agreed, without a twinge of remorse. "Thin, sir, very thin." And I'll make him drink every drop while I eat a poached egg and bacon right in front of him, she thought.

The landlord nodded and hurried down the hall, calling to Malcolm about his first command performance in the downstairs parlor. Kate remained outside the door, waiting for Davy to finish. "Never let it be said that Kate Billings was not flexible," she muttered under her breath. "Besides, Maria is jolly company, and I must see Phoebe act again."

Davy opened the door and motioned her inside, whispering, "He puts up a good front, but I know his head really aches."

"I'll do what I can for him," Kate said quietly. "Perhaps you could hurry up the landlady and her headache powders."

He nodded and clambered down the stairs. Without a sigh

Kate cast all propriety behind her and closed the door. She set the bowl down by the bed, glanced at her charge, and giggled in spite of her mixed feelings.

"You look as though you are drowning in that nightshirt," she said as she raised his head carefully and spread a towel on the pillow.

"Then I savor the experience," he replied. "It's comforting to know that there is someone wider and taller than I in the British Isles."

"You're being ridiculous, Lord Grayson," she began as she dabbed carefully around his ear. "I am certain more women prefer well-fed men to those sprites of fashion who appear rail-thin. Now, hold still."

He did as she said. "Do I take that to mean that you prefer well-padded men, dear wife?"

Kate blushed, set her lips in a firm line, and dug a little deeper around the wound. The marquess yelped. "I am not 'your dear wife,' " she replied. "And I was merely making a harmless observation."

He put his hand up to stop her. "I apologize. But I do need to call you something for the duration of the little farce, for it appears that for propriety's sake you are the wife of Hal Hampton, which, by the way, really is my name, or one of them, at any rate."

Kate sat down and looked at him. "You may call me Kate, I suppose. Only yesterday I was a respectable lady on her way to a governess's post."

"And now you've fallen into a real den of thieves."

She shook her head. "No! I like these people." Kate sighed and dipped the cloth in the water again. "I only hope I know what I am doing." She wiped away the crusted bloodstains on his face. "It appears to me that you're the one in danger."

"Only from women with heaving bosoms and candlesticks," he said promptly.

"Don't remind me!" she said, her face fiery. "Turn over and

let me survey the damage I did. And kindly do not refer to my 'heaving bosom,' Lord Grayson. All of us have some trials in life."

He grinned and obliged her, turning onto his stomach and moving over as an invitation to sit on the bed. Kate sat down, peering close and wincing at the sight of the wound. She dabbed at it until the dried blood was dissolved, and examined the results. "It is but a small cut, my lord. When the swelling goes down, it shouldn't give you any trouble." She touched his neck, her fingers gentle this time. "Well, it might rub against your shirt collar while it is healing, if you are a slave to the fashion of elaborate neckcloths. I am sure the sacrifice of fashion will be only temporary. It wasn't a death blow."

Hal thought of the torture of fashionable excesses that Wilding had put him through since his return from Spain and dismissed them with a grunt. "I can easily forgo the pleasure of seeing myself trussed up like a Ubangi," he said.

Kate nodded. She wrung out the cloth and placed it over the cut. "Now lie there. This should help the swelling." She returned to her chair by the bed, pulling it closer, and folded her hands in her lap. "Now tell me, my lord, how you came to know who I was, and what it all means."

"My lips are sealed until you quit calling me my lord. It's Hal to you, remember?"

"It seems so improper," she protested.

From his stomach Hal managed a glance around the room. "There is nothing proper about any of this, Kate. I insist."

"Oh, very well! Hal!" she exclaimed. "You are exasperating."

"Usually I am compliant to a marked degree and very much a lazy sort of fellow. I was beginning to disgust myself, until I, too, fell in with the Traveling Bladesworths."

Kate laughed, her good humor restored. "I am sufficiently chastised, sir! And didn't Malcolm Bladesworth just abjure me to be more flexible? Now tell me, Hal, and no more putting off. How do you know who I am?"

"We share the same solicitor, my dear. When I told Abner Sheffield I was traveling north to visit my friend Pinky D'Urst outside of Leeds, he asked me to give you a message. He described you, of course, with that wondrous mane of black hair. That was easy. And there is that heaving bosom which you told me not to speak of. The hard part was figuring out what you were doing with the Bladesworths. I had thought you were going to the Leavitts." Hal took off the cloth and turned over onto his back. "Here, good wife, fluff up these pillows. I'm really not a supine sort of fellow when I am conversing with family members."

Flashing him a warning glance, she helped him sit up, reaching across him for the other pillow and plumping it behind him. "I was destined for the Leavitts, but I learned something about Squire Leavitt while I was traveling on the mail coach that made me …" She paused, groping for the right word. "Reconsider."

"And?"

She looked at Hal, considering him. "I've never been raised to speak of such things, sir, but I heard that Squire Leavitt was a noted lecher, and I was afraid." The words came out in a rush. She looked down at her hands, embarrassed at such plain speaking. "It's difficult to be on one's own, sir," she continued, her voice barely audible.

To her surprise Hal reached out and took hold of her hand. "We both seem to be experiencing difficulties on our own. Perhaps it's just as well we combined forces with the Bladesworths."

Her hands were cold and his were warm, and she did feel inclined to not pull away. "I may have still gone to Leavitt Hall, but I made a mistake and got off at Wickfield instead of Wakefield, and there was Gerald Broussard waiting to pick up an actress. I assumed he was from Leavitt Hall, and he assumed I was the actress. The rest you can figure out."

Hal patted her hand and released it. "These strange people

are so persuasive." He sank a little lower on the pillow and closed his eyes. "And so kind." In another moment he was asleep.

Kate watched him, pulling up the covers higher against the room's chill. She put the back of her hand to his forehead. He was warm, but not burning up. Likely he would recover without mishap. Surely this trouble with his heir would be quickly resolved, and he would resume his normal life. And I suppose this whole episode will be something to recount to your friends, Lord Grayson, she thought as she pulled the chair closer. "Are you asleep?" she whispered.

No answer. Drat, she said to herself. I still do not know why Abner Sheffield wanted my attention. Perhaps he found new debts. The thought propelled her from the chair. She paced in front of the window for a lengthy time, then stopped her restless wandering to lean her head against the window frame. "Well, they can't squeeze blood out of a turnip," she said. "I suppose there is debtor's prison." She shuddered and turned from the window.

Hal was awake again and watching her. "Did someone just dance on your grave?" he asked, his voice kind.

She tried to keep her tone light. "No, silly. I was imagining that Mr. Sheffield wanted to tell me that there were more debts, and that I was bound for Newgate." Tears came to her eyes. "Please tell me the worst."

"Sorry I dozed off. Sit down! You make me fidgety," he ordered, but his tone was mild. "Do you still have a Giotto sketch in your possession?"She stared at him. "Yes, I do. Abner told me to toss it on a bonfire somewhere, because it was worthless, but I couldn't do it."

"Thank goodness for that!" Hal exclaimed. "I have glad tidings for you, Mrs. Hampton. Your Giotto is worth a little fortune."

Kate opened her mouth in disbelief and threw herself on her knees by the bed, grasping his arm. "Are you sure?"

"This seems to be the season for confusion. It appears that Abner mixed up your sketch with another and gave you erroneous information. It's only a little fortune, though," Hal assured her. "It would probably only keep my rascally nephew in neckcloths and tight pantaloons for a year or two, but I think it would be enough for you to maintain a frugal household." He watched her reaction. "At least, until you find yourself a husband, my dear Miss Billings."

She bowed her head over his arm and burst into hearty tears. With an effort Hal rested his other hand on her head. Her hair was soft and curled loose on her neck. Touched as never before, he fingered the curls as she sobbed into his arm. How terrifying your future must have appeared, he thought, and how ladylike you were about it.

Someone scratched on the door, and it opened. The innkeeper's wife stood there, holding a covered tray. Kate raised her tear-stained face from Hal's arm.

"No need in carrying on so, lovey. I'm sure he'll be right as a trivet in a day or two!" the woman exclaimed as she set the tray on the bedside table. She winked and poked Hal in the ribs. "Of course, you'll have to go easy on him for a few nights!"

With a groan Kate put her head back down on Hal's arm.

"She's shy about those things," Hal explained. "We've only been married a little while."

The landlady laughed and poked Hal again. "It's the shy ones you have to look out for, gov'nur."

"How well I know," Hal replied fervently, and Kate resisted the urge to bite his arm.

"Here's them powders, now," the landlady said. "When your little lady gets around to it, she can put some in this glass for you, and you'll sleep like a baby."

"Thank you."

The landlady watched Kate another moment. "Do you think she'll be all right?" she asked Hal in a loud whisper.

"I'm sure of it."

When the landlady closed the door behind her, Kate raised her head from Hal's arm. "You are completely unscrupulous, my lord."

"Me?" he asked innocently. "I was merely being an agreeable husband. You will be easy on me, won't you?"

Kate glared at him. "I won't dignify that vulgar remark with a reply." She found the powders and dumped them in the water glass, stirring furiously. "Drink this," she commanded. She thrust the glass at him, then pulled it back. "No, first tell me what my Giotto is worth."

"Somewhere in the neighborhood of four thousand pounds, if I remember right," Hal said.

Kate sank into the chair again.

"If you want to look in my wallet, Abner gave me the name of an art dealer here in Leeds who can verify that amount. He'll probably try to buy it from you. Now don't be such a watering pot! You'll dilute the headache powders," said Hal, reaching for the glass, which was tipped at a precarious angle.

Wordlessly she put her arm carefully around his shoulders and helped him drink the potion, then removed one pillow and eased him down. She sank back into the chair, her eyes on Lord Grayson, but her mind miles away. If I am prudent, I can manage for years, she thought, a smile on her face. I'll never again be at the mercy of such dubious characters as Squire Leavitt.

"This is such good news, Hal," she said at last. "You cannot imagine. If I buy a little place in Kent, I can have a garden, and a cow, and …"

Hal put his hand on her arm. "You don't want to rush into anything, Kate," he said, his voice already starting to slur. His eyelids drooped, and he struggled to keep them open. "Think about it. Please."

Kate was on her feet and over to the bureau. She looked back at the marquess, startled at the intensity of his words. "In your wallet, you say?" she asked. He was asleep, his hand still stretched out toward her. You dear man, she thought. Was ever anyone's news more welcome?

She found the paper in a moment and opened it. "'Socrates Cratch,'" she read out loud. "'Dealer in fine art and gentlemen's estates.'" The direction was unfamiliar to her, but she could ask the landlord. She pocketed the little paper. I can be out of here by nightfall and on my way back to London, she thought.

She picked up the bonnet she had flung aside before she began to tend to Lord Grayson's wounds, and retied the bows firmly under her chin. I can practice such economy and never be dependent on anyone again. The thought felt so good that she said it out loud.

Before she left the room, she went to the bed and stood there, looking down at Lord Grayson, admiring his improbably long eyelashes. Why is it that some men are so blessed? she thought. It hardly seemed fair. She smoothed back the hair from his forehead and noted the shadowy whiskers on his face. "You could use a shave, Lord Grayson," she said softly. "Perhaps I will make that my last official duty as your wife before I fly this coop."

She rested her hand lightly against his cheek. To her great surprise he stirred and kissed her palm, then settled more comfortably in the bed. She stared at him, wondering if he was awake, then decided it was merely a dream. "What can you be thinking?" she asked and shook her head.

She closed the door quietly behind her and hurried down the stairs to see all the Bladesworths assembled in the dining room. Malcolm held out his hand to her. "Come, my dear, and join us!"

Ivy nodded and motioned her into the room. "We are all heading for the Banner Street Theatre in a moment. It will be a family expedition, since we have all worked so hard for this moment. The rest of the company will be there, too. Are you going out, too, my dear?"

Kate accepted the cup of tea that Ivy held out for her. She

took a sip, preparing a lie for these good people and not sure why. Surely the Bladesworths would rejoice at her good fortune. "I thought I would inquire of the landlord for an apothecary so I could purchase some strawberry salve for Lord Grayson's neck." She set down the cup, angered at herself for prevaricating. "I ... I'll be on my way."

"Certainly, my dear," said Ivy. "We will meet you back here with the best news."

"Oh, yes," Kate agreed fervently. "Wonderful news."

The landlord stood in the hall with her trunk. "I'll take it up to your room directly, Mrs. Hampton," he said.

"No, wait," she said and knelt on the floor by the trunk. The Giotto sketch was wrapped in oilcloth and preserved carefully in the bottom. She removed it. "Now you may take the trunk upstairs, sir. But first, can you direct me to Walton Street?"

The landlord gave her directions, and she hurried from the inn, the Giotto clutched in her hand, a smile on her face. I'll be an independent woman by nightfall, she thought.

7

THE OFFICE OF SOCRATES Cratch was in the very center of Leeds, next to the Corn Exchange. It amounted to nothing more than a shopfront to Kate's eyes, having one small, dusty window with tired curtains and the word "Cratch" over the little door in serviceable black letters. Clutching the Giotto to her breast, Kate knocked.

"Come." The voice was barely audible. Kate took a deep breath and opened the door. She was short enough not to have to stoop and was only grateful that Lord Grayson was not present. He probably would have banged his forehead on the sill and laid up yet another wound to her account.

A man as little and old as his office sat at a desk several sizes too large for him. His pince-nez drooped on the end of his nose. When he pushed it up and looked at her, his eyes seemed magnified as an insect's. His tidiness was at odds with the clutter about him in the cramped office. He was as neat as a pin.

Kate stepped forward, careful to avoid the piles of papers that formed a path from door to desk. "Mr. Cratch?"

He nodded, rose, and extended a hand. "The very same, my

dear." For all his apparent age, he twinkled surprisingly young eyes at her. "It has been, by my calculations, roughly two centuries since someone of your obvious pulchritude walked through that door. Do sit down, if you can find a space."

Kate stared at him and then laughed. "La, sir, you cannot be a day over eighty-five," she said, teasing in the same vein and wondering, at the same time, when she had suddenly become so saucy. It must have something to do with association with the Bladesworths. I am becoming flexible, Malcolm, she thought, and shook Cratch's hand.

He glared at her and then smiled to ameliorate the effect. "You are an astute observer, Miss …"

"Miss Billings," she supplied.

"I am eighty-three this month, you flippant baggage! It only seems like two hundred years. Ah, yes, move those books and sit down. Billings, did you say? Not Katherine Billings?"

Kate could only stare again. Why is it that everyone in this part of England seems to know my name? "Yes, Mr. Cratch. How do you know my name?"

He was looking at the rolled-up oilskin in her lap. "I'll even wager I know what is in that packet, Miss Billings. Stout angels bumbling through an Italian sky!" His voice was triumphant. He bowed to an imaginary audience and sat down again. "I rest my case."

Kate blinked. North England appeared to be populated entirely by eccentrics. "The mystery continues, sir," she said. "How do you know all these things? Do you read tea leaves or palms?"

He laughed and squirreled around his desk until he unearthed a sheet of paper. "I received this missive yesterday from my friend Abner Sheffield, who, I believe is your late father's solicitor, and also a surveyor of antiques?"

Kate nodded, mystified.

Down went the spectacles on Cratch's nose. He peered over them at the letter. "Among other tidings Abner assures me that

I might be blessed with a visit from a lady named Katherine Billings." He looked at her. "Provided that a certain Lord Grayson located her. I see that he must have. My dear friend and colleague Mr. Sheffield assured me that you would have something I was looking for, a sketch by Giotto."

He said the name lovingly, pronouncing it correctly like an Italian, and then gestured across the desk. "Come, come, my dear Miss Billings. Unroll it."

She did as he said, unrolling it carefully, and then standing back to look at it again herself. The angels still hovered over the barely roughed-in forms of two shepherds sleeping on the ground. The background was sketched in more prominently and displayed three Wise Men on Italian-looking camels.

Socrates Cratch clapped his hands in glee. "Ah, this is a treasure!" He pointed to the camels. "The actual mural does not contain these beasts, but Giotto mentioned them in one of his letters. Art scholars had been sure they did not exist." He clapped his hands again. "Miss Billings, this is a prize."

"My father gave it to me for my birthday," Kate said softly, taking back every distressing thought that had circulated through her brain about her father and his frippery ways, as far as art was concerned. "Indeed, it was his last gift to me."

Cratch nodded, his eyes kind. "Mr. Sheffield alluded to something about that in his letter. My condolences, Miss Billings, but I trust you will discover that you have been well provided for by your father."

After another long look at the sketch, Cratch rolled it up and handed it back to her. He sat at his desk again and clasped his hands together. "I am prepared to pay you handsomely for it. There is a pre-Renaissance scholar in Belgium who has a companion sketch, without camels." He leaned toward her across the huge desk. "Now, if this were the time of the Borgias, he would probably have you poisoned, to obtain his sketch." He laughed when she gasped. "But as it is, he is willing to bow to modern convention and pay you four thousand two hundred fifty pounds."

Kate leaned back from the force of the news. "That much!" she breathed. "Oh, Mr. Cratch, you can't imagine what that means to me!"

"I think I can, Miss Billings," he replied. "A lady of your obvious quality who traipses across town without an escort is likely down on her luck. You should be able to live quite comfortably on the interest, if you know how to keep household."

"Oh, I do," she declared and handed the sketch back across the desk. "Sir, I will sell it to you."

The little man clapped his hands again. "Well done, Miss Billings!"

In the matter of an hour's business the deed was done. For all his age and apparent decrepitude, Socrates Cratch let no flies rest on him. He produced official-looking documents, and she signed them after a careful reading, which had Cratch nodding his head in approval. "You're no ninnyhammer, Miss Billings," he chortled. "I expect you will be wise with this money."

"I must be, sir," she said quietly as she looked up from the document at long last and reached for the pen.

After more applause from Cratch she sat back while he scurried next door to the Corn Exchange, returning in surprisingly short time with the money. He handed it to her, eyeing the reticule on her arm.

"It'll never all fit in there, Miss Billings." He leaped up from the desk, energized by his good fortune, and rummaged in another corner of the tiny office. He produced a small canvas bag, covered with the dust of years. Kate coughed as he brushed off the bag and the dust rose in circles about the room.

"There you are, my dear. Plop the ready in the bag, and for the Lord's sake, look out for cutpurses!"

Kate did as she was told. "It will be safe as houses, Mr. Cratch," she assured him. "I intend to be very careful about my future." She held out her hand to him. "Thank you."

He shook it and held the door open for her. "Anytime you have another Giotto sketch, you need only remember Socrates Cratch. I plan to be here at least another one hundred years until 1918!"

Kate hurried back to the inn. It was noon and she was hungry, but she ignored the rumblings in her stomach. She thought about stopping at a tea house, but she had never taken a meal unescorted before and did not now. As she hurried along the crowded market streets, she thought about the lie she had told the Bladesworths and resolved to ease her mind in that regard. She asked directions of the nearest apothecary from a constable. It would only take a moment to buy the strawberry ointment she had claimed as the reason for her sojourn and return to the inn.

The apothecary shop was empty, and the druggist inclined to be garrulous. He commented upon the weather, the state of York's economy, the trouble with magistrates, and the difficulties of getting a really close shave from a barber while he blended a pot of the ointment. He handed the jar to her over the tall counter, and she stood on tiptoe to reach it.

"Of course, for all my troubles, I'm in better trim than that poor marquess, ain't I?"

Kate's hand froze on her reticule. "Poor marquess?" she managed finally as she removed a coin.

"Have you been living in a cave, missy?" he asked and leaned over the counter. "It seems a bloody riding coat and a riderless horse turned up near Wickfield. Belongs to a marquess, a blighted cove name of Lord Grayson, some aristo from Kent who lives in London." He took her money. "A Bow Street Runner has already been in here this morning, asking me to check with everyone who buys anything that might be used to doctor a wound."

Kate dropped the ointment in the satchel with the money.

"Heavens, sir," she said faintly. "Do they think he's alive and hidden somewhere?"

He shrugged. "Who knows? I think he's dead under some bush."

Kate turned to the door, hoping that the light in the shop was dim enough to hide the paleness of her complexion.

"One moment, miss!" the druggist called.

She stopped, rooted to the spot, then turned slowly on wooden legs.

"Say now, what are you using that ointment for?" he demanded, his brows drawing together in one line.

Kate resisted the urge to pick up her skirts and sprint from the store. She raised her chin and stared back at him, hoping that her heart really wasn't leaping about visibly in her chest. "I have a rash," she declared.

"Where, missy?" he insisted, his eyes boring into her.

"I refuse to tell you, sir," she said, her voice frosty, her knees knocking together.

To her relief he burst into loud laughter and winked at her. Kate fled the shop. She walked briskly, forcing herself not to look over her shoulder at Bow Street Runners, real or imagined, who were bearing down on her in platoons. They were probably circulating about Leeds, asking everyone if they knew the whereabouts of persons only recently arrived from Wakefield who might have seen something. It was only a matter of time before they arrived at the Scylla and Charybdis and questioned the landlord.

HAL WOKE UP TO an empty room, which suited him. His bladder was full to bursting. He sat up cautiously, waiting for his head to begin booming again. It was silent this time; there was only the threat of a dull ache by his ear and on the back of his neck. He stood up slowly, ready to grab the bedpost if the room started to revolve.

It did not. "Good," he said out loud, then knelt down as

though on eggshell knees to hunt for the chamber pot.

When he finished his business and slid the pot under the bed again, he was glad to crawl back between the sheets. I am either weak with hunger, he thought, or still not up to my best effort yet. I can only pray that when my darling Kate Billings and I eventually marry, she will not ever feel the need to thump me with a candlestick. I shall be a most compliant husband and lover.

The thought pleased him as nothing else had before. Making love to Kate Billings, no, Kate Tewksbury-Hampton, Lady Grayson, would be a most agreeable occupation. Hal chuckled.

I have saved myself through eight years of Spanish service for the king, and onerous imprisonment, holding out for marriage with someone I love, and not someone my family appoints. Married love is a modern notion, he thought. I have seen too many of my friends marry those chosen for them and then cheat without a qualm. Whatever the faults of my character, I am not a hypocrite.

He settled himself comfortably in the bed, pillow behind his head, hands folded over his stomach. There was no denying that he had been first attracted to her beauty. Lying in her lap all night, miserable beyond belief, he had still wanted to touch her bosom to see if it felt as soft as it looked. And when she leaned over him that morning to get the other pillow to prop behind his head, her amplitude had brushed his chest. He had wanted to grab her right then, except that his head pounded.

He thought of Amanda Braithwaite, his fiancée of eight years ago, who had waited for several years through his imprisonment, then given up and married another. She, too, was a beautiful woman. "But I was never tempted to make mad, impetuous love to her. Why is it?" he asked out loud.

There was no answer. He closed his eyes, a smile on his face. If it is not beauty, it must be character. He frowned and turned on his side, considering this new puzzle. No one could deny that Amanda had possessed furlongs and furlongs of character.

What was the difference? He considered Katherine Billings and then knew the answer to his riddle. It was her gallantry that held him captive. Here she was, poor and unescorted, and he wanted to protect her. Lord Grayson, who hadn't lifted a finger on anyone's behalf since his return from Spain, was ready to exert himself for a woman he hardly knew.

"Katherine Billings," he mused out loud, lingering over her name as over a good port after dinner. "You are a brave woman. I used to possess that quality. Perhaps I shall again."

Then another thought intruded, an unwelcome one that brought a frown to his face. Why the deuce did I ever tell her about the Giotto? he thought. So much for my plotting. She will be gone by nightfall.

He thought about possible solutions to this predicament, worrying it around in his head until it began to ache again. "This will never do," he said at last, closed his eyes resolutely, and kept them slammed shut until he slept.

Kate returned to the Scylla and Charybdis, hungry and out of breath hurrying from imaginary Bow Street Runners. She came into the inn cautiously, looking about her for suspicious characters. She peered into the taproom, but there was only a mild-looking young man thoughtfully nursing a pot of ale and staring out the window. This will never do, she thought. I am turning into a worrywart for nothing. I will be out of here by evening.

She started up the stairs, hoping for a moment to lie down before the Bladesworths returned and then stopped. She had no idea which rooms had been allotted to Phoebe and Maria, and she was not about to go back to Lord Grayson and tell him to move over so she could rest. The thought made her blush. She looked back down the stairs, toying with the idea of asking the landlady about the room arrangements. She abandoned that notion. It would appear suspicious in the extreme if the wife of Hal Hampton chose not to return to her husband's room. "What a bumble broth this is," she murmured out loud.

As she stood, hesitating, on the staircase, the landlady came from the kitchen, a tray in her hands. The woman, her hair frazzled about her face from the heat of the cooking stove, smiled and gestured with the tray.

"Mrs. Hampton, this is for your husband. Surely he feels like eating by now."

If he doesn't, I will, Kate thought as she accepted the tray with a smile. "You're so good to us," she said.

" 'Tis nothing, nothing at all," said the landlady. "I peeked in your room a few minutes ago, and there he was sitting up, with a deck of cards on the bed. I think he's ready for something besides gruel and sympathy." She winked at Kate. "But do go easy on him, lovey!"

Kate blushed and hurried up the steps as the landlady laughed. She tapped on the door, then opened it.

Lord Grayson looked up from the cards. "Ah ha! Food! I seem to remember food. What ho, good Kate?"

Kate set the tray on the chair by the bed while she scooped up the cards and then set it on his lap. "You'll have to share it, Lord Grayson," she said.

"Hal," he reminded her.

"Very well, then, Hal." Kate sat in the chair beside the bed and took a good look at Lord Grayson's head. There was no new blood from the wound by his ear, and the swelling seemed to be going down on the back of his neck. While he pounced on the slices of crisply cooked mutton with cries of delight, she took the strawberry ointment from the canvas bag and applied some to the back of his neck.

"There, now. That should help," she said and accepted the half-eaten plate of food from the marquess. She looked at it dubiously. "Are you sure you've had enough?"

"Positive," he said, as he grinned and slid back down in the bed. "Kate, you must look on this whole experience as high adventure."

"Malcolm tells me to be flexible," she said as she shoved

aside convention and ate the rest of the marquess's dinner. "Delicious."

Lord Grayson was observing her, and his expression was quixotic. "Well?" he demanded at last when she set the tray aside. "Well? Did you locate Sheffield's art appraiser?"

She nodded and touched the canvas bag at her feet. "Oh, Hal, he paid me 4,250 pounds. Imagine!" Kate laughed out loud. "When the Bladesworths return, I will thank them for their many kindnesses and take the next mail coach south."

"Oh."

Kate peered at the marquess. "That's all you can say?"

"Delighted for you."

Exasperated, Kate leaped to her feet and took a turn about the room, stopping before the bed. "You didn't really think I would remain here with the Bladesworths?" she asked when he said nothing.

"Well, I had hoped you would," he replied. "Besides all that, what will the landlady think when you leave me? She will lose all faith in young love."

Kate stamped her foot. "Lord Grayson! This is all a great fiction!"

Pointedly Lord Grayson turned his face to the wall. "This is our first quarrel," he said.

Kate stared at his back. "You are so provoking!" she exclaimed.

No reply.

There was a knock at the door. The landlady came into the room, carrying a tray with a can of hot, soapy water, a shaving brush, and razor, which she held out to Kate. Exasperated with herself, Kate took it.

"He'll feel much better after a good shave, Mrs. Hampton," said the landlady. She picked up the luncheon tray. "How long have you two dears been married?"

Kate took a deep breath, determined to confess. "You need to understand …"

"One week," came the voice from the bed.

Kate stopped in surprise. Would this man never quit?

"One quite splendid week," Lord Grayson amended.

The landlady sighed. "Summer is such a wonderful season for lovers." She was still sighing as she left the room.

Lord Grayson turned around. He sat up, caught the towel that Kate threw at him, and winked at her.

"I think I will slit your throat," she hissed as she lathered up his face.

"My dear, that would be so rude," he said serenely from under the shaving lather.

She took up the razor and sat on the bed. He winked at her again, and she burst out laughing.

"Much better!" he observed. "No sense in getting lathered up over a farce that surely can't continue much longer."

"You are so right," she agreed and turned his head to one side so she could begin. "I will put this all down to experience. Perhaps I will even write a guide for young ladies on how to avoid the pitfalls of traveling alone on the mail coach! Hold still now."

She shaved his face in silence, admiring, despite her irritation, Lord Grayson's rather fine, straight nose, and the pleasing way his mouth seemed to curve in a natural smile. Even with lather on it, it was a handsome face. She wondered again why he wasn't married. "It seems a pity," she said, speaking without realizing it.

"What does?" he asked as she wiped the lather off his face.

"Was I talking out loud?" she asked. "I was merely wondering how you've managed to escape Parson's Mousetrap."

Lord Grayson took the towel from around his neck and tossed it toward the door. "I was wondering that same thing about you."

Kate returned to the chair and smiled, her charity restored. "That's easy, my lord. Who on earth wants a woman with no dowry?"

By God, I do, he thought. You could come to me barefoot and in a shift, and it would be enough. "Surely you exaggerate," he protested, keeping his voice light.

"No, I do not," she assured him. "Nothing scares off a man faster than the news that the cupboard is bare."

"This doesn't speak well of my sex," he protested.

"It hardly matters," Kate replied, waving away his objections. "But I asked my question first. If you had a wife, my lord, and children, your nephew wouldn't be taking pot shots at you on the Great North Road."

"No, he wouldn't, would he?" the marquess agreed. "I was engaged once to a lovely lady." He chuckled and put his hands carefully behind his head. "It was all a wretched plot between her family and mine, one of those cradle conspiracies. Don't laugh! They let me in on it only at the last minute, when they couldn't keep it silent any longer, and they needed my signature."

Kate clapped her hands, completely diverted. "You can't be serious."

"Well, perhaps I am poking a little fun. But that was what it seemed like to me. It seemed that I woke up one morning after a night of too much whisky to read an announcement in the paper with my name in it. She even picked out the ring." He chuckled at the memory. "And stuck it right through my nose."

Kate laughed and shook her head. "You were entirely too complaisant, my lord!"

"Yes, wasn't I?" he agreed. "There was only one thing to do, and I owe my salvation to Napoleon. I went thankfully to war and eventually landed in prison. Praise God from whom all blessings flow! I did have the decency to help my men escape one at a time. It hardly seemed sporting for me to keep them incarcerated because I had no backbone."

Kate could only stare at him, her mouth open. "I do believe you are serious," she said at last.

"Never more so," he replied, his voice firm. "Dratted thing

was, she hung on for three years, pledging undying love and loyalty to the family fortune, I think. The week I got news of her marriage to another—my first lieutenant who escaped, by the way—the coast was clear. Funny how that worked out."

"But, why?" Kate asked finally when the silence stretched out. "My lord, you are a marquess. Surely you can do what you want."

"I wish it were so, Kate," he said. "You're overlooking family obligations and all that. I have observed that there is something about a title that brings out the worst in one's relatives. Of course, when I returned from Spain finally, they washed their hands of me, and only tolerate me because I bail them out of scrapes and keep them a step or two ahead of financial ruin."

Kate touched his arm. "Here I am, bemoaning the fact that I am alone in the world."

"Permit me one more pomposity, my dear. Being a marquess is a damnable business. I envy you your freedom." He patted her fingers, and she drew her hand away. "I think I'll cast my lot with the Bladesworths for a while yet, as long as it isn't too much of an exertion. Perhaps you could, too, as a favor to me."

She couldn't think of anything to say. When she did not respond, the marquess closed his eyes. When he was breathing evenly, Kate took off her shoes and curled up in the chair, tucking her feet under her. How odd, she thought. Here I have been feeling sorry for myself because things are far from perfect. At least I haven't a passel of relatives badgering me for money and shooting me to inherit.

She rested her chin on her hand. Where are the Bladesworths? she asked herself. The room filled with the shadows of deep afternoon as she sat thinking of their eccentricity and kindness. She knew she should still feel impatient to be off, but the thought of traveling alone again kept her from slumber.

Dusk settled on the room. The marquess sighed and changed position, groaning softly as he turned over. Kate reached out and touched the back of her hand to his neck. He was still too warm, but not as feverish as before. He should be fine by tomorrow, she thought.

But where are the Bladesworths? Kate got to her feet and stretched.

"Light the lamp, Kate," came the voice from the bed.

"You are so quiet, my lord!" Kate said, startled. "I didn't realize you were awake."

She lit a lamp on the bureau by the door and brought it to the bedside stand. Without a word she put her hand on the marquess's forehead and reached for the remaining headache powders. Lord Grayson put his hand over the glass.

"No, Kate. They make me drowsy. I am worried about the Bladesworths," he said simply. "Just sit by me and I'll feel better."

She did as he said, perching on the edge of the bed. He edged closer to her hip, as if drawing comfort from her presence, and she hadn't the heart to move away. She rested her hand on his chest. "I am sure they are all right."

"Then why do they not return?" the marquess fretted. "I fear something is wrong."

"Surely not," she said without conviction. "What could be wrong?"

They sat close together in silence. At last Kate got up and went to the window. The lamplighter was finishing his rounds on the street. She watched him shoulder his ladder and move away into the growing darkness toward another street.

As she stood by the window, hugging her arms, she saw the Bladesworths. They walked slowly, heads down, as if every step hurt. The younger Bladesworths, who had started out skipping beside their parents, plodded along, too, as though they had added forty years to their lives since that morning. Kate nearly opened the window to call to them, but there was something about their slow progress that brought an icy chill to her heart. She returned to the bed and sat down, her hand on Hal's shoulder. She shook him.

"I am awake," he said, protesting in that mild tone she was becoming familiar with. "What is it?"

"It's the Bladesworths." She leaned closer. "I fear something has gone terribly wrong, Hal."

He took her hand and held it in a firm grip. "We'll soon know, won't we?"

In a few moments they heard the Bladesworths on the stairs. Hal tightened his grip on her fingers. Someone knocked and the door opened.

Phoebe, white faced, ran into the room first. She threw herself down by Kate and burrowed her head in Kate's lap, sobbing. Kate's arms went around the weeping girl. Soon Maria was beside her, her tears mingling with her sister's. Hal patted her head, and then gripped Kate again, this time on her arm.

Kate bowed her head over the sobbing girls. "My dears, what can be the matter? Surely it is not the end of the world?"

"I fear it is, Kate," came Malcolm Bladesworth's voice from the doorway. "I fear it is." His voice had none of that theatrical brilliance she had already come to recognize. There was bitterness that made Kate grasp Hal's hand, even as his grip tightened.

Malcolm came into the room, Ivy beside him, her face a mask of shock.

"Good God, man, speak out," said Hal, his voice urgent.

It was a moment before Bladesworth could conquer the struggle within him that was so visible on his expressive face. "My partner has lost all our money. We haven't a farthing to buy the Banner Street Theatre." His voice shook. Ivy reached up and touched his face. He kissed her fingers, his eyes bleak.

"My dears, we are ruined."

8

PHOEBE BURST INTO LOUDER sobs. Tears in her own eyes, Kate kissed her and rested her cheek against the young woman's curls. "Oh, Malcolm," was all she could say.

On feet made of lead, Bladesworth crossed the room and sank heavily into the chair by Hal's bed. Without a word Ivy curled up in his lap and closed her eyes. He rested his hand on her hair, his eyes far away beyond the distant wall. Gerald and the little girls came into the room, shut the door, and sat on the floor.

"What happened, man?" Hal managed at last, his own voice unsteady.

It was a long moment before Malcolm could speak, and even then each word was a struggle. "We stopped at Crossett Row for Mr. Dawkins, who owns the theatre." Bladesworth kissed the top of Ivy's head, as if to get strength to continue. "I cannot believe how excited we were!"

The bitterness in his voice filled the room to overflowing. The girls sobbed louder. Ivy put her fingers on his lips for a moment, and then he continued, each word dragged from him.

"We waited all day for my partner to appear. Lord Grayson,

if you could have seen us, measuring the floor, calculating how much paint and gilt we would need for the walls! Oh, God, it tears me!"

He bowed his head over Ivy, his misery too great to continue. Gerald Broussard stepped out of the shadow by the door. His face wore a stricken expression so at odds with the brightness of his personality that Kate could only look away. He continued, his voice subdued, but under control.

"That … that infamous villain sent Monsieur Bladesworth a letter that arrived only an hour ago. He lost everything in bad investments."

"Everything?" Hal asked in disbelief.

"Everything."

"And he had not the courage to tell me in person!" Malcolm burst out. "He sent a letter!" He spit out each word as though it were poison.

As if on cue, the girls sobbed louder. Kate patted them, looking at Hal in mute appeal. Hal sat up, but did not relinquish his hold on Kate's arm.

"Where is the rest of your company, Malcolm?" he asked, more by way of diversion than from any desire to know.

Malcolm shook his head. "When that infamous letter arrived, they informed me that they could no longer stay."

"It is not their fault," Ivy whispered, sitting up on her husband's lap and running her hand up and down his arm. "They have to earn a living, too. I, for one, do not blame them."

Malcolm snorted. "I divided among them the receipts from the performances at Wickfield, so we truly are penniless." He sighed heavily. "I wonder if our landlord will be so generous when he realizes I cannot even pay this night's bill?"

"I can pay it," said Hal quietly. "Would to God I thought I dared contact Abner Sheffield for more, but as things stand with my nephew Algernon, I dare not. But I'll pay your shot here. I have enough for that."

They were all silent then. Gerald Broussard came closer and

sat on the end of the bed. Kate watched him. "You remained," she said. "Why?"

Gerald only smiled and looked down at the floor. "These people are not so easy to leave, as you may discover. Besides, Kate, I have nowhere else to go."

Kate could think of nothing to say. She looked down, too, embarrassed to meet Broussard's frank gaze, or run the risk of seeing the sorrow in Malcolm's eyes. I know there is still one more mail coach this evening, she thought, and despised herself for thinking it. She glanced at the canvas bag of money on the bureau, hoping that no one would call attention to it and ask her what she had. That's my future, she thought. She said nothing.

In another moment Ivy got off her husband's lap. She held out her arms to Phoebe and Maria and walked with them to the door. "Come girls. Perhaps things will seem better after a good night's sleep."

Gerald touched Phoebe's arm as she passed him, and blew her a kiss. The young woman managed a smile that reached no farther than her lips before it trembled and vanished. The other Bladesworths followed Ivy from the room, shutting the door quietly behind them. Hal propped a second pillow behind him and motioned Gerald into the chair.

"What will they do?" he asked, his voice still low, as though they were listening outside.

Gerald shook his head. "We've been through tough times. It is the way of actors. But this time ..." His voice trailed off. "I wish I knew." He leaned back and closed his eyes.

Suddenly the door swung open. With an oath Gerald leaped to his feet. Kate looked up in surprise as Malcolm bounded into the room, his finger to his lips. Ivy followed at his heels, her eyes wide with fear. She ran to Kate and pressed one of Malcolm's handkerchiefs into Kate's hands.

"Quick! Wind this around the marquess's head to hide the bullet track!"

Kate grabbed the handkerchief and wound it around Hal's head, neatly covering his ear. "What on earth?" he began and then stopped.

In the door stood the young man Kate had noticed in the taproom earlier that afternoon. He was neatly dressed in plain, serviceable clothes, but something about him, perhaps the nicety of his neckcloth or the rakish tilt to his hat, proclaimed London. Maybe it was the confident, almost arrogant way he walked across the room to Malcolm, who was standing in front of Kate as she tucked the end of the handkerchief into itself, shielding her actions.

"I am so glad you have arrived," the man said, holding out his card. When no one took it, but only stood watching him, he announced himself. "My name is Will Muggeridge. I am a runner, and I come to you from Bow Street." His tone was apologetic, regretful even. "I hate to disturb you at this late hour, but the landlord tells me you were near Wickfield last night."

He came closer. Kate rested her hand on Hal's shoulder, and he reached up and covered her fingers with his own. In a moment she felt him slide his signet ring onto her finger and turn the crest around. She slid her hand behind his neck and under the edge of his nightshirt, praying that the runner's attention was on Malcolm.

Muggeridge addressed Malcolm, who sat in the chair Broussard had vacated. He appeared at ease, affable, as he patted his lap and Ivy sat down again. He stretched out his legs as though he sat in his own sitting room. "Ah, yes, we performed *Taming of the Shrew* last night in that village. The natives are receptive to Shakespeare, my good man."

Muggeridge stretched his thin lips across his teeth in the appearance of a smile. "I am relieved to know that, sir," he said. "I have a matter of some gravity to discuss with you."

Malcolm waved his hand in a broad gesture. "Say on, sir." Muggeridge pocketed his card again. "I am interested in the whereabouts of one Lord Grayson, of Grayson, Kent, whose riderless horse was found near Wickfield last night. The saddle, I might add, had blood upon it."

Ivy gasped and covered her mouth with her hand. Malcolm clucked his tongue. "Dear, dear, sir. It sounds like dirty work to me. How does this concern us?"

"I am wondering if you may have seen anything suspicious in Wickfield that night. We have reason to suspect that the marquess has been abducted by his valet and is being held captive for a ransom."

"That would be the most productive thing my valet ever did, then," Hal whispered to Kate, his lips barely moving.

Malcolm looked at Gerald, who shrugged. "I saw nothing, monsieur," Broussard said.

"And you, sir?" The runner was looking at Hal now. He came closer to the bed. "Have you been injured?"

Hal put his hand to the back of his neck and winced. "This comes from stumbling around backstage in the dark, my dear Mr. Muggeridge."

"He is such a clumsy dolt," Malcolm added, his voice filled with exasperation. "I do not know why we keep him in the company, except that he is a relative." He clapped his hands together. "We do not wish to waste your time. Perhaps you wish to question my daughters, Mr. Midden?"

"Muggeridge," said the runner patiently, his eyes on Hal. "Your daughters will keep, sir. I am looking for a tall man, with thinning hair. He is plump and inclined to be lazy."

Hal gave a start, and Kate pinched his shoulder.

Malcolm struck his palm on his hand. "I'd never have such a slow fellow in my troupe, sir!"

The runner only smiled, his eyes still on Hal, who sighed and removed a pillow, lowering himself back to the bed. Kate sat beside him.

The man looked at his fingernails. "I hear around Leeds that your little scheme to buy a certain theatre has fallen through.

You sound like a man in need of money, sir, if I may be so crass." He looked at Hal again. "Comfortable, sir?" he asked, his tone so unctuous that Kate itched to slap him.

"I'm tired," Hal complained. "Do wish you would go bother someone else."

"In good time, sir. Your name?"

"Hal Hampton."

"Hampton. Hampton. That seems to be one of the names of the gentry mort I am looking for, Henry Tewksbury-Hampton."

"Small world," Hal said, his eyes closing. "However, mine is Harold, not Henry."

"Oh, is it?" After another long minute the runner turned his attention back to Malcolm. "The man who engaged Bow Street's services is offering a tidy reward for any news of Lord Grayson's whereabouts."

Malcolm raised his eyebrows in inquiry.

"Five hundred pounds, sir. It wouldn't buy you a theatre, but it would see you on your way again."

Under her hand Kate felt Hal stiffen. Malcolm whistled softly. "Five hundred pounds?" he asked, his voice reverential. "Just for news of some fubsy layabout?"

Kate looked at Malcolm, her heart in her throat. Good God, she thought, I believe he is considering it. He will surrender Hal to the runner and claim the reward. And how do any of us know that the runner has been sent by Sheffield? It could be Algernon, trying to locate him so he could kill him. She moved involuntarily, but Hal gripped her fingers again and forced her to stay where she was. She couldn't look at Malcolm.

Malcolm ushered Ivy to her feet again and stood up. He clapped his arm around the runner, gave him a quick shake that almost lifted the smaller man off the ground, and released him. "My good man, I would love to help you, I really would, but I haven't the slightest information that could be of any possible benefit."

Kate let out her breath slowly. She put her free hand to her cheek, feeling the color there, ashamed that she ever considered for even a moment that Malcolm Bladesworth would betray a man for money, no matter how badly he needed it.

The runner nodded and showed all his teeth in what only the truly charitable would call a smile. He turned his attention back to Hal. "You, then, sir." He brought the lamp closer to Hal's face, standing over him and looking down for such a lengthy time that the marquess opened his eyes.

The runner set the lamp back on the bedside table. "Sir, you certainly fit the description of the man I am looking for. And you have the same name, or one of them. How odd."

Hal raised himself up on one elbow. "If I were the marquess, you don't really think I would be so slow as to use the same name, do you?"

"That might be just the thing you would do," the runner replied. "Sir, I wonder if I could observe the extent of your injuries. Pardon me, madam, but would you move?" he asked Kate.

It would have been an easy matter for her to step aside. The runner could unwind the handkerchief and discover the bullet wound. He would have his marquess, and she could be on her way back to London. Instead she clutched Lord Grayson's hand to her breast, ignored his appreciative sigh, and took a deep breath. She caught Malcolm's approving glance and found her strength.

"Sir! I beg you! This is my husband, and I wish you would leave him alone! His head aches."

The runner blinked. "This is your husband?" he asked, his voice filled with disbelief.

"Yes," she snapped. "Didn't the landlord tell you downstairs that this room was taken by Mr. and Mrs. Hal Hampton? We are part of the Bladesworth troupe." Tears came to her eyes. "Though I suppose we will have to leave the troupe, too, now that Mr. Bladesworth cannot buy the theatre. Was there ever such a dilemma?" She threw herself down on the marquess's chest, wrapping her arms around him and sobbing into the cavernous folds of Malcolm Bladesworth's nightshirt.

Hal's hand came up and caressed the back of her neck as she lay sprawled across his chest. He kissed the top of her head. "There, there, my dearest Kate. I'll be all right soon." He sighed, and his voice caught in a little moan. "Mr. Muggeridge, could you hand me that glass of headache powders?"

The runner put his hands on his hips. He stared down at the marquess, his lips tight together in a thin line. After Kate slipped the signet ring off her finger and left it under Lord Grayson's back, she ran her hand over his face as he kissed her fingers, and nestled her hand by his neck. The marquess put his arms around her, holding her tight.

"Muggeridge, we wish to be left alone now." He kissed Kate again. "Kindly oblige us, and take the Bladesworths with you as you close the door. Quietly, please. My head is pounding."

"Very well," said the runner, biting off his words and looking around him. "You won't have any objections if I remain in the vicinity?"

Malcolm clapped him on the shoulder again. "It's a free country, laddie. I wish we could help you, truly I do."

Without another word, the runner stalked from the room. Malcolm rolled his eyes after him and motioned for Ivy and Gerald to follow. Kate looked up from the marquess's ample chest. Bladesworth put his finger to his lips and winked. "Good night, my dears," he boomed as he closed the door behind him.

Hal groaned. "That voice!"

Kate sat up quickly, straightening her clothes. "You didn't need to kiss me so many times," she protested.

The marquess reached under his back, pulled out his signet ring and dropped it in her lap. "It seemed what the situation called for, especially when you draped yourself all over me like that. Hide that thing somewhere, will you?"

She placed it in the canvas bag, then pushed the bag under the bed. She was relieved to have the money out of her sight. Its presence was becoming almost a reproach. With a sigh of her own Kate sat down in the chair.

The marquess put his hands under his head. "So Sheffield says I am plump and inclined to be lazy? Well, he is right."

Kate rested her chin in her hand and looked at him thoughtfully. "Sir, you are assuming that Abner Sheffield sent the runner. Could it have been your nephew, trying to find you so he can finish the deed?"

Hal considered. "I wouldn't have thought so, but who knows?"

"Your relatives are distressing," Kate said with a shudder. "I rejoice that I know none of them, sir. They seem a plaguey lot."

"Oh, they are," he agreed. "I shall happily hole up with the Bladesworth Traveling Company and not see them for a summer. I can scarcely imagine anything more agreeable."

Kate sat in silence, thinking of Malcolm and his refusal to betray the marquess. Her eyelids began to droop and her whole body sagged, heavy with sleep. As her chin slipped forward on her hand, she jerked upright. The marquess cleared his throat.

"You know, Kate, this is a delicate situation," he began, picking his way among the words. "Under other circumstances, I would advise you to find Phoebe and Maria's room, but as things stand, I fear that nosy runner is camped within easy sight of this door. If you leave, his suspicions will be answered."

"I am well aware of the impropriety of this situation," she said crisply, putting her knees close together and her hands in her lap. "My father is probably somersaulting in his grave! My reputation is in tatters, but it is of no account. We don't run in the same circles, my lord, and unless you decide to announce this frolic to your friends, it will never come to anyone's attention. I, for one, do not intend to say a word about it."

"You mean you wouldn't even be tempted to tell your grandchildren about this evening's work someday?"

"Never! I will make myself as comfortable as I can in this chair, sir, and bid you good night." Kate shut her eyes resolutely.

"And I will not hear of that," said the marquess. "Kate, go ask the landlady for some more blankets. I will make a pallet for myself on the floor and you can have the bed."

Kate gasped and leaped to her feet. "But, my lord, it will still be warm!"

The marquess laughed, even as he held both hands to his head. "Kate, you are the most difficult of bedfellows! We are roughing it tonight. Surely the runner will be gone tomorrow, and—"

"—and so will I," Kate exclaimed. She went to the door and opened it a crack. "Your wife is going to find a more pressing engagement calling her to the south tomorrow. I leave it to your fertile imagination to think of something to tell the landlady."

She stepped onto the landing and saw the runner seated at the foot of the stairs, his chair tipped back and his eyes wide open. He nodded to her and tipped the chair down as she descended the stairs, her heart thumping in her chest.

"Is something the matter, Mrs. Hampton?" he asked, his voice oily with solicitude.

Again resisting the urge to scrape her fingernails across his face, she smiled at the runner. "No, sir, nothing at all. I merely want some more blankets from the innkeep."

"Cold, Mrs. Hampton?" he asked.

Don't call me that, you dolt, she wanted to shout, but she kept her hands clutched tightly in front of her and swept past him with all the dignity she could muster. The innkeep, his expression bemused, supplied her with two more blankets, and she stalked past the runner, eyes ahead, and up the stairs. She forced herself to move slowly, even though she felt his eyes boring into her back as she climbed the stairs.

She closed the door of the room with relief. The marquess was sitting in the chair, a blanket around his bare legs. "I wish you would take the bed," he said.

"Well, I will not," she replied and made herself a pallet as far away from the bed as possible.

"Stubborn woman," the marquess said. He blew out the lamp, and she heard him climb back into bed. It another moment the extra pillow whistled past her and landed on the floor by the pallet. "It's not warm," he said.

Kate put her hand on her mouth so he would not hear her chuckle. "Now face the wall and close your eyes," she commanded in her best governess voice.

"Yes, ma'am," he said.

In a rush of skirts she hurried out of her dress, lay down, and covered herself with the blanket. The floor was hard, but it was such a relief to stretch out. She patted the pillow into a shape of her liking and sank her head into it. The pillow was not warm, but it did smell of the shaving soap that she had lathered on the marquess's face that afternoon. "When in Rome," she murmured.

"Excellent, my good wife," came Hal's voice from the bed. "You are becoming flexible."

He was silent then, and she thought he slept. Her eyes were closing when he spoke again.

"Kate, I was sure Malcolm would betray me. I mean, I would have done it for five hundred pounds, if I had a family to feed. Churlish, wasn't I?" His voice was sleepy.

"No more than I, my lord," was her quiet reply. "I think we do not know these people very well."

There was no answer, but only the faintly reassuring sound of the marquess's even breathing. Kate turned onto her side, trying to find a soft spot on the boards. What a dreadful brew I have stirred for myself, she thought. What a relief it will be to put this behind me tomorrow.

If she thought she would sleep, she was sadly mistaken. Even though her body cried out for rest, she remained acutely aware of the marquess's presence. As eccentric as her upbringing was, with Papa dragging her from England to Rome and then to Florence to follow the trail of art, she had managed to avoid all hints of compromise. And here she was now, sleeping in the same room with a man who was not even a relative. Surely I cannot sink any lower, she thought.

The hours dragged by. Somewhere from a nearby church, she heard a clock toll the time. At three o'clock, unable to lie on the floor any longer, Kate rose quietly, wrapped a blanket around her, and tiptoed to the marquess's bed. He lay on his back, his hands resting on his chest in a shaft of moonlight. She sat in the chair, admiring the length of his fingers, and the capable look to them. I wonder if he plays the piano, she thought. He should. Or, at least, he should make sure that his children do someday, if they have hands like his. I wonder why Sheffield called him plump and lazy? He may be a little overstuffed, but he is tall. And lazy? Time will tell, she thought and then reminded herself. But I will not be here to find out just how lazy he is.

She leaned back in the chair. If I remained here, I would put him to work. I hope Malcolm does. Her eyes closed then, and she dozed a few minutes.When she woke, dawn had reached the windows. The shaft of moonlight was gone, and the marquess was in shadow. She listened to his steady breathing, then reached out her hand to touch his forehead. She smiled to herself. He was cool now.

Quietly she glided on stockinged feet back to her pallet and pulled on her dress and shoes. She combed her long hair as she sat in the window seat, looking out at the town. Farmers were already bringing their produce to market. Soon the day would begin. Nightfall would find her far to the south, her future safely in her hands and no longer at the whim of an employer or the strange company she had fallen into.

She retrieved the canvas bag from under the bed and tied her bonnet firmly under her chin. There was no question about moving her trunk. That would only call attention to herself. When she was settled in her own place in Kent, she would send Malcolm some money to forward it to her.

She opened the door slowly, pausing at each squeak and

looking back at the bed, and then hurried into the hallway, which was still dim with night. She took a deep breath and held it, hoping that the runner was still not guarding the foot of the stairs. She let out her breath. The chair was empty.

Kate hurried down the stairs and out into the inn yard. She would walk toward the marketplace, and ask where else in town the mail coach stopped.

"The King's Rest on Crossett Row," said a woman with a basket of eggs over her arm. "Four streets south but one."

Kate nodded her thanks and hurried on. As she walked, the canvas bag on her arm seemed to grow heavier with each step. "Bladesworth's Banner Street Theatre," seemed to rumble through her mind until she kept time with the cadence. "Bladesworth's Banner Street Theatre."

She stopped. "This will never do," she said out loud and then looked around to make sure that no one had heard her. She looked up. It was Crossett Row. Wasn't that where the owner of the Banner Street Theatre lived? She shook herself mentally. You are being absurd, Katherine Billings, she told herself.

She passed a row of houses, and there it was beside the door in discreet letters: WILLIAM DAWKINS. She stopped again. That was the name of the theatre owner. Kate rested her hand on the gate, then looked down the street at the sound of a coachman blowing his yard of tin. She hurried toward the inn, breaking into a run, and not looking back at the Dawkins's residence, where lights had come on and the day was beginning.

9

WHEN THE ROOM WAS bright with morning sun, Hal opened his eyes to the sound of his stomach growling. Despite the noise of his stomach gnawing on his backbone, he felt content. His head did not hurt beyond an occasional twinge, and he was perfectly at charity with the world in general and his mattress in particular. He settled himself into it more appreciatively and then gave a guilty start. Poor Kate, he thought, suffering on those bare boards. Well, I did offer to trade with her, and that was damned nice of me.

He looked over at Kate's pallet by the window and frowned. She was gone. The blankets had been folded neatly, and the pillow placed on top. He looked around. Her trunk was still there, but her bonnet was no longer on the bureau. As he squinted closer at the bureau top, he saw his signet ring, which she must have removed from the canvas bag.

"Damn," he said out loud with plenty of feeling. Miss Billings had left him, after all, and he had no idea how to locate her. He sat up in the bed that was suddenly no longer satisfactory, threw back the covers, and got to his feet. He waited a moment, testing his balance, then walked carefully to the window seat.

He seated himself and looked down on the inn yard, his heart heavy, despite the sound of birds singing and lilacs in bloom just outside the window.

I need a runner of my own, he thought, someone who can locate a stubborn woman who probably does not wish to be found. He arranged the folds of Malcolm Bladesworth's nightshirt about him, trying to remember what little he knew about Kate Billings. She had mentioned a little place in Kent and a garden and a cow. Good Lord, he thought, that could be almost any little small holding in Kent, and it was a large shire. His family seat was there, but he had vowed several years ago to remain in London, principally to avoid his scavenging relatives who also resided close by. "Odd's fish," he said, "if I promised any of that greedy crew a bit of land, a cow, and garden implements, they would scream such ill usage!"

He smiled as he gazed down on the lilac bushes, then pushed the window open so he could smell them. "Kate, you are stubborn *and* independent! Why couldn't I have fallen in love with a brainless beauty who would require no exertion?"

It was the question of the decade, and he had no answer for it. Why do the seasons change, he wondered to himself. I don't understand that, either.

Someone knocked on the door. Hal looked up expectantly, his heart pounding more rapidly. Dear God, let it be Kate, he thought.

"Come," he said, acutely aware that his nightshirt was sizes too big, his face in need of a shave, and his feet bare.

Ivy Bladesworth pushed open the door. She looked around the room quickly, her face falling when she saw that Kate was not there. She came in and shut the door quickly behind her.

"That dratted runner is still in the hall," she said, her exasperation evident. "Kate is gone?"

He nodded, but did not move from the window seat.

Ivy came closer and put the clothing over her arm onto the bed. "When she did not come down for breakfast, we feared it must be so, because she is not the sort of woman to remain in a room with a single gentleman."

"Well, you are right," he agreed. "I have no idea when she left, or where she has gone, and it pains me."

Ivy cocked her head to one side and regarded him with sympathy. "Lord Grayson, you aren't falling in love so quickly, are you?"

He nodded, wondering how easy it was to share his feelings with someone his relatives would probably cross the street to avoid, and yet relieved to speak of it to a person who obviously cared.

"Oh, dear," she said, perching on the arm of the chair. "This has certainly been an uncomfortable forty-eight hours for you."

"That it has, Mrs. Bladesworth," Hal replied. He was silent a moment, intrigued by the thought that her state was far worse than his, and she did not seem to be repining about it. "But what of you, madam? What are your plans?"

Ivy shrugged. "At the moment we do not have any plans."

She waved her hand in an airy gesture. "Perhaps we will tell our butler to remove the knocker from the door and retreat to our country estate for the summer!" She sobered immediately and folded her hands in her lap. "If you have any suggestions, we are perfectly at leisure to entertain them."

She sat in silence then, looking down at her hands, until he cleared his throat. Ivy glanced up then, apology written on her face. "And here you are, sitting in Gargantua's nightshirt, wishing I would leave!"

He was thinking nothing of the sort, but was remembering his own airy communication to his butler just last week. So many people are worse off than I, he thought, but how much more gallant they are. Looking at Ivy Bladesworth, one would never know that her world has crashed down on her.

He smiled at her. "No, madam, I was merely thinking how kind you have been to me. And is that my shirt, washed and pressed?"

Ivy looked where he pointed. "And mended, I might add, my lord. We did the best we could with your riding leathers, and Davy has shined your boots to a fare-thee-well and left them outside the door."

The marquis nodded his approval. "I suppose I would not cut much of a dash in London with this wardrobe. But then, I never was a man milliner. Dash it all, Mrs. Bladesworth, why did she have to leave?"

His words sounded like whining to his own ears, like a child disappointed over a promised outing or toy. He had envisioned a leisurely summer with the Bladesworths and Kate Billings. He would patiently let love unfold until it was a full-blown flower. There would be no relatives and no cares. Somehow he would find a way to get his wardrobe from Pinky D'Urst, and when the time was ripe, he would declare the emergency over and his life no longer in danger. By then Kate would have been his for the plucking.

But Ivy was speaking. "I have discovered, my lord, that plans only exist to be changed." She stood up and squared her shoulders. "Ah, well, come to luncheon, Lord Grayson. Perhaps things will appear more sanguine over barley soup."

"Perhaps," he agreed. "At any rate, surely we can drink to the disappearance of Mr. Muggeridge, Bow Street's Finest."

Ivy paused at the door, her hand on the knob. "He is still with us, my lord, rather like a putrid sore throat or … or a creditor."

"What can he possibly want?" Hal asked.

"Who knows? Malcolm thinks we should invite him to take his meals with us!"

Hal snorted. "By all means! Perhaps he will fall wondrously in love with … with Maria and leave Bow Street for a life on the wicked stage."

After Ivy left, Hal thoughtfully pulled on his clothes. The way things stood now, it would be an easy matter to drop enough of his blunt with the landlord to pay everyone's shot and then hire a post chaise to take him in comfort to D'Urst Hall. He could be there by dinnertime. Perhaps in the softer light of evening, Pinky's sister would not seem so formidable. "And this will make my relatives so happy," he said out loud, loathing himself.

His words sent him back to the window, where he finished buttoning his shirt. He ran a finger around the neck and smiled in spite of his petulance. It seemed looser, somehow. He patted his stomach. Soon I will be weak from hunger and thin as a pikestaff, a victim of the heartless Kate Billings, who abandons husbands like some people discard nail filings.

He leaned out to close the window against the relentless good cheer of summer, and there was Kate Billings now, walking slowly back to the Scylla, looking as dejected as the Bladesworths only last night. As he watched, she wiped her hand across her eyes. He looked closer. The canvas bag containing her money was gone.

"Blast and damn," he said softly, but not without a little satisfaction. "Kate, did someone take your money? Poor honey. Are you stuck with us?" The thought made him wish to caper about, except that he feared the effect of too sudden motion on his tender skull. She disappeared into the inn, and he hurriedly tucked him shirttails into his pants and opened the door.

The runner had resumed his place at the foot of the stairs.

He stood up when Kate, her eyes on the stairs, swept past him.

"One moment, Mrs. Hampton," he began, his voice heavy with sarcasm, "I would like a word with you."

Damn you, Hal thought. Why must men pick on defenseless ladies?

As the marquess watched, wondering if he should come to her rescue, the runner took Kate by the arm. Without a word she slapped him with the back of her hand, and he collapsed in the chair, his eyes wide and his hand to his flaming cheek.

His eyes wide, too, Hal chuckled as his hand went

involuntarily to the back of his neck. "Muggeridge, I could have told you what happens to coves who trouble Kate Billings. What a brick you are, my darling girl," he said under his breath as she started slowly up the stairs.

To his utter amazement, when she saw him, she burst into tears, gathered up her skirts, and ran the rest of the way. To his complete gratification she threw herself into his arms and nearly bowled him over backward through the open door. "Oh, Hal!" she wailed out loud, her voice carrying far enough to suit even Malcolm Bladesworth. "You won't believe what I have done!"

Doors opened all down the hall. Hal recovered quickly. He grabbed Kate up in his arms, closed the door with his foot, and carried her into the room, while she sobbed into his shirt.

It was useless to ask for an explanation when she was in such a state. Hal sat with her in the window seat, cuddling her close while she cried, and breathing in the intoxicating combination of lavender and sunshine in her hair. Her body was warm and softer than he ever could have dreamed. He wanted to kiss her, but she was sobbing and hiccupping, and his shirt-front was soaked. He was content to rest his hand on her hair and murmur nonsensical things.

In a few moments she stopped crying, but did not raise herself from his chest. On the contrary she settled in more comfortably, until he wondered if she slept. He was about to speak when she gave a squeak and sat up.

"Oh, I am sorry!" she declared, her hands to her face. "You must think me dreadfully forward."

He thought her a darling, but he could not say so, not then. She dug around in her reticule for her handkerchief and blew her nose heartily. "I am taking dreadful advantage of you, sir," she managed to say at last.

Hal owned to a twinge of conscience and took his hand from around her waist, where it seemed to fit so well. "Oh, well, damsels in distress, and all that," he stammered. "Tell me,

Kate, if you can. What happened?"

To his ineffable pleasure, she leaned against him again. It was almost as though she could not bear to speak and look him in the face. Her words were muffled in his damp shirt. "I cannot believe what I did. I must have been crazy."

There was a long silence. Finally Kate seemed to gain possession of herself. She sat up and got off his lap, settling herself in the window seat with him, her eyes on his face, this time with an expression that he could not fathom.

"I was going to leave," she began, never taking her eyes from his face. She raised her hands, as if to protest her words, and then settled them in her lap. "I mean, I had bought the ticket and was only waiting for the others in front of me to board the mail coach. Then it was my turn." Her voice faltered, but she did not drop her gaze. "Suddenly it seemed the basest kind of cowardice to leave the Bladesworths, especially when I had the means to help them." She touched his arm, but he did not move, fearful of shattering the intimacy that seemed to have settled around them like a nimbus. "I could think only how Malcolm had rejected the offer of reward for news of your whereabouts."

"I own I have been thinking about that, too," he murmured.

She clasped her hands together again until the knuckles were white, and then relaxed and gazed out the window, breaking the spell. "I went to William Dawkins's house and convinced him to sell me the Banner Street Theatre," she said in a rush of words.

Whatever he had been expecting to hear, Kate's quiet words confounded him. Impulsively he took her chin in his hands and turned her face toward him. "You did what?" he asked, carefully enunciating each word.

Tears started in her eyes again. "You heard me," she whispered. "I just spent my future on the Banner Street Theatre."

He dropped his hand, then leaned forward and touched her

forehead with his. “Kate, you are an incredible woman.”

She looked out the window again. “Thank you, sir, for not calling me a fool.”

“Never that,” he said, his voice as quiet as hers, “although I must admit this takes my breath away.”

“Mine, too,” she agreed. “Lord Grayson, I have spent my life in obedient compliance with the whims of a somewhat eccentric parent.” She looked at him, as if to gauge his reaction. “I do not wish to appear in any way disrespectful of the dead, because I am not.”

“I understand, Kate.” He took hold of her hands. “I hope I am not being forward myself when I say that I am not put here to judge you.”

She smiled. “We judge ourselves harshly enough, do we not, my lord? Thank you for your forbearance. I told myself that I would never be a child of chance again. When Mr. Cratch handed me all that money yesterday, I had my entire course plotted out, right down to the shingles on the roof of my little small holding in Kent.”

“Then why did you change your mind?” he asked. He released her hands and leaned back. Please tell me it is because you find me irresistible, and you cannot draw another breath without me close by. He grinned at the absurdity of his thought.

“Must you grin in that perfectly odious way?” she asked, but there was a touch of humor in her voice. “Well, really, why should you not? This whole episode is quite, quite absurd. I did it because it seemed like a good idea at the time.” She drew her knees up and rested her chin on them. “Of course, each step I took back here convinced me otherwise, but it was too late.” She reached out her hand to him impulsively. “Oh, please say that you will help me!”

“This sounds like work,” he teased, taking her hand.

“It will be,” she assured him. “Mr. Dawkins insisted on walking me through the theatre, which suffers from serious neglect. I defy even the most haunted of houses to boast more cobwebs! But Hal, it *is* a fine old building, with sound floors and walls." She squeezed his fingers, in her enthusiasm. "Of course, the curtain wants repair, and it all reeks of bat soil."

She sprang up then and went to her trunk, rummaging around until she found some paper and a pencil. "I believe I will put you on a tall ladder, and you can make short work of the bats and—"

"Wait!" Hal exclaimed, holding up both hands. "What makes you think I know anything about bat removal?" He shuddered. "Good God, woman, you are presuming a great deal."

Kate hurried back to the window seat. "Perhaps we can smoke them out," she said, frowning over the paper. "And we will need to wash down everything and paint it all." She looked up from her notes. "And I will make you manager, Hal."

Lord Grayson shook his head and took the pencil from her fingers. "No, you will not, my dear. *You* are in charge. I will happily serve as your assistant, but this is your venture."

She looked at him for a long moment, and he watched doubt and uncertainty chase themselves across her expressive features. She began to chew on her lower lip. How full your lips are, he thought. I wonder if they feel as good as they look.

Kate set the paper aside and took a deep breath. "Lord Grayson—"

"Hal," he corrected.

"Hal, I have never been in charge of anything before in my life. I've only done what I am told to do."

"What better time to learn leadership than now?" he asked and handed the pencil back. He picked up the paper she had set aside. "I suggest you write down everyone's name and decide how you want to use them."

She started to write, then stopped. "Oh, dear, I've not told anyone I bought the theatre! Perhaps that should be my first move." She went to the door and Hal followed. Kate paused before she opened the door and looked back at the marquess with frightened eyes. "Hal, suppose they will have nothing to do with my scheme? I will be stuck with a theatre."

"And bats," he added, taking her hand. "Let's go find out, shall we?" When she tried to pull her hand away, he grasped it more firmly. "My dear, we must be the loving couple for the omnipresent runner, drat his carcass."

"So we must," she agreed and opened the door.

The runner still sat in his chair at the foot of the stairs, his hand to his face, which bore red finger marks. He glared up at Kate. "I could prefer charges against you," he muttered.

Hal wrapped both arms around Kate's waist and pulled her back against him. "If you touch her again, you'll rue more than finger marks on your face, Muggeridge," he said.

The runner rose to his feet in one smooth motion, as though pulled upright by invisible wires. "Is that a threat?" he asked, his voice low.

Hal shook his head. "Nay, sir, it is a promise." He released Kate, took her hand, and hurried her down the hall.

"Very impressive," she said, skipping to keep up with his long stride. "Although you don't need to hold me so close."

Hal looked back at her and grinned. "Be quiet, wife. We have a very skeptical runner to impress." He knocked on the door. "And let us hope the Bladesworths like your scheme."

"They must," she said, moving closer until her shoulder touched his arm. "Oh, they have to."

Malcolm Bladesworth was silent during Kate's recitation of the events of the morning, only motioning his other children into the little room while she explained her purchase of the Banner Street Theatre. No one spoke when she finished.Hal watched Katherine, moved by the dignity of her quiet presence. They sat close together, and he could feel her leg trembling, but none of her fears registered on her face. He wanted to put his arm around her, but there was no runner to use as an excuse.

Malcolm finally cleared his throat. "Kate, the theatre is a risky business," he said, and there was nothing encouraging in his voice.

"Then we will have to make it pay," Kate said simply. "Malcolm, I would like you to be my artistic manager. I depend upon you to make this the most wonderful theatre in the north part of England. It must be."

After another long moment of silence Malcolm held out his hand. "Done, lady."

They ate a thoughtful dinner in the taproom, no one speaking much. The runner watched from a corner table. Hal rested his arm along the back of Kate's chair, noticing the way she picked at her food. He leaned closer to her. "You couldn't keep a sparrow alive on what you are consuming, Mrs. Hampton. Do make a better effort."

Kate made a face at him. "Don't bully me, sir!" She started to say something else, but changed her mind. "That confounded runner!" Instead she smiled sweetly at Hal, exclaimed, "Yes, dear," in loving tones that carried to the corner table.

Malcolm finished first. He folded his napkin and patted his ample stomach. "Kate, it is still light. I suggest we take a look at your purchase. Do you have the key?"

They walked in companionable silence along streets deserted by shopkeepers and tradesmen for dinner tables all over Leeds. Hal strolled in perfect charity with the world, Kate's arm resting on his. Bladesworth couldn't help himself. He hurried ahead with Ivy running and skipping to keep up. When they were half a block ahead, Hal noticed that Gerald Broussard took Phoebe by the hand.

"Is there a budding romance among the youngsters?" he asked Kate.

"You're just noticing?" she asked. "Phoebe may be only sixteen, but I think people grow up quickly in the theatre. I believe I will go back to my room tonight and pick out my own gray hairs. I have probably sprouted a whole head of them only since this morning."

He looked down at the soft ebony curls that peeked from

under her bonnet. "Not a gray hair in sight, Mrs. Hampton."

"You need not call me that when the runner is not around!" she protested.

Hal gestured with his head. "My dear, he is following us."

Kate sighed and tightened her grip on his arm. "What is his game, sir?" she whispered.

"I wish I knew."

The theatre was swathed in deep shadows when Malcolm took the large key from Kate and let them in. The younger Bladesworths lighted the lanterns they had brought along and set them on the stage.

Hal looked around him, noting the cobwebs that festooned the curtains, ropes, and pulleys. As he stood contemplating the vast darkness of the auditorium, he felt more than heard a sudden rush of wind by his ear and a strangled cry from Kate, who leaped toward him and grabbed his arm. It was a perfect opportunity to put his arm around her.

"It is only one of those infamous bats you expect me to conjure away, Kate."

She waited a long moment before releasing him from an iron grip. "Let that be your first duty."

Malcolm let himself off the stage and walked into the darkness of the auditorium. When they could no longer see him, he called from the blackness. "Phoebe, favor us," was all he said.

Phoebe Bladesworth stepped forward toward the makeshift footlights made of lanterns from the inn. "What will it be, Father?" she asked, shading her eyes and trying to catch a glimpse of her parent in the gloom.

"Let it be Kate's choice," came the voice. "It is her theatre."

Hal felt Kate start. "It *is* my theatre, isn't it?" she asked, her voice filled with wonder. "Oh, Hal." She was silent only a moment before he felt her draw herself together. She stepped away from him toward Phoebe.

"Let it be something from Shakespeare, my dear," she said.

Phoebe smiled at Kate and blew her a kiss. "Let it be Portia then, from *The Merchant of Venice.* 'The quality of mercy is not strain'd; It droppeth as the gentle rain from heaven …' "

Her voice carried, clear and lovely, to the back wall that no one could see in the darkness. When she finished, all were silent, still caught in the power of her talent, plain to see, even on a dusty stage, half-hidden in gathering gloom, with bats circling and swooping.

A bat dived too close and broke the spell. Phoebe dodged backward into Broussard's waiting arms. He whisked out an imaginary sword and sparred with the bats while the younger Bladesworths giggled. When Malcolm returned to the stage, Ivy clapped her hands.

"Come, children. Let us leave this 'nest of …' "

" '… dead and contagion and unnatural sleep,' " the Bladesworths all shouted in unison.

They started from the stage. Davy Bladesworth handed Kate a small box. "I found this in the corner." He grinned. "I am sure it is treasure."

While Hal held a lantern, Kate opened the box. Costume jewelry spilled out. She laughed as the children gathered it up, decking themselves with glass jewels and brooches that winked in the light.

"How is it that these tawdry bits look so real on stage?" Kate asked Malcolm.

He bowed. "It is because we govern the magic, my dear."

Hal handed Malcolm the lantern. He rummaged in the box and found a gilt ring. "Hold out your hand, Mrs. Hampton," he ordered.

With a laugh she did as he said. He grasped her slender hand, wondering to himself at the exquisite fragility of her bones, the delicacy of her touch that seemed to fuel a fire in him.

"This is for the benefit of our dear friend the runner," he said as he slipped on the plain band.

"And I pronounce you man and wife," Malcolm intoned. "What the theatre has joined together, let no pesky runner put asunder."

They laughed and left the theatre, admiring the stars that blazed overhead in the summer sky and breathing in the fragrance of lilacs that seemed to fill the market town.

Malcolm stood still for a moment, his arm about his wife's shoulders, looking back at the theatre. "The Bladesworths have come to roost," he murmured to no one in particular. He glanced over at Kate and Hal. "My dear, we will go no more a-roving. We'll make it pay."

"We'll have to," said Kate fervently.

Hal was hoping that the runner would be back in his customary position at the foot of the stairs when they returned, so it would be out of the question for Kate to dare spend the night anywhere else. He regarded the seated man with a benevolence bordering on charity as he nodded to him and gave Kate his arm up the stairs.

"Ah, my dear, we must spend another night together," he commented as he showed her into the room. "Only this time, I insist that you have the bed. My head has not ached since early this morning."

Kate stood in the middle of the room. "This is so improper," she said, her voice filled with doubt.

"But I do not know what we can do about it," Hal finished helpfully. "I will take a glass of stout below stairs while you, well, you know ..." He left the room before she could think of any more objections.

When he returned, the room was dark and Kate was in bed. She had made up the pallet on the floor by the window and folded Malcolm's huge nightshirt on top of the pillow. Quietly he got into the nightshirt and lay down. This reminds me of my days in the Peninsula, he thought to himself as he tried to find a friendly board.

The room was quiet as moonlight settled over the bed. He

could see Kate's hands on the covers, folded together tightly. In another moment he heard muffled sobs.

"Kate, don't cry," he said, his voice gentle. "You know I will never breathe a word of this to anyone."

The sound of her weeping tore at his heart. "Kate, please don't!" he implored, sitting up on the pallet. "What is the matter?"

He did not think she would answer him.

"I am afraid," she said at last. "Oh, Hal, I am afraid this will be a huge disaster." She sobbed louder.

He had heard women cry before. His fiancée had cried when he left for the war. His mother and sisters had hung on him and wept, and it had caused him the acutest feelings of ill usage. But this was different. Kate cried as a child would cry who was afraid of the dark. It was the hopeless sound of someone used to shedding tears alone.

You can only slap me, he thought, as he walked quietly to the bed and sat down next to Kate. He gathered her in his arms, and she did not object as he held her close. He let her cry until she was worn out, then he wiped her eyes, made her blow her nose, and lie down. He sat in the chair, his hand resting on her hair until she slept.

He returned to the pallet and lay down. The moonlight streamed in the window. He glanced over at the sleeping woman. The gilt ring on her hand glittered for an instant, and then she rolled over. He watched the graceful curve of her back and hips and felt a wonderful contentment he had never known before.

She needs me, he thought, as his eyes closed. I hope she will love me, too.

10

WHEN KATE WOKE, THE room was empty. She sighed with relief and snuggled back into the covers, pulling them up to her chin and relaxing completely in that boneless way of cats and small children. The window was open, and the scent of lilacs drifted toward her. She sniffed appreciatively, glorying in the fragrance of early summer, pleased to be in England again after so many Italian springs, dedicated to the pursuit of art and cheap lodgings.

Kate turned on her side and tucked her hand under her cheek. Not that Italian springs were unpleasant—far from it; but they came with a dazzle of tropical color and a slap of humidity and no subtlety. No, summer in Yorkshire was infinitely preferable. She breathed deeply of the smell of shaving soap still on the pillow and closed her eyes, imagining what it would be like to wake up with a man lying beside her.

There was no one in the room, but she blushed anyway, and then turned even more fiery as she permitted one stray thought to lead to another. She wondered how nice it would be to make love in the morning, with the smell of lilacs and the scent of shaving soap, and a soft mattress underneath. I could enjoy that, she thought, especially if the man were somebody solid like Lord Grayson, someone a girl could hang onto.

"Goodness," she scolded out loud and sat up, folding her hands in front of her. Her eyes caught the glimmer of the gold-colored band on her left hand. She turned it around on her finger and noted with a chuckle that it was already turning her finger green. So much for theatre magic, she thought. Someday I would like to have a real gold ring, and a husband to love, and perhaps children.

It was all a mystery to her, how such things happened. She allowed herself the luxury of a great stretch as she contemplated the wonder of it. Certainly marriages were still arranged.

She chuckled again, thinking of Lord Grayson and his strenuous efforts to avoid his family's selection. If I am to marry, she thought as she dangled her bare legs over the edge of the bed, it will be due entirely to my own exertions. But I am not lazy like Lord Grayson. Perhaps when this theatre scheme pays, I will have the time to cast my own net.

She frowned. "*If* this pays," she amended. "If I do not lose my bonnet, pelisse, petticoat, and stockings in the bargain and end up without a sixpence to scratch with!"

The thought was not a pleasant one to wrestle with in bed. Kate got up and pulled on her clothes, wishing that she could shake the wrinkles from her dress hoping that tonight there would be time for a good wash in a tub. As she threw on her clothes, she thought of the Baths of Caracalla where Roman ladies used to lie naked in the water and lull away their cares until they must have been pink and wrinkled. There were slaves to dry them, and dress them, and fix their hair, and tell them lies about how fine they looked.

All I have is a mirror, and it does not lie, Kate thought as she brushed her unfashionably long hair, braided it, and wound it around her head. It tells me I have a mass of hair, a stubborn jaw and ordinary lips that no one has ever taken the trouble to kiss. She ran her fingers over her cheekbones. Well, at least I have never thrown out spots, she thought. And even though I am twenty-six, I do not have any wrinkles yet.

She glanced at the bureau top, which was littered with Hal's shaving gear. It must be Malcolm's razor, or Gerald's, she thought as she carefully wiped the blade clean and closed it. Hal has nothing except the clothes he stands in. She shook out the shaving brush and put a lid on the soap. It must be pleasant to have a valet tend to your every need and never have to worry about picking up after yourself.

Lord Grayson's signet ring still rested on the dresser. Kate put it on her finger, twirling it around and around. He was so careless! It would never do for the Bow Street Runner to prowl in here and find a lord's ring. She pocketed the ring and went to the window to straighten the blankets that Lord Grayson had left in a jumble on the floor.

"Sir, you are most definitely not accustomed to tidying things for yourself," she said as she folded the blankets and put them on the bed. Her conscience tweaked her as she folded Malcolm's nightshirt and added it to the pile. She had spent two nights alone in the same room with a grown man she was not in any way related to. Kate sank onto the bed and thought of the milkmaid on the mail coach, warning her of Squire Leavitt. What on earth would she say if she knew of this? What would anyone say?

Kate told herself again that it did not matter. Once Lord Grayson regained his customary station, surely he would not mention this to anyone. I will certainly never repeat it to a soul, she promised herself. Not that it matters, she thought, as she ran her fingers over the nightshirt collar. Was there ever a nobody more unknown than Kate Billings?

There was a knock at the door, and she hurried to open it, hoping that it might be Hal. She would give him a little scold about his untidiness. She opened the door upon Phoebe and Maria, dressed in faded garments with their hair done up in turbans.

"Come, Kate. We are off to tackle the Banner Street Theatre. *Your* Banner Street Theatre," said Maria, taking her by the arm. "And here is a cloth to wind around your hair. It is fearfully dusty there."

Kate accepted the scarf and wound it around her head. "Have the others gone ahead?" she asked, peeking into the hall.

"Yes," said Phoebe, "even your husband."

"He is *not* my husband!" Kate protested.

"He is as long as the Bow Street Runner refuses to budge," Phoebe replied, and then laughed as she poked Maria. "And who do you think sent Mr. Muggeridge over to the theatre to help Hal with the bats?"

"Maria!"

Maria blushed rosily. "If Will insists on hanging around like a fly at a midden, we ought to use him."

"Will, is it? She wouldn't say that if he were skinny, bald, and queer as Dick's hatband," Phoebe whispered to Kate, her eyes twinkling at her sister's discomfort, and loud enough to be overheard.

"I am sure that thrilled my husband," Kate replied, her voice heavy with sarcasm. She almost pulled the door closed before Phoebe stopped her.

"No, wait. Davy is coming to get your trunk and anything else that belongs to either you or Lord Grayson." She laughed at Kate's mystified expression. "No, silly, we are not camping out in Leeds park! There are rooms and rooms at the theatre. We will stay there."

Kate shuddered. "With the bats?"

Maria tugged at Kate's arm again. "Kate, now that you are part of the theatre, you must be open to a little more adventure."

Phoebe waltzed across the room, picked up her father's nightshirt, and held it in her arms. "Or you could stay here with Lord Grayson."

Kate snatched up the nightshirt and stuffed it in her trunk, along with the razor and shaving soap. "I will take my chances with the bats!"

"What, does he snore?" Maria teased. "Or sleepwalk?" Both girls giggled behind their hands.

"Well no, but ..." Kate closed her trunk with a firm click. "Maria, you are entirely too jolly for *my* own good!"

They started down the stairs. "I think it is perfectly romantic," Phoebe said.

"Oh, you would," Maria quizzed. "And I suppose Monsieur Broussard will write a play about this and cast you as the beautiful governess forced to compromise herself by two nights in a bedroom with an unmarried man. Gerald will be the French bachelor, of course."

Kate stopped on the stairs. "Please don't tease about this," she pleaded suddenly, alive to the implication.

Maria took her arm more gently this time. "I am sorry, Kate," she said, her voice contrite. "I am sure by autumn that you will look back on all this and laugh, too."

"I hope you are right," Kate replied quietly.

While it couldn't be said that dust was actually rising into the air over the Banner Street Theatre, the old building already had a less abandoned look to it, seen in the cheerful light of midmorning. Davy waved to them from the seat of the prop wagon as his little brother and sisters carried in the last of the wigs, swords, and Yorick's skull.

"I'm off for the finale," he told his sisters. He flicked the reins across the backs of the two horses. "And then it's goodbye to Troilus and Cressida here. Papa sold them to the innkeep."

Maria stopped and ran her hand along Cressida's flank. She looked up at her brother. "Davy, we certainly will have crossed the Rubicon then, won't we?"

He nodded and motioned her back from the horse. "The Bladesworths are here to stay," he declared. "I hope Leeds is ready for us."

So do I, thought Kate as she entered the theatre.

Many lamps were glowing in the building now, and Malcolm Bladesworth was lighting the last candle on the first tier of the chandelier. He waved a cheery greeting to Kate and his daughters and motioned for Gerald, rope in hand on the edge of the stage, to raise the chandelier. It rose on squeaky pulleys and took away some of the shadows.

"Very good, very good," Malcolm boomed. "Tie it off, Gerald. Mustn't waste any more tallow." He gestured grandly across the broad stage that was strewn with props, boxes, and bat leavings. 'There isn't anything we can't perform on this stage, with enough actors." He chucked Kate under the chin. "We might even make some money, my dear."

Kate took his arm. "Malcolm, I know I have bought this theatre, but I know nothing about the business. I want you to organize it the way you want. Tell me what to do, and I will do it. I have three hundred pounds left from the purchase price. We'll have to stretch that until it screams."

"I've sold my horses, and your good husband paid our shot at the inn."

"My good … oh, yes."

Malcolm patted her arm and leaned closer. "And as long as the runner thinks he needs to know Hal's business, you'd better be the devoted wife, my 'super-dainty Kate.' "

Kate sighed. "Why won't that dratted runner leave?"

But Malcolm was gone, calling to his little ones to carry the props offstage, and then shouting for Ivy to "soothe his fever'd brow with a gentle kiss, a fairy's gossamer touch."

Kate smiled in spite of her discomfort. How do these eccentric, unregimented dears get from day to day? she asked herself.

"Madam, I feel extremely ill-used."

The voice was Hal's. Its cheerful tone belied the marquess's stringent words and carried well on the stage. But where was he? Kate looked up, raising her hand against the candlelight's glow, and laughed.

"Lord ... Lord knows how you have grown so gray, my love," she stammered, recovering herself. The runner stood beside Hal on the catwalk that ran the length of the stage. "And you, Mr. Muggeridge."

Hal leaned down, resting his arms on the railing. "His name is Will, my dearest love. He had promised me that he will never lay another hand on you, and I have promised him that you will never plant him a facer again, even if you are sorely provoked." He turned to the runner, his expression virtuous. "Since our nuptials, she had taught me many wicked things, sir, but I draw the line at fisticuffs."

Kate gasped. The runner laughed, and she looked at him in surprise. I must be the only sane person in all of Yorkshire, she thought, as she glared at the two men. But what was it Malcolm, and then Phoebe this morning, had said about being adventurous? What have I to lose, she thought. My dignity? My reputation? That drooped down to my ankles the first night I spent alone with Lord Grayson."I shall tell you what I think," she declared. "Where is the ladder, Hal?"

He pointed off the stage. "It is but a very narrow stair, my dear. Do have a care."

She nodded at him, pleased somehow that he did not warn her off the stairs, or remonstrate with her. He stayed where he was, arms draped over the railing, his hair powdered gray with bat soil, perfectly at ease. I could almost like you, she thought, if that were even a consideration, which it is not.

She found the stairs easily, and with one hand on her skirts, she climbed up to the catwalk. Heights had no terrors for her. She had climbed to the top of the Parthenon with Papa once in the moonlight to look over Athens, asleep far below. She smiled, even as the pungent bat soil tickled her nostrils and made her sneeze. I am as eccentric as all the rest.

The catwalk swayed a little, and she sucked in her breath. Hal held out his hand to her, and she took it gratefully.

"If it can hold a fubsy fellow like me, it can hold a sprite like you, Kate," he said. "Wouldn't you agree, sir?"

The runner had moved off a few paces. He nodded, his eyes wary again, watching them. Kate ignored him. She let Hal put his arm around her waist.

"Now, tell me, sir, why you are so ill-used?" Her voice was soft, loverlike, and he leaned closer to hear her.

"Because I had planned to spend this summer acting for Malcolm Bladesworth and making love to you, not dodging bats in dusty halls," he reminded her. He winked and pinched her waist. "Some could accuse you of being eccentric in buying this bat-filled barn, Mrs. Hampton."

Kate turned slightly so the runner could get a good view. She wiped off a spot on Hal's cheek and kissed him. "Only an eccentric would marry you, my lord." She dared the runner to say anything.

He looked back at her, his stare equally level. "Do you always call him 'my lord,' Mrs. Hampton?"

"Sometimes I even call him 'Your Grace,' or 'Your Excellency,' she replied, and kissed Hal again, wishing he would not inch his hand up so. "You must excuse us, Will, if we act a little loverlike."

Will bowed and the catwalk swayed. "You may act all you choose, Mrs. Hampton, but I do not believe a word you say." He nodded to Hal and stepped around them. "But I will play along with your little game as long as it suits you."

The runner walked across the catwalk and down the narrow stairs. Hal did not release his hold on her.

"Do mind your fingers," Kate whispered to him, a smile on her face for the benefit of the runner, who watched now from the stage. "You are trying me sorely."

Hal grinned at her. "Tell me who climbed up to the catwalk, then, my dear." Before she could say anything else, he kissed her.

It was a gentle kiss, a mild one completely in tune with mid-morning, and the two littlest Bladesworth girls applauding below and Maria giggling. He kissed her again, and this time there was something more. Kate couldn't have explained it to a jury, but she wanted suddenly to kiss him back.

Before she followed through on her urge, he stepped back and took her face in both hands. "Perhaps I am not so ill-used, after all," he murmured.

The applause continued from below. Hal bowed and waved regally to their audience. Laughing, he clasped her hand and led her off the catwalk. In the half light of the wings, still high above the stage, she turned to him. "You are such a rascal," she whispered.

"Hush, my dear," he said, his composure irritating beyond belief. "Mustn't let the runner hear you." He edged her toward the steep stairway. "You go first. If I should chance to slip, then you can break my fall."

She glared at him and then laughed in spite of herself. "You are also absurd," she muttered as she descended to the stage below. She paused halfway down and looked up at the marquess. "I still do not understand why you cannot tell the runner who you are!"

"What, and have all my worried relatives descend on me like a downpour, cut up my peace, and ruin my summer?" he whispered back. "And, dear wife, we still do not know if this runner was sent by Algernon or Abner Sheffield. Suggest to me how I can ask him without arousing suspicion, and I will do it."

She was silent a moment, and then continued down the stairs. "I suppose you are right," she said finally, "but I don't like it."

When she regained the stage again, it was an easy matter to abandon Lord Grayson to his own devices, and, with Phoebe and Maria, tackle the rooms that would become their living quarters.

"Mama says that we girls can stay in one room, Gerald, my brothers, and Lord Grays … Hal, in another, and she and Papa in the third." Phoebe put her hands on her hips. "Maria, you are *not* to suggest to Will Muggeridge that he join us!"

"I would never," Maria declared with some heat. "But you must own that he is helpful."

They washed down walls and scrubbed floors all morning, pausing at noon for a luncheon of bread, meat, and cheese spread on a blanket on the stage, and washed down with cool water from the well behind the theatre. It was easy for Kate to avoid the marquess and sit with Phoebe and Maria. She ignored the runner's pointed glances at her when she did not join her husband on his side of the stage.

When the last crumb had been brushed away, no one felt inclined to rise. With a sigh Hal lay down on the stage. He patted the boards beside him. "Come here, wife," he said. "Rest your head a moment."

Kate gritted her teeth. The man was so flagrant! I will give him such a scold when we are alone tonight, she vowed as she pretended not to hear Maria's infernal giggling, walked across the stage with all the dignity she could muster, and plumped herself down beside Hal. He spread his arm out obligingly, and she had no choice but to lie down next to him. He cuddled her in closer. "Very good, my dear," he murmured, and then whispered in her ear. "Relax. I won't bite."

"You are a complete scoundrel," she whispered back. "I think you are taking vast advantage of this situation with the runner."

"Of course I am," he replied, his composure unruffled. "So would any man with blood flowing through his veins—however sluggishly—and the remotest semblance of a heartbeat. Be quiet, now, and for goodness sake, relax. You feel like a board."

"And you smell vilely of bats," she said. Kate turned pointedly away from him and rested her cheek on his outstretched arm. He was more comfortable than she would ever have admitted, and her eyes began to close.

They opened at the sound of firm footsteps on the stage. Malcolm Bladesworth, his longish hair wrapped in a turban like his daughters', sat down next to her.

"Something has occurred to me, Kate," he said, his voice booming out portentously. The others looked up expectantly. "We are few in number," he began, and his family nodded. The runner gazed at them in faint amusement. "In fact, as I have been sweeping out bat leavings, I am struck by something."

"You, too, sir?" Hal said, laughed, and slapped Kate on the hip. "Do not stand under bats. It does terrible things to one's dignity and makes one prematurely gray."

Gerald laughed out loud and ruefully dusted at his hair. "We have all been struck by something, monsieur."

Malcolm waved his arms about in the grand gestures that Kate was becoming familiar with. "No! No, you simpletons! Do you realize that we do not have enough actors to present a significant play?"

The Bladesworths were silent a moment, mentally counting their number. "What about *Love Withheld*?" Phoebe ventured.

Malcolm shook his head.

"*The Saracen*?" Davy asked.

"*Beaux Stratagem*?" Maria suggested.

"No, no, and yet again, no," Malcolm. "And I can think of nothing by Shakespeare, either." He looked at Kate. "My dear Kate, this is a dilemma I had not considered until now. Our other actors deserted us like rats from a drowning ship, and we haven't enough money to spare among our remaining company to tempt the Devil, much less an actor."

Kate turned onto her back and stared at the chandelier that winked overhead. Hal's arm tightened around her, and she scooted in closer. "Dear me, this is a problem," she said softly. "Malcolm, we could clean and scrub and refurbish to a fare-thee-well and still be unable to open."

"I am afraid that is so, Kate," he said.

Kate closed her eyes. Somewhere behind her closed lids, tears began to gather. I will not cry, she thought fiercely. Could I plead with Mr. Dawkins to take the theatre back? He would never do it. It had been empty for years, an eyesore on Banner

Street, which no one wanted. She reached up for Hal's hand that grasped her shoulder and twined her fingers in his.

"I wish I had access to Abner Sheffield," he whispered in her ear. "My present resources are far from sanguine, or I could get us out of this muddle."

"No, Hal, it is my problem, not yours," she said out loud. "I must find a solution." She sat up and drew up her legs into her favorite thinking position. Resting her chin on her knees, she stared straight ahead.

Gerald Broussard was in her line of sight. He lounged carelessly on the edge of the stage, his leg dangling off, contemplating her. She gazed back and then began to smile. Startled, Gerald smiled back at her, and then he seemed to understand without words, what she wanted.

"I will do it, Madame Hampton," he said. "Do you trust me that much?"

"It seems that I have to," she replied and then turned to the others.

"Gerald will write us a play," she said. "It will be a play using only such actors as we have."

"Gerald?" Malcolm roared, ignoring Ivy's hand on his arms. "My dear, he only dabbles in words!"

"Well, then, he will have to dabble in earnest now," Kate replied. She got to her feet and shook the dust from her dress onto Hal, who coughed and then grabbed her by the ankle.

She shrieked and then tugged at his hair until he let go. "Madam wife, it is thin enough!" he protested. "Would you snatch me completely bald?"

"The thought had occurred to me," she replied, her composure restored. "Monsieur Broussard, I absolve you of all further housekeeping duties. You are to devote yourself to a play."

Broussard extended his leg and bowed gracefully. "Madam, we will open in six weeks' time."

11

DINNER WAS A QUIET affair, eaten again on the stage, which by now had been swept clear of bat leavings and scrubbed until the boards squeaked. Using the charm that had probably mollified many a reluctant merchant and creditor, Ivy had convinced the bakery two doors down to allow them cooking facilities. She and the younger Bladesworths produced a hot meal that brought cries of delight from Malcolm.

He clapped his arm around his wife. "I don't know how she does it, Hal, but we have never starved." He kissed her cheek. "An enviable achievement, considering the precarious nature of our profession."

"And look at this," Ivy said with a flourish, as her youngest daughter walked carefully onto the stage, "and all for the promise of tickets to our opening performance."

It was a cake of three layers, frosted white and decorated with sugared violets and roses of marchpane. Maria hurried to steady the cake as it threatened to topple off the plate. They set it on a wooden crate amid exclamations and applause.

Malcolm kissed his wife again. "Ivy, dearest, this goes beyond your previous achievements."

"It was luck," she said modestly. "I happened to be in the shop when news came that a groom had cried off and there would be no wedding feast."

"One hates to take pleasure in the misfortunes of others, but how well we have benefited," Phoebe declared. "And who should do the honors?"

"I suggest our newest married couple," said Malcolm.

Kate blushed and protested, but took the knife from Phoebe.

"Well, do your duty," Malcolm reminded the marquess, who joined Kate and grasped the knife, too, resting his hand lightly on hers, his other hand around her waist.

They cut through the cake, Kate with her tongue between her teeth, intent on slicing through roses and violets, and Hal with his eyes on Kate.

"Do not stare at me so," she whispered, "or I shall make a mistake."

"Some would say you already have, by marrying an actor," he said, loud enough for the runner to hear as he sat on the edge of the stage, apart from the others.

The remark called for some reply. "I know my own mind," she said softly, as tears filled her eyes. Why am I so missish, she asked herself, as the marquess kissed her cheek. Is it because this is so improbable? Or is it because I am such a fool? I couldn't possibly love him; I don't even know him.

The cake was delicious by everyone's account, so Kate could not imagine why it tasted like sawdust to her. She watched the others: Phoebe and Gerald sitting together, smiling messages meant for only each other; Maria shyly offering cake to the runner; and Ivy and Malcolm leaning against each other, with their little girls close by, concentrating on their rare treat. If this theatre fails, she thought, these dear people will be without resources and at the mercy of the parish workhouse. She set down the rest of her cake.

"Excuse me, but I am going for a walk," she mumbled and hurried from the stage.

The night air revived her spirits somewhat as she put distance between herself and the theatre. She found a tree with a low limb and hiked herself into it, resting her cheek against the cool, rough bark and watching the stars through the leaves as they began to wink on in the evening sky. She was used to solitude; Papa never seemed to realize how the hours passed when he was inhaling the special air of old cathedrals and art galleries. Solitude was the quiet friend of her childhood.

But tonight was different somehow. She felt lonely. She thought of Malcolm and Ivy, living a difficult life, always on the edge of disaster, but facing it together with a certain gallantry that she knew would never be hers, not as present conditions prevailed. She looked down at her hands and twisted the wedding ring on her finger, wishing she could cast away the impossible burden she had saddled upon herself.

"A penny for your thoughts, wife."

Hal stood, hands in pockets, just below her at the base of the tree. Without an invitation he pulled himself into the tree, too.

Her heart full of misery, but her voice light, she held up her ring finger in the moonlight. "Beware hasty weddings and cheap rings," she joked. "It is turning my finger quite green."

Hal looked and shook his head. "That comes from hanging about with Captain Sharps and other shady coves. You really ought to keep better company."

She sighed and said nothing. He nudged her shoulder.

"You can tell me, Kate," was all he said.

"My burdens aren't yours," she replied. "I am sure you'll resolve this difficulty with your nephew and soon return to your own pursuits. And I have stuck myself with this theatre and I am afraid."

"That was last night's theme, if I remember," he said and took her hand.

She glanced down to see the Bow Street Runner strolling by. Yes, by all means, she thought, carry on this stupid deception. Will Muggeridge tipped his hat to her.

"Do you return to your lodgings at the Scylla and Charybdis?" he asked.

Hal draped his arm around Kate's shoulder and tugged her close. "No, my dear sir. We are staying at the theatre with the others."

"Not much privacy there for a newly wed couple," Will said.

"Economy is the key word here," Hal replied.

The runner threw back his head and laughed. "This must be a new experience for you, my lord," he said when he could speak again.

"Whatever do you mean?" Hal asked.

The runner struck a sulphur off his boot and lighted the pipe he held cradled in his hand against the slight breeze. He stoked it slowly until the bowl gave off a steady red glow. "I can humor you, my lord, as long as you want, but I know who you are."

"You'll have to prove it," was Hal's quiet reply.

The runner shrugged, tipped his hat to Kate again, and walked slowly toward the inn. Hal released Kate, and she jumped down from her perch. She started briskly toward the theatre and then stopped and turned to Hal. "You probably should tell him who you are. I am sure Mr. Muggeridge wants only to escort you in safety back to London."

"What, and miss all this fun?"

Kate whirled around and increased her speed. Hal grabbed her arm. She turned to face him again, wishing he would not hold her so close.

"We are only an amusement to you, sir," she snapped. "You will tease and play to alleviate whatever boredom you are feeling, and then when you are tired of this entertainment, you will be gone. This is a serious matter!"

"More than you know," he murmured, pulled her in close suddenly with his hand on her neck, and kissed her.

It was the sort of kiss she had read about in those fervid romances that Papa so deplored, but which kept her company when he would not. The reality of Hal's lips on hers covered her like a warm bath or a rainy walk in Italy's hot summers. He was much too close for her to keep her eyes open, but she wanted to jump outside her skin and see this thing that was happening to her.

Too soon he was releasing her, even though he still held her close. She kept her eyes shut and breathed in the fragrance of his skin and the elusive odor of bay rum that lingered improbably, even under the layers of theatre dust that coated them both.

"There, now," he said, as if she were a student and he the teacher. "You needed kissing." He touched her chin, released her, and started toward the theatre. He turned around, hands in his pockets again, and walked backward.

"By the way, Mrs. Hampton, that was a wise decision you made," he said, his voice cheerful.

"Wh … what?" she asked, opening her eyes and wishing the moment would linger.

"Gerald Broussard will write you a good play, I am sure of it. Good night, my dear. Don't stay outside too long."

With a wave of his hand he turned around and soon vanished in the shadows. She watched him go, then went quietly back to the tree and sat there until she felt entirely composed and a little sleepy.

The wedding cake had been put away when she returned, and but one lantern burned on the well-swept stage. She fingered the curtains. Tomorrow these must come down, she thought, so we can mend them. I shall send Hal and Davy for paint and ask Ivy what we can do about that cavern that Mr. Dawkins called the front lobby. And Gerald can find himself a quiet place free from Phoebe and all other distractions and write a play.

She walked to the middle of the stage and set the lantern down in front of her, trying to imagine a row of lights and people in the audience, waiting to be entertained. The dream eluded her; all she could see were empty seats deep in dust and a bat wheeling overhead, amusing itself with flying tricks.

She picked up the lantern and found the sleeping room for the Bladesworth girls. Someone had made up a pallet for her on the floor. Accompanied by a huge yawn that seemed to go on and on, she shucked off her dress, lay down, and slept more peacefully than she would have believed possible.

Kate woke to the sight of the smallest Bladesworth daughter rising from a tub of water to be draped about with a towel by Ivy. What a welcome sight, she thought, her hands behind her head.

"The baker loaned us his tub," Ivy explained as she dried off her little one. "I fear you are the last to use the water, but we can promise you first rights on the next bath."

"Anything will be welcome," Kate said as she sat up and rubbed the back of her neck. She had wakened from a disconcerting dream, with Hal pulling her close, his hand on her neck, reeling her in like a fish on a line. He was about to kiss her when he dissolved into the Bow Street Runner, and then Mr. Cratch, who scolded her for wasting her inheritance on actors and vagabonds.

The water was tepid and didn't bear close inspection, but it was better than nothing. After five other bathers she could not bring herself to wash her hair, too. It would have to manage with a vigorous brushing. Her clean dress felt good as she smoothed its folds over her hips and looked about for her slippers.

Her eyes alive with good humor, Ivy handed her a large white apron.

"The baker?" Kate teased and laughed along with Ivy. "It seems that you have an admirer, Mrs. Bladesworth."

She nodded. "And I will cultivate him, too! He already has said that he will see that our handbills go along with each of his orders."

"What a wonderful idea," Kate exclaimed as she tied on the apron. "Ivy, I appoint you to cultivate all the shops along Banner Street. Where are the men?"

Ivy handed her a bun still slightly warm from the baker's oven. "Malcolm is determined to arrange the prop room to his liking; Davy, Hal, and our friend the runner are washing down the walls; and Gerald is in the balcony with a large supply of ink and foolscap. And my girls are mending the curtain."

Kate joined Phoebe and Maria on the stage, where they bent over the curtain, needle in hand. She scrutinized the curtain until Phoebe looked up.

"When we are big success, a new curtain will have to be our first purchase." She said it calmly in a matter-of-fact tone that made Kate blush with the memory of her own doubts. She raised her beautiful eyes to the balcony and sighed. "Gerald says I am not to pester him."

"I do not believe that was the word he used," her sister corrected.

Phoebe made no remark, but lowered her eyes and returned to the curtain. Kate found a long tear and seated herself cross-legged on the floor. "How does Gerald Broussard come to be with your company?"

"Oh, he has always been with us," Maria replied. "You have never heard of the Broussards?"

"Silly, Kate does not travel in theatrical circles," Phoebe said. "The Broussards were a well-known French troupe, who had the misfortune to enjoy friendly ties with the aristos. They fled after Louis lost his head. Papa knew them and invited them to travel with us. We have always known Gerald."

Kate looked up from the curtain. "Where are his parents?"

Phoebe sighed. "They thought to return to France, once Napoleon was in power, but were drowned in a Channel crossing. Gerald had remained behind with us to tidy up some business and escaped death."

"It is so sad," Kate exclaimed.

"But so romantic, don't you think?" Maria asked. "Almost as romantic as you and Hal," she teased.

"Oh, heavens!" Kate scoffed. "Don't let your imagination run you in circles."

"Why else would he stay?" Phoebe asked. "Surely he could elude this runner and avoid the clutches of his odious nephew. I think he loves you."

Kate ignored their laughter and then bent over her work again. He wanted to stay with the Bladesworths, did he? She wondered again how long before he would tire of the exertion. Hadn't Abner Sheffield said he was lazy?

She sewed in silence, listening as Maria and Phoebe traded lines from Shakespeare plays, correcting each other when memory failed them, and laughing when they mixed up roles with plays. She could see Davy and the runner washing down the walls, but where was Hal?

After an hour when her back was beginning to ache, she heard a familiar weighty tread on the stage. Hal stood behind her, observing her efforts. He was dressed in a handsome garb a little out of fashion, but which elegantly suited his tall frame.

"Sir, wherever did you get such an outfit? Am I ruined now and my fortunes depleted?" she asked, beaming up at him.

He turned around for her benefit and pulled open the coat to reveal a waistcoat of startling hue. "Your father is a complete hand," he told the Bladesworth sisters. "He came up with this creation from the depths of the costume wardrobe. I defy anyone not to see this waistcoat from the back row."

Phoebe nodded and threaded the needle again. "Sir Hugo Dreadmore from *Least Said, Soonest Mended*. He is a great villain and meets a suitable end in the fifth act."

Hal bowed. "I am not familiar with that play, but I am sure he is killed for his wardrobe. The toils of fashion have never been my problem, so let us hope I can avoid his fate." He pulled something from his watch pocket and dropped it casually in

Kate's lap. "Here you are, good wife. Something that won't turn your finger green."

It was a ring, slim and gold. Kate held it up to the light, exclaiming with pleasure at the delicate flowers etched in the band. "I am sure you shouldn't have done this," she said, wanting to scold him, but touched by his thoughtfulness. She took off the gilt ring and replaced it with the gold one. The fit was perfect. "You know you cannot afford this right now," she said, her voice low.

Hal accepted the gilt ring from her. "My dear, I may be living on the cheap this summer, but I am not entirely dead to duty. It was only a simple matter of pawning my signet ring."

"You didn't!" She spoke too loud, and the runner looked up from the wall he was cleaning, his face alert. She lowered her voice. "That must have been difficult for you."

"Not at all, not at all. And do you know, with that pawn, I was able to purchase enough paint for the interior of this bat haven. *And* two painters to go with it." He bowed to Kate and flicked her cheek idly with his finger. "You see, I am still lazy, wife."

"Hardly, sir," she murmured, her head bent over the curtain to hide her blush. "Is it better to work harder or think smarter?"

He grinned at her, knelt down with less effort than he would have expended two weeks ago, and brushed the top of her head with a kiss. "I am beginning to think that marrying you was the smartest thing I ever did."

"We are *not* married," she whispered back, striving for emphasis even as she presented a smiling face for the benefit of the runner, who had stopped washing the walls and was trying to appear that he was not listening.

To her intense aggravation Hal's grin only deepened as he took hold of her left hand. He turned it this way and that until the dull glow of the ring caught fire. "It would appear that we are, my dear."

As quickly as she dared, especially with the runner so intent upon her business, she pulled free from the marquess's grasp, attacked the curtain more fiercely with her needle, and jabbed her leg. "Ow!" she exclaimed and rubbed her thigh.

Hal continued to kneel beside her, his face full of sympathy. "What, wife, should I kiss it to make it better?"

Kate gasped. "Don't let that thought even cross your mind!" she hissed, wishing the runner would mind his own business so she could give Hal Hampton the massive scold he deserved. "I suspect you are far, far more dangerous to my peace than Squire Leavitt ever would have been!"

Hal threw back his head and laughed, got to his feet, patted Kate on the head, and strolled off the stage, whistling to himself. At the edge of the stage he blew her a kiss, to Maria's delight.

"He is a complete hand!" she said.

"He is a rascal!" Kate insisted, still rubbing her thigh. "Why does he flirt with me like this?"

"Perhaps it is because he loves you," Maria said in a matter-of-fact voice as she reeled off another length of thread.

"Do you think so, sister?" Phoebe asked, her eyes on the balcony, where Gerald sat with his back to them, hunched over a sawhorse table Malcolm had created for him.

"I am certain of it," Maria replied firmly.

"Then he must be all about in his head," Kate reported, picking up her needle again.

Although the thought was a pleasant one, she never would have admitted that fact to Maria. It might be disturbing, she thought, if I were susceptible to his charms—oh, why on earth is that man not married already; what can the young ladies of the *ton* be thinking?—but I am not. As it is, I can find it flattering that a marquess thinks I am worth flirting with.

She smoothed down the curtain and tucked in several more blind stitches. Still, she thought, it would be nice to marry someday, and maybe if I am lucky enough, I will marry someone like the marquess, who is intelligent, handsome, and has kindness to spare. I wonder how scarce such men are?

"Do you think he is handsome?" she asked Phoebe suddenly.

Phoebe was still gazing at the balcony, with the longing obvious in her eyes and in the way she held herself. "Who, Gerald?" she asked.

"Silly!" Maria exclaimed. "Everyone knows Gerald is handsomer than Apollo. I think she means the marquess."

After another sigh in the direction of the balcony Phoebe dragged her attention back to the stage. "I suppose he is, Kate. He has nice facial structure. He will be fun to make up, don't you think, Maria?"

Maria nodded. "He has particularly fine, well-defined lips."

They are especially nice lips, Kate thought, remembering last night. Well-trained too. She blushed again and ducked her head over the curtain, but not before Maria noticed.

"Kate," she whispered, her eyes lively. "Has he kissed you?"

She nodded, too embarrassed to look up. The sisters laughed and Phoebe leaned closer, her voice conspiratorial. "Did you like it?"

Kate nodded again. "I think, more than I should have," she said, her voice quiet.

To her relief neither of the sisters quizzed her further. Her calm statement earned a sigh from Maria, and a long glance at the balcony from Phoebe. I really must think of something else, Kate thought. If only he were not so attractive, it would be easy. If only he would not smile so at me, or touch my hand that way he does, or put his arm around my waist and tug me in close to where I seem to fit.

Kate threw down her needle in disgust, repented immediately, and crawling around on all fours, patted the curtain until she found it again. She heard heavy footsteps on the stage and looked around expectantly.

It was Malcolm. She stuck the needle in the pincushion as he walked around, surveying the day's work. He beamed at his daughters. "Well done, my dears," he boomed, his voice carrying beyond the back row and into the lobby. "Think you, if this venture fails, I shall hire you out as seamstresses, and we shall cheat the poorhouse yet!"

The Bladesworth sisters giggled and bent over their sewing again. Kate watched them, struck by their calm acceptance of the situation. They are not afraid, she thought suddenly. They have always lived precariously, and it does not frighten them anymore. She thought of her own life with Papa, never knowing his true financial condition until he was dead and Abner Sheffield was pouring reality into her lap all at once. She winced even now at the shock and surprise—anger, too. Admit it, she thought, that had been her final parting gift from the father she loved, but who remained a mystery. Phoebe and Maria have no such surprises awaiting them, she told herself. I wonder if they realize how lucky they are? I have been a fool to think myself their superior.

She looked up at Malcolm, surprised at how blurry he appeared. He held out his hand to her and lifted her to her feet. "Come, my super-dainty Kate and let me show you what I am doing to your theatre."

"It is our theatre," she said, winking back her tears. "Yours and mine." She gestured toward the sisters, who were watching her with all the good nature that was their special gift. "I may supply the money, sir, but yours is the heart. For this I thank you."

To her amazement Malcolm's eyes filled with tears. She watched as he whipped out a massive handkerchief, flourished it around his eyes, and then blew his nose. "It appears we are all in debt to each other," he said from the depths of the handkerchief. In another moment he had recovered his composure. He held out his arm to Kate, and she took it, mystified.

As she hurried to keep up with both his enthusiasm and his long legs, Malcolm Bladesworth showed her the careful arrangement of prop rooms, makeup tables, and wardrobe closet. "This could be the finest theatre in all the provinces," he said, the pride unmistakable in his voice. "Now if only Gerald can write us a play."

THE PLAY WAS DONE in three days, three days in which Gerald, unshaven and a little desperate about the eyes, left the balcony only for sleep, food, and trips to the necessary out back. During those three days Phoebe drooped and pined and would only trade lines with Maria if they were death-bed scenes, or passages equally gloomy. Her own doubts returning, Kate spent the time in the wardrobe room, reinforcing seams already sound, or tightening buttons completely anchored. Like the others she avoided the stage and the sight of Gerald sitting so quietly in the balcony, hunched over the sawhorse desk, writing and writing. Only Hal appeared oblivious to the tension. Wearing his leathers, old painter's shirt open at the neck, and whistling to himself, he joined the journeymen working swiftly in the lobby. He seemed to have no fear of tall ladders.

"I do not know why you have to be so careless of your person," Kate complained one afternoon as she passed through the lobby and quickly averted her eyes from the sight of the marquess leaning out at the top of the ladder to reach an elusive swirl in the design overhead.

He looked about to make sure the runner was not in sight. "Wife, I do it only in case the marquess business should suddenly slack off. Everyone should have a trade. Consider Louis of France before his appointment with Dr. Guillotin. He was a clockmaker."

Kate stood below, her hands on her hips. "You worry me!" she declared.

He beamed down at her. "Do I?" He flicked a little paint in her direction and chuckled when she shrieked and jumped back. "In any event should I plummet to the floor below, and pressed to your wonderful bosom, gasp out my life in your lap, you can report to Abner Sheffield that I was not lazy."

"What you are is a sore trial," was all she could think to say.

"But I am so much fun, Katie, my love," he said cheerfully. "You'll see."

"I will not!" she exclaimed and marched from the lobby as he laughed.

Three nights later, when dinner was over, and the runner had not yet returned to the inn, Gerald emerged from the balcony, scruffy and haggard, but with a certain quiet triumph in his handsome brown eyes that no one could mistake. He strode into the sparsely furnished chamber that Malcolm had dubbed the green room, and plopped a sheaf of papers into Malcolm's lap as he sat playing jackstraws with his younger daughters.

"Monsieur, you see before you a play," he said, his face tired and enthusiastic at the same time. "It is a farce in five acts, using as many people as we have." He bowed elegantly to the youngest daughters. "Even you, too, *mes amis*. You can't begin too young in the theatre."

He rested his hand on Malcolm's shoulder. "You, sir, and you, dear Madame Bladesworth, are the parents of five hopeful daughters, three of age, and two much younger." He gestured at the runner and the Marquess, who were engaged in a game of cards, and slapped himself in the chest. "And we are the suitors." He turned to Davy. "You, my lad, will be a particularly slimy brother."

"Capital!" Davy exclaimed.

"He needn't even act," Maria teased and shrieked as she dodged the pillow he threw.

"Now only tell me there will be sword fights, and I shall be quite content!" Davy continued.

"Of course!" Gerald looked at the marquess. "Hal, can you fence?"

"Not in years, lad," Hal replied. "Where *is* that ace?" While the runner looked on in amusement, Hal tipped Will's cards down. "There it is!" He threw down his hand and the runner laughed. "Well, sir, if you will not cheat, then I must! Fencing, you say? When do we begin?"

12

KATE BILLINGS DRIFTED TO sleep listening to the sound of the men laughing in the green room over Gerald's play. She tucked her hands under her cheek, closed her eyes, and smiled at the warmth of Lord Grayson's laughter. It was the full-bodied sound of someone enjoying himself, and it pleased her. I wonder what your life was like before you fell in with the Bladesworths, she thought. It hope it wasn't as lonely as mine.

Her own had been sterile enough lately, full as it was with worry over her new situation and fear of the future. And now I am the owner of a theatre, God help us, and I have friends, and I have been kissed. Considering that only three weeks ago she had been on her way to Leavitt Hall and a dubious future, it seemed a fair exchange. Now if only we can make this theatre pay, she thought as she let loose of the day. She tried to worry about it some more but the memory of Hal's kiss wouldn't let her. Her lips curved into a smile.

She was dreaming what it would be like to wake up in his arms when someone shook her gently.

"Kate? Are you asleep?"

The voice was low, but she would have recognized it in a roomful of whispers. The marquess shook her again, then rested the back of his hand against her throat, right against her pulse. "Kate?" he whispered in her ear.

Kate opened her eyes and reached for the marquess's hand. He twined his fingers in hers, and she knew she was not dreaming. She could barely see him as he knelt beside her pallet on the floor, but there was just the faintest lingering odor of bay rum, and his fingers in hers, so long and fine-boned, were already as familiar to her as her own.

She watched him in the dark, wondered briefly what he would do if she pulled him down closer to her, and then sat up quickly, amazed at the direction her thoughts continued to take. He released her hand, then settled back on his haunches.

"Whatever is it?" she whispered.

He laughed low in his throat. "This play is too good to waste until morning. Get up and listen to some of the lines, my dear Kate."

She was fully awake now and regretting her impish thoughts. "I am not your dear Kate," she argued, keeping her voice low. "Surely the runner is gone by now."

"That he is, but I suppose I am in the habit of calling you 'my dear Kate.' " He hesitated, as if he wanted to say something more, and then his voice lightened. "I am sure it will pass."

"Of course it will," she agreed, grateful for the dark. Don't be an idiot, she told herself as the marquess rose and pulled her to her feet.

"Wait! I am only in my nightgown!"

"And it is a very pretty one, if I remember, dear Kate," he whispered. "A little bow at the neck and rather a pleasant shade of blue? Flannel or something equally daunting?"

"You are outrageous," she returned, fumbling for her robe, and wishing he would not stand so close.

"I suppose I am," he replied. "But considering that three weeks ago I was the most boring person I knew, it must be an improvement. Come now, unless you would rather waste your time sleeping."

Buttoning her robe, she followed him into the green room. Gerald, his face tired, but his eyes still lively, looked up and nodded to her. "Let us entertain you," he said, gesturing to one of Malcolm's prop boxes serving as a stool.

She sat, pulling her robe about her, and wishing her feet were not bare and her hair tumbled down her back to her waist. "I am sure I look a sight," she murmured, embarrassed at her appearance.

The marquess sat down on the floor next to her. "I ask you, Gerald, is there any way to understand women? Here sits Katherine Billings, looking her grandest, and she complains that she is an antidote."

Kate's retort was drowned out by giggles from the doorway. Phoebe and Maria, herded along by their brother, Davy, came into the room. "Brothers are the curse of the earth," Maria said as she yawned, but Phoebe had already seated herself by Gerald. "Let us hurry with this. Papa will have a fit if he finds us up at th—"

"Papa will do what?" asked Malcolm from the doorway, clad in nightshirt and paisley robe of intricate design and eyepopping color, suitable for a sultan or an actor. He rubbed his hands together. "Some things cannot wait until morning. Who do you think told Davy and Hal here to roust the females! Come, Gerald, let us read, only not in too animated a fashion. I do not wish to waken dear Ivy."

"Oh, you do not!" Ivy scolded from the doorway. "Then you should stay in bed and not go lumbering about, if you do not wish to waken dear Ivy!"

"I am always quieter than a mouse," Malcolm replied, his expression morose, his voice ill-used.

"That is a vast fiction, but we will overlook it," Ivy said, seating herself beside her husband.

"I have given the major share of the lines to Phoebe and

Maria," Gerald explained, his eyes on Kate. "They are scheming to find a suitor for you, Kate, so they will be free to marry their lovers."

"The fewer lines the better," Kate replied.

"As long as she wears that wonderful corset," the marquess added.

"You try me, my lord," Kate said, glaring at the man who sat at her feet, looking much too cheerful for one o'clock in the morning.

"Of course Lord Grayson will be your suitor," Gerald continued smoothly.

Kate rolled her eyes, but said nothing.

"Only he is a bumbling, clumsy fellow with nothing to recommend him."

Kate laughed and prodded the marquess with her bare foot. "'A hit, a palpable hit,'" she quoted and stood up and bowed when all the Bladesworths applauded.

Maria was looking over Gerald's shoulder at the manuscript in his hand. "Am I to assume that you are Phoebe's would-be suitor?"

"*Mais oui*," Gerald replied. Malcolm harrumphed, and Phoebe, adorable in nightgown, robe, and disheveled hair, blushed.

"Very well, then, who is to be my suitor?" Maria asked.

Gerald sighed and looked at the marquess. "Lord Grayson, I regret this, but I am going to have to ask Will Muggeridge to join us, if he will."

"Gerald!" Kate exclaimed. "As it is, he dogs our every footsteps!"

"I know, and I am sorry for that, but the Muse beckoned, and what could I do? Oh, and there is one more part that wants filling, but it is a small one. We need to procure a vicar to marry you and the marquess in the fifth act."

"Gerald, what are you doing!" she demanded.

"Excellent!" said the marquess. "And to think that we already have the ring! Let us read this charming confection that grows more palatable by the minute."

Kate glowered at him, and he grinned back.

Gerald was eyeing the marquess, too, only he was not smiling. "My lord, you may not like this." He paused and then proceeded slowly, picking through his words like a housewife at a farmer's market. "I mean, Lord Grayson, would you be offended to play a buffoon? I really should ask."

All were silent, looking at the marquess, who considered the matter in silence. He shook his head finally. "My dear Gerald, considering that I have been a buffoon for the past seven years at least, who better to play one?"

After sorting out parts, they began the play, passing the manuscript from hand to hand, quickly caught up in the magic of *Married Well, or, Love in Strange Guises*. It was funny, Kate admitted, a delightful comedy of mistaken identity, desperate lovers, and Squire Antonionus Pinchbeck, bumbling his way through a courtship with the very proper Miss Agatha Rowbottom, eldest and most brainless daughter of a wealthy brewer.

Gerald had crafted well, using his resources, with no one left over. "And see here," he said, "during this fifth act, we have a play within a play, so it won't be out of character for one of the cast members to open or close the curtains, or perform other stage business."

"Wonderful!" declared Maria, clapping her hands. "And here Papa thought you were just another handsome actor! You own you must take that back, Papa."

Malcolm harrumphed, "We shall see, sir!"

Gerald's face fell.

"But so far, I am delighted," Malcolm hastened to add. "And now, this final act."

"*Oui*, Monsieur Bladesworth," Gerald said, his enthusiasm bounding up again. "You see, Miss Rowbottom has no idea that she is really being married in this farce, which they are performing for their friends."

"Delightful," murmured the marquess. "What a clever idea."

"And the curtain closes with the spinster married off to the bumbler, and the other two couples free to make their own matches," Gerald finished triumphantly "Davy, can you continue to fill in as Maria's lover, just for tonight?"

Maria made a face as Davy bowed deeply before her.

"And Monsieur Bladesworth, you will play our vicar just for now, as well as the brewer?"

"Of course, lad."

They read the fifth act, Malcolm laughing so hard that they had to stop and fan him on one occasion, while Ivy sent Phoebe scurrying for a glass of water. Kate did her best with the part of Agatha Rowbottom, struggling against the laughter that bubbled to the surface over the plight of this befuddled spinster. May I never be so foolish, she thought to herself as she listened to Malcolm, reading the vicar's lines, marry her off without her knowledge to Antonionus Pinchbeck.

Hal Hampton did his best with the role and finally flopped back on the floor, succumbing to a wave of helpless laughter. He held his hands to his midsection. "My stomach hurts, I have laughed so hard," he managed finally. "Gerald, you are going to commit theatrical murder among the unsuspecting citizens of Leeds!"

"No one ever died of laughter," the Frenchman replied with a pleased grin on his face.

And then it was over. They sat, exhausted, just looking at each other and giggling as the bells from St. Giles down the street tolled three times. Ivy Bladesworth moved first, rising, stretching, and holding her hands out to her daughters.

"Come, girls, let us go to bed. A few hours sleep should see us with steady enough hands to begin copying parts." She touched Gerald on the shoulder as she passed him. "Gerald, this is a triumph. Your dear papa would have been so proud of you."

Gerald only smiled at her, too tired to speak. He gathered up the manuscript and placed it carefully on the packing box that served as a table. He sat down, rolled up his sleeves, and pulled the inkwell closer.

"Surely this can wait until you have had a little sleep," Hal protested.

Gerald shook his head. "I must begin copying now," he said. "We have less than four weeks before we open."

"Then I will help you," the marquess said and pulled a sheaf of blank papers toward himself.

Kate smiled at him from the doorway. "This smacks of unnecessary exertion," she teased. "What would Abner Sheffield say if he could see you now?"

Hal dipped his pen in the ink and began to copy the manuscript on the packing crate between the two men. "He would be grateful that I am at last rendering some useful service to the nation. Go to bed, Miss Agatha Rowbottom, with no arguments, or I will carry you there myself."

At his words, which sounded more like a caress than a command, Hal looked over his shoulder at her. There was something in his expression that told her he would do just that, if she should argue with him.

"Very well, sir," she said, wondering at the emotions that tumbled over her. I must be very tired, she thought.

She went back to the bedroom and lay down on her pallet. Phoebe lay on the pallet beside her, her eyes wide open, staring at the ceiling, her profile beautiful in the fading darkness. She put out her hand and touched Kate.

"Do you think it is wonderful?" she asked, her voice a low murmur.

"Oh, I do," Kate whispered back. "You were so right about Gerald."

Phoebe closed her eyes. "I have always known he was special," she said simply.

Kate closed her eyes, too, but she heard Phoebe tossing about, and opened them again. Phoebe, raised up on her elbow, was looking at her. She leaned closer.

"Kate, he has asked me to marry him after the play opens."

"Phoebe!"

The young woman put her finger to her lips and cast a meaningful glance at Maria, who slept on her other side. "Shhh, Kate! I have not said anything to Maria about this, but I wanted you to know." She faltered and looked away. "Perhaps you could drop a hint to Papa … Oh, Kate, I fear he will be displeased."

"You are but sixteen, Phoebe," Kate reminded. "Surely Malcolm would want you to wait a few years."

"I am sixteen and I know my own mind. I will have Gerald, and none other."

She lay back down again. Kate watched her, noting the resolution of her jaw and the firm line of her lips. "You are so sure," she said. It was more a statement than a question. "How can you know?"

"It is something a woman just knows," Phoebe replied, her voice softer now. In another moment she slept.

Kate closed her eyes. I wonder if it is so simple, she thought.

It seemed only minutes later that she woke to the sound of the birds chattering at the squirrels on the ground. Kate looked around. Everyone still slumbered. Quietly she got up and put on her robe, letting herself into the hall.

A bat swooped past her head, just missing her. Kate put her hand to her mouth, frozen to the spot, until it undulated gracefully away. I must remind Gerald to add bats to his plot, she thought ruefully, else how can we explain them to our theatregoers?

The door to the green room was open, and she peeked in. Gerald lay on the floor, covered with Hal Hampton's coat, snoring peacefully. The marquess still sat at the table, steadily copying the play. Kate rested her head against the doorframe and watched him dip the pen in the ink, careful not to blotch the paper, as he continued Gerald's work. He had a broad back, one that looked capable to bearing any burden. Abner Sheffield must have been crazy to think him a useless ornament to society, she thought.

Kate tiptoed into the room, careful not to waken Gerald. She padded quietly on bare feet to the table and stood a moment behind the marquess. She hesitated and then rested her hand on his shoulder.

He seemed not to be startled by her unannounced presence, but only looked at her hand on his shoulder. He rested the pen on the table. "Do you know, Kate, you would make my joy complete if you would put your other hand on my shoulder and rub … ah, yes."

She laughed softly as she rubbed his shoulders, pushing the heels of her hands against the back of his neck until he sighed with pleasure. "Don't stop," he urged when she let up on the pressure.

"I should abandon you to your discomfort," she said, her voice light. "That would serve you right for staying awake all this time, hunched over a packing crate." She continued to knead his shoulders, enjoying the warmth of his skin and the surprising resistance of his muscles. "I do wish you would relax."

"Maybe someday," he said quixotically.

She rubbed his shoulders in silence until her hands were tired. She stopped, but did not remove her hands. It should have surprised her, but it did not, when he leaned back and rested his head against her bosom. She was silent, scarcely breathing. When he did not move, she slowly looked around to see his face.

The marquess was asleep, resting against her breasts, looking as comfortable as if he slept in his own bed. She watched him and then slowly brought her arms around until they encircled his neck. She rested her chin on the top of his head for a moment, wondering if she had ever felt so content before, and knowing the moment would pass too quickly.

Sensing that he was waking up, she quickly moved away and rested her hands lightly on his shoulders again. She rubbed his shoulders until she was sure he was awake. "Dear me," he said, passing a hand in front of his eyes. "I must have dozed off. What a pleasant dream I had," he said, his voice quiet. "At least, I think I was dreaming."

"I am sure you were, my lord," she said. "And now it is morning."

He nodded and picked up the pen again. Kate turned to tiptoe from the room, so as not to awaken Gerald, but the Frenchman was awake, a smile on his face. As she left the room, he winked at her.

13

THEY BEGAN IN EARNEST the following day when the parts were all copied and everyone rested. Hal approached the runner about joining the cast of *Married Well.*

"Only think what an excellent opportunity this will be for you to keep me in sight," he said, when Will Muggeridge came to continue washing the walls. "And it will add new horizons to scrubbing bat leavings and dangling from tall ladders."

Will regarded the marquess thoughtfully. "I cannot imagine you would want me at such close quarters."

The marquess shook his head. He reached for Kate's hand and kissed her fingers one at a time. "We need you, sir. That is all, although I, for one, wonder why you are not chasing up leads in your search for the late and apparently unlamented Lord Grayson. Wouldn't you agree, wife?"

"Wh ... what?" Kate asked, her mind on his kisses planted so lightly on her fingers that seemed to sink into her heart and settle there.

The runner laughed. "I suppose I must humor the eccentricities of the aristocracy. I can certainly play along with you, my lord. And you, Mistress Hampton," he added, the sarcasm unmistakable.

The marquess bowed. "Very well, sir. But I do insist that you call me Hal. After all, it is my name." He pulled Kate close. "And it's good enough for my wife."

Kate smiled shyly at the runner and put her arm about Hal's waist. "Of course it is, my love," she said. At her words the marquess tightened his grip on her. He did not release her, even when the runner strolled away to join Maria, who held out a script for him.

"That is the first time you have called me such an endearment," he said, his voice soft. "I could almost think you meant it."

Kate took his hand off her waist. "Then I suppose I am getting into the spirit of this little adventure, Hal," she replied. "When the runner is about, you will be 'my love this' and 'my darling that.' " She looked into his eyes. "Isn't that what you want?"

"You know it is," he said. "Only …"

"Only what?" she asked. "What more can there be, sir?"

To her amazement the marquess took her by the hand and dragged her into the shadows off the stage. His hands on her shoulders, he pushed her up against the wall and held her there. She held her breath, wishing her heart would not crash so hard against her ribs.

"Tell me something, Kate," he said finally, after he had observed her for a moment. "Do you like me?"

His question surprised her. There was nothing loverlike in his tone, so she relaxed and considered him. It required only a moment's thought. "Why, yes, I do," she said, her eyes merry.

There was a considerable pause, while several emotions crossed his face as she watched. "Why?" he asked finally. His voice was soft, and he was standing so close to her, but she did not fear an improper advance. He seemed to want information more than kisses.

She went down the mental list that had been in her mind,

for some reason or other, for nearly a week. "Because you are a hard worker, and thoughtful. And you are nice to look at, and you have beautiful hands, and I like the way you listen when other people talk, even when they must be boring you."

"Do I bore you?" he asked. He released her and leaned up against the wall next to her.

"Heavens, no," she said. "I do not think you could."

She watched in amusement as he shoved his hands in his pockets and brought out the pocket linings. "Suppose I told you that the Grayson family was in debt to the eyebrows, and I was doing a dance with the cent percenters?"

Kate laughed softly. "With what I know of your character, I would suspect that you would find a way to pay them off and get out of debt and lead a more profitable life."

"Really? Well, suppose I told you that I was richer than Croesus."

"Then I would wish you the careful spending of it." Kate took a deep breath and touched his shoulder. "Hal, what can this possibly have to do with me?"

To her relief he seemed to relax. "I just wondered. Abner Sheffield seems to feel that I have turned into a useless fribble."

Kate straightened up and faced him, suddenly angry with their solicitor. "Then Mr. Sheffield is all about in his head! I think you should get a new solicitor."

"But Abner has known me all my life," Hal insisted, "and you only three weeks. How can you be so sure about my character?"

She paused and leaned against the wall again. Their shoulders touched, but she did not move away, as good manners would dictate. "I do not pretend to understand it, Hal. I just know that he is wrong." She thought a moment. "Perhaps I know you better. Now, don't tease me anymore about this!"

Without another word Hal grabbed her by the shoulders again, pulled her in close, and planted a loud, smacking kiss on her forehead. "Bless you, Miss … Mrs. Hampton!" he exclaimed.

From the stage the others applauded at the sound of his kiss, and then Gerald, his voice filled with amusement, called to them: "And now, Hamptons, if you are quite through … We have a play to learn!"

They rehearsed singly and in pairs—the marquess, the runner, and Gerald trading lines as they washed walls; Maria, Phoebe, and Kate as they sewed the curtain and then repainted the gilt on the chandeliers. They quizzed each other as they sat at meals, walked to church on Sunday, and shopped in the market. Kate gulped as her funds dwindled lower and lower with each excursion to the baker or the butcher, but thrust images of the poorhouse from her mind and doggedly worked on her lines, wishing she had the easy facility for memorization that the others possessed.

"It is a trial to me," she admitted to Hal one afternoon as they sat together in the tree that had become their favorite memorization spot. "Why are they so good at this, and we stumble and stutter over each line?"

"It *is* a chore," Hal agreed, "but, then, we have not been learning lines since we were first burped and breeched, as the Bladesworths have. Have you ever tried to count the parts they have memorized from other plays? They quote them all the time."

"It is quite beyond me," Kate said. "All I want to do is learn this one part." She nudged Hal and giggled as he grabbed the branch to retain his balance. "Oh, and look, Gerald showed me how to appear as the simple Miss Rowbottom. I merely let my mouth hang open as though I am catching flies."

Hal laughed at her attempt. "And you must open your eyes wide and stare adoringly at me if I should ever utter anything resembling a witticism. Ah, yes! That is the look. Trust me on this, Kate. And if you would flutter about and pick at my sleeve and gaze at me …" His voice trailed off, and he looked away, shaking his head.

Impulsively Kate took his hand and squeezed it. "I'm sorry.

I am certain I never knew that being such a catch on the Marriage Mart would be a chafing duty."

He turned his hand over and wound his fingers in hers. "You can't imagine what it is like, wondering if any woman is truly sincere, or just lusting after my money and title. I confess to a rising cynicism."

The sun came out from behind a cloud, and Kate raised her face to its warmth. "Well, I have never had such worries, sir. Who in the world wants a twenty-six-year-old spinster with no fortune?" She laughed and gave him another nudge. "Any man I would attract would have to be entirely serious, Hal!"

He joined in her laughter. "Twenty-six? I would have thought twenty-eight, at the very least!"

She pushed him from the limb, but he landed gracefully on his feet, grabbed her ankle, pulled her off, and caught her in a froth of petticoats and shrieks.

"I am a ripe thirty-five," he confessed as he tried to dodge her hands reaching to pull his hair. "And don't do that! I have little enough as it is."

"Very well, oh Ancient of Days," she teased. "Now, let me down. I don't want to put any undo strain on your heart."

"Kate, you already have," he whispered as he set her down.

She looked at him, so suddenly serious, and did not know what to say. A breeze sprang up and snatched away some of the manuscript. Grateful for the diversion, she hurried after the pages. Hal remained where he was, watching her, a half smile on his face. When she retrieved the last page, she headed for the theatre, knowing that he still gazed at her, and wishing he would not.

After a night spent tossing and turning about on her thin mattress, Kate decided that it would be best for her to spend less time in the solitary company of the marquess. Thank the Lord they had at least proceeded to the point of full company rehearsals. They would work long hours, and perhaps she would be so tired that she would not dream about Hal Hampton anymore.

Nothing worked, even though the marquess played a most unattractive character, a bumbling, fumbling suitor as liable to trip over a horse as a floor tile. Under Malcolm's patient direction, he stuttered and floundered about, a woman's worst nightmare as Antonionus Pinchbeck, but she could see only Hal Hampton, a man she loved and wanted with all her heart. It was a longing more powerful than anything she had ever experienced, and it left her shaken, frustrated, and almost ill.

She found herself bursting into tears over the smallest difficulty, and it chafed her to lie and say that she was merely worried over finances, or the success of the theatre, and that it would pass. She knew her feelings for the marquess would never pass. She knew that when the summer was over, and he exerted himself to contact Sheffield, or admit the obvious to the runner, Hal Hampton would be gone. In his place would be Lord Henry Tewksbury-Hampton, marquess of Grayson, and he would be heading back to London and out of her life. Whatever mild flirtation he had undertaken for his own trifling amusement—surely it could be nothing more—would be soon forgotten.

It was impossible to avoid Hal, and her cup ran over with misery. There was the runner, more of a friend now, after several weeks of rehearsal, but still demanding, by his presence, that she continue her fiction as Hal Hampton's loving bride. Her heart cracked and snapped as she forced herself to flirt with Hal. It was the performance of her life, one that caused her the most acute compound of ecstasy and misery.

She dared not back out of the venture. It would mean the ruin of the Bladesworths and all they dreamed of. Ivy and her little daughters, between rehearsals, had seen to it that nearly every mercantile establishment in Leeds exhibited the theatre bill for *Well Married* that Maria and the runner—their heads together, their concentration intense—had labored over. The poster, so cleverly drawn, seemed to mock her from every street. Her heart twisting into knots, she smiled and answered questions about the play from townspeople who accosted her on the street as she strolled in the evening hours, her arm tucked into Hal's, carrying on the pretense that seared her heart like a heated brand.

If Hal noticed anything different about her, he chose to keep it to himself, and she was grateful. She wished she had the courage to ask him his thoughts, but that much bravery failed her. Even more painful would be the acknowledgment that it was only a summer flirtation, with nothing meant. If he were to laugh away her love, it would be more than she could bear. Better not to know, she decided, not while there remained some glimmer that she could still extricate herself from this bumble broth and pick up the pieces before her heart was even more seriously involved. Recovery was still possible. It must be.

And then the painters reached the stage.

"Mama, I cannot bear it," Phoebe said one morning as the fumes seemed to fill every inch of space around them. "Can we not escape this?"

Ivy looked at Malcolm. "Husband, I suggest that we send them into the woods with a picnic and the fencing foils."

"Capital!" Malcolm said and mopped his streaming face. "And Ivy and I will stroll over to the silk warehouse to look at fabric." He nodded to Gerald. "You can help these two swordsmen improve their faulty choreography. We cannot have them capering about like Russian circus bears." He smiled at Hal. "Even Squire Pinchbeck should not be without some rudimentary agility."

Hal bowed and winked at Kate. "Good wife, bring along a blanket so I may rest my head in your lap after such exertion done in the name of art."

"Certainly, my love," Kate said.

The littlest Bladesworths leading the way, and Davy laboring with the hamper, they left the theatre, crossed the river, and headed into the trees. Hal and the runner walked together, carrying the foils and trading lines, while Kate and the sisters walked behind them, enjoying the paint-free air and each other's company.

As they left the path and looked for a spot among the trees, Maria tucked her arm through Kate's and motioned for her to lean closer.

"Do I imagine things, Kate, or does our friend the marquess appear to be considerably less flabby?" she asked, careful to keep her voice low. "I mean, walking behind him has become a pleasant experience, don't you agree?"

"He does have a nice swing to his walk," Kate agreed, hard put not to laugh.

"I wasn't referring to the swing," Maria said, "but to the … Kate, he looks awfully good in those wardrobe room castoffs."

"Well, perhaps a trifle snug still," she said.

"Exactly!" said Maria.

She tried to smother her laughter by turning it into a coughing spell. Hal turned around, looked at Maria's red-faced exertions, and shook his head. "I won't ask, and you won't tell," he murmured. "Maria, you are a certifiable rascal. We shall leave it at that."

And thank goodness, Kate thought, as Maria went off in a gale of merriment. Hal had trimmed down to a high level of appeal. Taken with a natural grace not often found in the very tall, he had already been turning female heads in Leeds, or so Kate had observed on their nightly walks. She sighed and forced her thoughts into other, more seemly channels.

They took their time eating, Hal lounging about on the grass close by and filching food from her plate, laughing at Davy's jokes, and letting the little girls tie his shoes into knots, pretending he did not see them. To their delight he took a few steps and fell down, before "noticing." Davy stood up and headed for the river, removing his shirt, intent on a swim.

When the marquess had retied his shoes, the runner tossed him a foil.

"We had better practice before Gerald and Phoebe discover a rare bird that must be followed."

Gerald took Phoebe by the hand and kissed it. "You are already too late, sir! I seem to hear nature whispering. Remember, practice makes perfect."

Phoebe blushed becomingly and clung to his sleeve. "We need to concentrate on our lines in solitude," she said with some dignity and then ruined the effect by sticking out her tongue when Maria laughed.

The runner watched them go. "Now then, Hal," he began, turning back to the business at hand. "*En garde.*" They touched foils and circled gracefully about, Maria shouting reminders about remaining open to the audience and watching their upstage hands. Kate drew the little Bladesworths close to her to watch. They lolled in the welcome shade, far enough back to avoid any chance encounters, even with buttoned foils. Maria watched in amusement as the men parried, tried to remember their lines, and then laughed at their clumsy attempts.

Hal stopped for a few minutes and shaded his eyes with his hand so he could see them in the shadows. "Dear wife, it is rather like patting one's head and rubbing one's stomach." He turned to the runner. "Will, why don't we just spill out the dialogue fast, and then fight it out?"

With a wild yell Will lunged at the marquess, who grinned and prepared to meet his mock attack. Suddenly two horsemen burst into the clearing, charging straight at the runner. As Kate watched in horrified paralysis, one of the riders kicked out at Will's head. The runner dropped to the ground without a sound, still clutching the foil. Maria gasped and tried to rise, but Kate grabbed her and pulled her down beside her little sisters.

Hal only had time to look at her, say her name, and then the horsemen were on him. He struck out, but one rider leaned over and enveloped him in a blanket while the other struck him with a dark object. As he collapsed, one rider gathered him up and helped the other sling the unconscious marquess across his knees. They were gone before Kate had time to draw another breath.

The clearing was silent. Only a puff of dust on the path and Will, groaning and trying to rise, indicated that anyone had been there at all. With a strangled cry Maria ran to the runner, throwing herself down beside him and clutching him to her. Ordering the little ones to stay where they were, Kate hurried to Will. Blood dribbled from a cut on his forehead, and a welt was already rising. He blinked and stared at her.

Tears streaming down her face, Maria dabbed at the cut with the hem of her dress. "Kate, do something!" she pleaded. "Call for Gerald! Oh, where is Davy?"

As she spoke, Davy came running from the river, his hair wet, clutching his pants, which were still unbuttoned. He took in the scene before him, his eyes wide. "Kate! I saw two men riding across the bridge. Was that Hal with them?"

She nodded, unable to speak. Maria looked up from Will. "Kate, it must be his nephew, and it is just as he feared! Do you think they will kill him?"

"Good God, I hope not," she said and leaped to her feet, screaming for Gerald.

In another moment Gerald and Phoebe ran into the clearing. Will was getting to his feet, helped by Maria and Davy. The little Bladesworths still clung to each other, crying. "Got to get back," Will gasped. "Someone has kidnapped Hal Hampton!"

Kate, her mind a curious blank, ran to gather up the picnic hamper. As she bent over, the ground seemed to spin about. For the first time in her life, she fainted.

14

"BLAST YOU, ALGIE, I don't know why you had to hit him so hard!"

"Well, you try to wrap up someone that size in a blanket and send him off gently to the arms of Morpheus! And I don't know why I am elected to do all the rascally things."

"Because you started this, you blockhead."

Hal groaned and the voices stopped, except that their words seemed to echo in the cavern that used to be his head. Even with his eyes closed he could feel the brightness of the lights through his eyelids, and he did not feel inclined to open them.

Someone shook him. He struck out with all his strength and managed a light tap across his own face.

"See here, Uncle, I wish you would open your eyes. We have rescued you."

A rescue? Was that what it was? Hal reached up gingerly to touch his head, knowing that it must be laid open, with his brains, what few remained, exposed to view. All he felt was a significant bump behind his left ear and the growing conviction that he had been safer in Spain during three years of incarceration than he was in Yorkshire. He opened his eyes, wincing against the light.

Faces swam into focus as he watched them. At first there were two of Algernon Mannerly, and the thought of Algie as a twin made him shudder.

"Oh, here, you are cold," said a voice, the body just beyond his vision. Before he could protest, he was bundled in yet another blanket. He looked down at the hands that patted the blanket into place. The hands, freckled but shapely, were definitely not Algie's. With a sense of real foreboding he shifted slightly in the bed, and his worst fears were confirmed.

It was Pinky D'Urst's sister Florence, she of the long nose and longer chin. The fact that she eyed him with tender consternation was little comfort. His eyes dropped lower. Yes, she was as flat-chested as he remembered. There was none of Kate Billings's bounty. He closed his eyes again, weary beyond measure.

"Come now, Henry, where's your gratitude? Maybe Algie and I bungled it a bit, but at least you're out of the clutches of that low-life theatre troupe. Can't imagine how you fell into such company and what hold they have over you. We'll prefer charges, if you wish."

Pinky D'Urst's voice was hearty and loud and grated on his ears. He opened his eyes again to gaze at his best friend, Thaddeus D'Urst, he of the pale hair and rabbity complexion. Pinky sat on the end of the bed, dressed in riding clothes and tapping his whip against his boots.

Hal struggled to sit up, as Florence D'Urst, all flutterings and twitterings, pushed two pillows under his head. He stared hard at the whip. "Is that what you hit me with, Pinky? I call that infamous."

Pinky laughed, a well-fed sound entirely in keeping with his over-stuffed person. "Lord, no! Algie used a blackjack. He didn't want to bungle it."

Hal groaned again as Algie pulled up a chair to the bed. The squeak of the chair on the wooden floor rocketed right to his brain and banged against the bump on his head. "So glad to hear it," he muttered when the throbbing subsided.

"I knew you would be grateful," Algie burst forth, leaning close to his uncle. "From the looks of things, we got there not a moment too soon. That shady character appeared about ready to run you through." With a smile of vast satisfaction on his normally vacuous face, Algernon Mannerly sat back, as if waiting for his uncle to shower him with appreciation.

The marquess could only stare at his nephew and heir. I simply must convince Kate Billings to marry me at once and start breeding immediately, he thought, else this idiot might someday succeed to the family title. He paused, trying to straighten out his brain enough to select well-chosen words.

Algernon mistook his hesitation. He reached for his uncle's hand. "You don't need to thank me, Uncle. I was glad to do it."

"Don't be so kind to yourself, Algie," he murmured, pulling his hand away. "I was merely trying to discover a socially correct way to break the news to you that you are an ass, and will always be an ass. I regret that there seems to be no polite way to put that. Pardon me, Miss D'Urst."

Florence D'Urst squeaked and retreated to stand beside her brother, her face fiery. "Really, Lord Grayson," she said.

"Yes, really," he retorted, out of humor with all of them. "Did it ever occur to you, Algie, that I have no desire to be rescued? We were rehearsing a play." He paused a moment, struggling to untangle the events of that noon. "You didn't do any damage to that young man, did you, Pinky?"

"Other than give him a three-day headache, I doubt it," Pinky said. "Henry, what's gotten into you? We have been waiting nearly a month for you to arrive, and then we hear stories in Leeds about a missing marquess who fits your description. And out of the blue, Algernon shows up with a wild story about shooting you on the Great North Road."

"It was only a prank," Algernon interrupted, his voice sulky.

Hal sighed. "I don't have time to talk about it!" He threw back the covers and stood up, clad only in his long-tailed shirt. He clutched the bedpost, while Florence shrieked again and galloped into the hall.

"I am going back," he said, gritting his teeth against the dizziness and the added distraction of Florence in mild hysterics outside the door. "Really, Pinky, hasn't she ever seen a man's bare legs before?"

"I should hope not!" Pinky exclaimed.

"Well, they aren't too bad," Hal said, smiling for the first time. "I've trimmed down a bit since we last met, Pinky. Can you tell?"

"Henry!" Pinky burst out. "Have you lost your mind?"

Hal sat down on the bed, looking around for his pants. "No, actually, I think I've found it. Algie, are those my pants on the chair over there? Do something useful for the first time today and hand them over. Good God, what time is it?"

He caught the breeches Algie threw at him and tugged them on. "You two clunches can dashed well un-rescue me! There is a whole bunch of people at the Banner Street Theatre who are probably out of their minds with worry about me." He tucked in his shirt and buttoned his pants. "I might add, Algie, that they need me."

Pinky leaped to his feet and paced back and forth, the riding crop twitching behind his back. "Next you will tell us there is a woman involved."

Hal found his stockings and shoes and pulled them on. "Actually, there is. She is a managing female with absolutely eyepopping bosoms, a beautiful face, and excellent brains. She's inclined to worry too much and is yet a little timid to take charge. I intend to dedicate my life to giving her nothing further to worry about more than where to send our sons to school and the color of come-out dresses for our daughters."

Slightly out of breath, Pinky stopped his pacing. "You can't be dreaming of marrying a theatre doxy!"

Hal grasped the front of Pinky's coat and lifted him off the ground. "If you weren't my friend, I would call you out for that, Pinky! She's no dollymop. Trust me with better sense than that." He set Pinky back on his feet. "H'mm, I couldn't have done that a month ago, fancy." He shook his finger at his friend, who glared back at him. "You will leave me alone for another week until this play opens, and then things should have settled out the way I want."

He eyed Algernon. "Well, are you taking me back to Leeds, nephew? Think about your answer, because I am fully prepared to cut you off without a farthing right now."

"You've gone mad, Uncle," Algernon said, even as he helped the marquess into his coat.

"Not mad, Algie," Hal said. He regarded his nephew with an expression approaching affection. "Do you know, I have discovered there are people who like me, one in particular. She even gave me reasons why, which was more than you could ever do. And they don't include my money."

"I, for one, hope you regain your senses," Pinky said.

"I have, Pinky, I already have. I have no desire to flee from this particular romantic attachment and into a Spanish dungeon." He patted his friend's shoulder. "Now, don't stiffen up so! Trust me." He chuckled. "They are forever saying that. Yes, trust me. You'll like my choice. Good day to you, Pinky."

Pinky D'Urst shook his head, but he appeared less irritated. "Well, if you are dead set on steering this course, at least let me loan you some money. You look as though you could use some."

Hal nodded, his eyes merry. "Actually I could use some of the ready, Pink. I need to purchase a special license, and I fear they are not cheap."

"I wouldn't know," Pinky replied, his voice virtuous.

"Amanda and I let them call the banns like normal people! I wish you would reconsider. This sounds too rackety by half."

"I wouldn't dream of it. Thanks, Pinky. Now, remember, give me at least a week."

HAL AND ALGERNON RODE toward Leeds as the sun was setting, trotting along in silence at first. Hal's head ached with a life all its own, but he clung grimly to the reins. Algernon sat stiff and prim for much of the journey, his eyes straight ahead. As they approached Leeds, he unbent enough to glance at his uncle. He cleared his throat.

"See here, Uncle, I tried to find you again, I really did. Have you any idea how many little roads there are in Yorkshire? Each of them seemed to lead off to someone's smallholding or pasture."

Hal leaned over and touched his nephew's knee. "That is precisely what I thought happened. Algie, you haven't the sense of direction of a chicken's egg, have you?"

His words were kind enough, and Algernon sighed audibly and shook his head. "I tried to find you."

"I know. I am truly glad you did not, or I never would have had this adventure." He slowed his horse. "Tell, me Algie. How did you find me?"

For the first time Algie grinned. "Uncle, I went to a pawn shop to spout my watch, and there was your ring with the Grayson family crest." He glanced at his uncle, and there was some affection in the look, as well as relief. "You can imagine I thought the worst! But when the proprietor described you as the seller, I knew you were alive, at least. It was only a matter of asking about town."

He was silent then as they rode to Leeds's outskirts. Hal reined his horse, dismounted, and handed the reins to his nephew. Algernon reached out impulsively and touched his uncle's shoulder. "Be careful, sir." He gathered the reins in one hand. "One week, and that is enough. You may not credit this, but my mother is worried about you, too."

Hal laughed and then pressed his hand to his head. "You

have my permission to tell my sister not to worry, but nothing more."

Algernon nodded. He touched his hand to his hat and wheeled his horse around. "One week, uncle."

Hal stood in the street, watching until his nephew was out of sight. I hope he will return to D'Urst Hall, he thought. Maybe Florence will look good to him. He stood another moment, Kate Billings on his mind, until his desire for her quite cast his headache into the shadow. He wanted her more than propriety dictated. "I have become so unfashionable in Yorkshire," he said out loud, looking at the poster advertising *Well Married*. "Can it be good for the health of the nation for a marquess to actually want to marry and bed his own wife?"

He laughed softly to himself, pressed his hand to his head again, and let himself into the theatre. He stood inside the door, stopped by another thought. I wonder if she feels for me even a tenth of what I feel for her, he asked himself. That would be more than a man could hope for, but I shall ask it anyway. Each blow to my head this summer has only made me more optimistic.

The stage, smelling freshly of paint, was wreathed in shadows. Out of habit he looked up toward the ceiling and noted to his satisfaction that the bats no longer wheeled and zoomed overhead. He looked around. So much for the bats; where was everybody? They should have been rehearsing.

He thought of the runner, remembering the blow Pinky had struck with his boot. God, I hope he is not really hurt, he thought. It was hard to credit it, but he had become genuinely fond of Will Muggeridge, even if Kate still had her reservations. Besides, the man had a natural talent for the stage.

"Malcolm? Kate?" he called out, his voice uncertain. He walked toward the green room. It hurt to raise his voice, but he called again, "Malcolm?"

The door to the green room banged open and the youngest Bladesworth daughters threw themselves on him, crying and clutching his legs. Surprised, he regained his balance and knelt to hug them. "My dears, I am quite all right," he assured them.

And then there was Malcolm, his frown replaced by a grin of enormous proportions, and Ivy, wiping tears from her eyes and clutching his arm, asking where he was hurt, and did he want anything to eat, all in the same breath.

"Come in, come in, lad," Malcolm said, taking his other arm. "So you escaped your kidnappers? How resourceful you have become."

"They were particularly inept," he said, "which is hardly surprising, considering that one of them was my nephew."

Malcolm frowned and shook his head. "It's a dirty business, lad. I'm glad you are safe with us again and out of the hands of those who would harm you."

Hal owned to a prick of conscience, but he easily discarded it. "What of Will? About the last thing I remember was one of those brigands giving him quite a kick." His hand went to his head.

"Oh, he's sleeping now, well-watched by Maria, Phoebe, Kate, and Gerald." He tugged the marquess down onto a packing-crate stool. "I vow Maria is hanging on Will's every breath and ready with a mirror to make sure he does not quit this earth without her knowledge. He'll be fine, Hal." He leaned forward in a conspiratory manner. "Kate's beside herself. I tried to jolly her out of the doldrums by teasing her that she was overacting as Hal Hampton's bereft wife, and we nearly came to blows. There is no understanding females."

Intensely gratified by this piece of news, Hal nodded. "I don't pretend to understand women, either, sir. Perhaps I should go find her and console her."

"Plenty of consolation is in order, Hal!" Malcolm stopped. "But I think I hear them now. Save yourself the trouble of going in search."

As the marquess waited, Kate came into the room, her eyes red-rimmed and filled with worry. She grasped a handkerchief that appeared to have been wrung from hand to hand until it was practically a rag. Every line of her body seemed to droop. Hal regarded her with a gaze approaching reverence. Is it possible that anyone cares for me that much? he thought as he got slowly to his feet and held out his arms for his dear Kate.

She gasped when she saw him, and before he had time to react, her eyes rolled back in her head and she sank to the floor. Gerald, walking behind, caught her as she fell. He lifted her into his arms and handed her to the marquess.

"That's the second time today, my lord," he said. "You seem to be having a startling effect on Miss Agatha Rowbottom."

Hal accepted the burden, amazed all over again at how light she was and moved almost to tears by his feelings for this woman in his arms whom he had known less than a month. She was everything to him. He would no more flee from her into a Spanish prison than vault to the moon. What is this power, he thought, as he gazed at her face. It fairly takes my breath away.

"Lad, carry her into our room," Malcolm said. He laughed and shook his finger at the marquess. "And don't bring her out again until she is much happier!"

"Carte blanche, if I ever heard it," Gerald murmured under his breath. "Would to God he would feel that way about Phoebe and me."

Hal followed Bladesworth down the hall and into the room he shared with Ivy. The marquess set her on the bed as though she were made of eggshells and tissue paper and took the lamp from Malcolm. The actor stood there a moment more, looking down at Kate.

"She cried all day when she thought none of us was looking."

"I'm not sure I am worth that," Hal whispered.

"No man is, laddie," Malcolm replied, his own voice soft for a change, "but somehow they take us, even at our worst."

Malcolm closed the door quietly behind him. Hal placed the lamp on the table and sat down on the bed next to Kate.

He unbuttoned the front of her dress, each fastener like butter in his fingers. He found a sheaf of papers on the bureau, and holding her shirtwaist open, began to fan her with it. She was still well-covered by her chemise, but the outline of her breasts was so inviting that he turned the fan on himself.

"Kate, I love you," he said, his voice almost inaudible to his own ears. I love you when you're happy, and when you're worried and trying not to let anyone know, and when you're peeved with me, and especially when there is a look in your eye that says you wish I would kiss you and maybe do something more—even though you are too much a lady ever to admit it."

He leaned over her and kissed her. To his delight she raised her hand to his cheek. He kissed her again and then let his lips rest against her skin where the chemise curved over her bosom. Her flesh was warm and smelled of lavender and Kate. Her hand went to his hair, and with a strength that he wouldn't have credited in one so dainty, she pulled him closer. He held his breath in wonder as she slowly kissed his ear, his neck, and then his lips, each kiss longer than the one before.

She sighed and opened her eyes. "I didn't think I was dreaming," she said, her lips so close to his mouth that he almost felt her words before he heard them, a sign of love that made the room even hotter.

He didn't want her to stop, but she stiffened her arms and held him off. "I was so afraid for you," she said, her eyes on his. With another sigh that seemed to come from her toes and all the way up her body, she twined her fingers around his back and hugged him to her. His arms encircled her, and as she clung to him, he marveled how a grip so strong could feel so yielding at the same time.

He lay down next to her, resting his head on her breasts, pillowed there as she gently stroked his face. "I was afraid I would never see you again, Hal," she said. "It was almost more than I could bear."

He could hear the anguish in her voice. If he had any

reservations about the depth of her feelings, they vanished in another wave of desire that flowed over him. I have met my match, he thought, as he touched her breasts, tentatively at first, and then with more assurance. I shall come to know this woman more thoroughly than I know myself, he told himself as he cupped her warm flesh and kissed her again.

That she was his for the taking he had no doubt. His inner sense that grew warmer by the moment told him that she would do whatever he wanted. It was an awesome power he had never possessed before, and he closed his eyes against it. As he lay there in her arms, she touched his face, and he opened his eyes to a glimmer of gold from the wedding ring he had given her.

"Kate, will you marry me? I love you." He spoke quickly, impulsively.

Her hand stopped its caress of his face and he almost cried out in disappointment. It was as though his words, spoken in love, were a basin of cold water tipped over them both. As he nearly groaned out loud, she slowly untangled herself from his embrace, tugged her skirt down below her knees where it had crept up, and struggled to sit up. He had no choice as a gentleman but to allow her to move.

"Oh, Kate, please …" he pleaded. Please what, he thought wildly as, with trembling fingers, she began to button her dress. Let me make love to you right now? Let me just lie here and talk to you? Let me plead my case, even as I see you turn away? What did I say?

There were tears in her eyes as she pulled her tangled hair back from her face and swung her legs over the side of the bed. "I love you, too, Hal," she said, her face turned resolutely away from his. Her voice faltered. He reached for her hand, wanting contact with her any way he could get it now, but she would not let him touch her. "I can't even fathom how much I love you. There aren't words, only deeds, and we can't do that."

"Kate, we can if we are married!" he pleaded, his voice rising."No!" The word was wrenched from her. She looked at him then, her eyes huge and beautiful. "Only imagine what your family would think? No one would ever understand."

She got to her feet, swayed, and leaned against the wall. "I can't imagine what came over me," she said, shaking her head as he reached to steady her. "If you don't have any sense at all, then I must. No, Hal. Not now, not ever. You would come to despise our unequal birth."

"By the infernal, I would not!" he snapped. "And who said it was unequal? I know you are from a good family. I know …" He stopped. She wasn't listening to him. While all the protests filled his heart, she began to cry. It was the most hopeless sound he had ever heard, and it chilled him to the marrow.

God grant me a little wisdom, he pleaded. Without a word he helped her back to the bed, made her lie down, and covered her with a light blanket. The air had turned cool quite suddenly. "Don't, Kate," he whispered. He stood looking at her for a long moment, then touched her hair. "I do not require that you trade your dignity. I am sorry I spoke so."

Without another word he let himself from the bedroom. He closed the door and leaned against it a moment, bereft of all energy. I have left my strength behind in that room, he thought, and then forced himself to remain calm. I must think.

He came back into the green room, where only Malcolm and Ivy waited now. They sat close together, holding hands, and the pain of his own empty hands washed all over him again.

Malcolm looked up from his contemplation of his wife. "May we wish you happy?" he asked.

The marquess shook his head. "No, you may not. Kate insists on being sensible."

Hal sat down. The knot on his head, which he had forgotten about, began to throb again. He felt old and tired as he rested his head in his hands. "Malcolm, this may require some creative planning."

When he looked up again, the Bladesworths were gone. He heard Kate's quiet tread past the green room, where she hesitated and then moved on. He thought about everything, and nothing, and when he finally stood up to go to bed, he was feeling quite creative, indeed. And audacious, still very much in love with Mrs. Hal Hampton. "There is more than one way to skin a wife," he said and managed a smile he did not quite feel. "If you have thrown down the gauntlet, well then, I have picked it up."

15

TO SAY THAT THE week before the opening of *Well Married* was purgatory would have been to put a rosy gloss on the matter. In all the history of the world, Kate Billings knew there never could have been a more terrible span of seven days.

The first morning was difficult enough, as she lay on her pallet and mentally kicked herself for ever letting the marquess know how much she cared. I must be an idiot, she thought, and her face burned from the memory of her behavior the night before. Could I actually have kissed him like that, and not once, but over and over? He could have taken me right then in the Bladesworths' bed, and I would have let him, without a single complaint. I did everything but spread my legs.

That it was shameful behavior, she was acutely conscious. Her own upbringing may have been casually eccentric, but she knew better than to allow a man to fondle her that way and offer no objections. Had it been anyone else, she would never have come so close to abandoning her virtue. But it was Hal, and she would have done anything for him.

The others still slept, so she got up in silence, unable to lie quietly under such torment. As she dressed, she glanced over at Maria's bed. It was empty. She must already have gone to see about the runner. "Will, you are in good hands," she said softly as she straightened the blankets on Maria's bed, which looked as rumpled and restless as her own twisted sheets.

During all those interminable hours yesterday everyone had seen a different Maria. With no joking or wisecracks she had stayed close to Will's side, keeping a cool cloth pressed to the bump on his forehead and murmuring to him quietly when he opened his eyes. She would not leave his side until he was fully conscious, and only then did she allow Phoebe to cajole her into eating dinner. Before the rest of them had scarcely begun, she was finished and back at Will's side, holding his hand, saying nothing, but speaking volumes with her eyes.

Malcolm had watched her go and then turned to Ivy. "My dear, our little girls are growing up," was all he said.

But I am grown, Kate thought as she left the bedroom without a sound, tiptoeing on stockinged feet and carrying her shoes. She went to the stage, avoiding the green room and the next room where the men slept, and sat down on the apron, looking out over the empty chairs. The paint smell was strong, but not unpleasant. Today they would move some plants into the lobby and hope for the arrival of the lobby carpet Ivy had purchased for a song and the price of a billboard in the merchant's shop window.

It is my theatre, she thought, and felt a spark of pride. It was a beautiful building, with cream-colored walls, elegant gilt chandeliers and sconces. If the curtain was shabby and patched in places, no one would notice when the play began. We will spin our little story for their entertainment and portray people we are not. They will laugh and forget their own problems, large and small, for a few hours, and then we will all go back and become the people we were before the play began.

And through all this theatre magic, I must remember who I am, she reminded herself. I am a twenty-six-year-old spinster with no prospects beyond this theatre, which may succeed or may fail, depending on the whims of chance. I am in love with someone who can do much better for himself, if he will only give it a little exertion.

She looked at the ring on her left hand and took it off. Her hand seemed bare without Hal's ring. "Oh, God," she whispered out loud. "How can I bear this?" He would probably want the ring back when his adventure was over and he returned to life in London. He could take the ring, but already, after only a month of wearing the wedding band, the skin underneath was whiter than the rest of her fingers. Somehow, whether on or off her fingers, the wedding band would be there to tease her.

She put the ring back on her finger. Drat the marquess, anyway. She had felt nothing beyond a casual interest at first, and a certain guilt at striking him with a candlestick. And then they were thrown into a closer relationship to protect him from the runner, who seemed to know everything anyway, and his nephew Algernon, who was out to do him harm. How did he become so attractive to her?

He was tall and inclined to plumpness and had none of the robust good looks of Gerald Broussard or even Will. She had to smile, in spite of herself. Lord Grayson was not in the image of any girl's prayers for a husband. But he was kind, willing to try new things, and not embarrassed of making a fool of himself on stage, as she was. He always seemed to have time for her, and when she was with him—even in a crowd of Bladesworths, as was usually the case—she felt as though they were the only ones in the room. And after those breathless moments last night, she knew how much he wanted her.

I must speak to him, she thought. I must apologize for my unseemly behavior and beg his pardon, and pray that he hurries up and returns to London before I embarrass myself again. Kate put on her shoes and got to her feet. She heard someone in the wings and held her breath. Don't let it be Hal, she prayed. I am not ready yet. I must compose myself.

It was Davy. He waved her a cheerful greeting.

"Is Will feeling more the thing?" she asked as he came closer.

"He'll do. Said his head pounds like a drum." He made a face. "He and Maria are making such sheep's eyes at each other! It's enough to put me off my feed!"

Kate laughed. "And Maria is standing sentinel?"

Davy nodded. "I would rather be raking old leaves outside than watching the two of them." He jumped off the front of the stage, heading toward the entrance.

"Wait, Davy," she called. "Could you … could you ask the marquess to come out? I need to speak to him."

Davy stopped. "He's already up, dressed, and out, Kate. Said he had something important to do that couldn't wait."

Inwardly sighing with relief, she waved Davy on. If he is wise, he is renting himself a post chaise for a speedy return to London, she thought, and then corrected herself. He would never leave before the play, not when so many depended on him. Fresh doubts assailed her. Hadn't Abner Sheffield said he was lazy and inclined to frivolity? Wouldn't it be entirely in character for him to abandon ship at this point? I will not consider such a thing, she told herself, but doubts continued to pinch at her. Surely he would not leave everyone in the lurch, not when they needed Antonionus Pinchbeck to woo Agatha Rowbottom?

She kept her fears to herself through breakfast and a brief visit with Will, who was protesting Maria's loving tyranny over him.

"Kate, tell her that I am perfectly able to be up!" he insisted. "It is only a small bump!"

Kate twinkled her eyes at Maria, who smiled back. "I wouldn't dream of interfering," she said. "Whatever Maria says, that will I agree to."

Maria put her hands possessively on Will's chest. "And Maria says he is not to stir until this evening's rehearsal."

"There you have it, sir," Kate replied. "You can petition no higher tribunal."

As the morning wore on and Hal did not return, Kate joined Ivy and Phoebe in the wardrobe room, where the women were putting the final touches on a coat for Squire Pinchbeck. Ivy patted the seat beside her and put the suit coat in her lap. "Since this is for your fubsy suitor, you can sew his buttons," Ivy said, handing her a needle and thread.

"My fubsy … I tell you, he is not my suitor!" Kate burst out, close to tears.

Ivy patted her hand. "In the play, my dear, in the play," she soothed.

"Oh yes, the play," Kate mumbled as she bent over the coat. The women were kind enough to overlook her outburst as they spoke of trivialities and then traded lines.

The hours dragged by. Kate was about to rip her hair out by the roots when the marquess strolled into the room. He nodded to the ladies. "Malcolm told me you wanted to see me for a fitting," he said to Ivy, so casual that Kate wanted to rake her fingernails down his face.

"Help him into the coat, will you, Kate?" Ivy said. "Oh, I do believe I hear Malcolm." She handed Kate a chalk marker. "If it is too large, mark where the seams should fall." She left the room. Phoebe followed a moment later, murmuring something about finding Maria, who probably had no wish to be found.

They were alone in the wardrobe room. Kate looked about for escape, but the marquess was removing his coat. He held out his arms while Kate, her face red, helped him into the costume. It fit well across the shoulders without a crease. She patted the material into place, thinking of last night, with her arms locked tight across his back, pressing him to her.

The sleeves were a trifle long, so she marked them with chalk, angry that her hand was shaking. She knelt to pin the coat's hem, which hung to his knees in fashionable Georgian style. "Lord Grayson, I must apologize for last night," she began, her mouth full of pins and not daring to look him in the face.

"I won't listen to a word until you take those pins out of your mouth," he said, a touch of humor in his voice. "I mean, what kind of an example will you set for our daughters if you carry pins in your mouth as you teach them to sew?"

She spit out the pins and sat back on her heels, gaping at him in amazement. "You cannot possibly be serious!" she exclaimed.

"Well, of course I am," he replied, the amusement deepening. "After all, children do tend to imitate their parents, and I know you will be a careful mother. It's just a little bad habit."

She stood up and stamped her foot. "You great big looby, I am trying to apologize for my unseemly behavior last night, and you speak of our children? Sir, have you been in the sun too long?"

He took her by the arms. "My dearest Kate, you have nothing to apologize for."

"I behaved like a... a... a light-skirt," she whispered, breaking free of his grasp. "I am so ashamed."

"I thought it entirely appropriate and altogether endearing," he said, his voice soft. "You behaved like a woman in love."

"I am nothing of the kind!" she exclaimed.

He was silent, watching her. "Very well, then, have it your way," he said at last, his good humor unruffled. He removed the coat carefully, looking out for pins. "You are more contrary than Balaam's ass, but I shall overlook it. I am sure I have faults unnumbered that you will have to wink at, once we are leg-shackled."

She knelt to pick up the pins, unable to look him in the eyes. Hot tears stung her eyes. "You are so provoking, Lord Grayson! We will not be married. I told you that last night."

She could feel his eyes on her, but she could not bear to look up. "We shall see," he said. He patted her on the hip as she crept along on all fours, searching for the pins she had scattered about. "By the way, the runner is about, so be more loving, dear wife."

Another pat, this one more of a caress, and he was gone. She sat down on the floor, amazed at his audacity, wondering how he could make a joke out of the heavy events of last night, and then grateful that he could tease so lightly. She discovered, to her peace of mind, that it was impossible to remain embarrassed.

She pulled the coat into her lap and continued with the buttons. Listening for a moment to make sure that no one was coming, she lifted the coat to her nose and sniffed the collar lining. It smelled of bay rum. "Oh, Hal," she whispered into the fragrant fabric. "You are so dear to me."

THEY ASSEMBLED THAT NIGHT for the first complete run-through. "Now, remember," Malcolm admonished. "We will stop at nothing!"

Gerald raised his hand. "There is one problem."

"Only one? You are an optimist," said Malcolm, and the cast laughed.

"We still do not have a vicar for the fifth act," Gerald reminded Bladesworth. "One or the other of us has been reading the part, but we do need to fill it."

"Let me make the arrangement," the marquess spoke up. "I met someone this morning who will do the part, if I ask him nicely enough."

Malcolm nodded. "It is a simple matter. All he has to do is read the marriage lines. We can steer him around the stage."

Where have I heard that before, Kate thought, and smiled. She looked at the others, some in costume, some in parts of costumes, and remembered her first treading of the boards with the indomitable, unique, one and only Bladesworth Traveling Company. Was it only six weeks ago? Surely not. I must have known you darlings forever.

The play began, the runner and Gerald in front of the

curtain, extolling the virtues of the Rowbottom daughters and bemoaning the fact that neither could marry until the oldest was wed. And then the marquess, squinting in spectacles and tripping over shoes too large, stumbled onstage as Antonionus Pinchbeck, and the act was off and running. There were several long pauses, where Malcolm would glare at the guilty party and do a ponderous hornpipe until the line was picked up, but no one resorted to the promptbook.

Malcolm played the vicar for the first time in rehearsal, holding out paper, pen, and ink for her to sign her name to the marriage lines. Kate looked at the blank sheet and poised the pen over it. "Sign your real name, Kate," Malcolm whispered. "That way you won't fumble over it."

She did as he said and passed the page to the marquess, who dropped his spectacles several times and bumbled about before doing the same. The littlest Bladesworths broke character and giggled at his antics, and Malcolm glared at them. "Mind yourselves, missies," he warned them over the dialogue that continued around him. "This is our bread and butter."

The bells in the church steeple were chiming midnight when the fifth act closed. The runner, still weak from his encounter with Pinky D'Urst's boot, had been dismissed earlier and helped back to the inn by Davy. The rest of the cast, exhausted, assembled on the stage, the little girls asleep as soon as they rested against their mother. They sat, waiting for Malcolm to pronounce judgment.

He looked around the stage at each person in turn, his gaze resting finally on Gerald.

"Gerald Broussard, I do believe we have a play. I cannot begin to express my gratitude."

The others applauded. The little girls woke at the sound of clapping, looked about them in pleasure, and went back to sleep.

"It is only the first of many that I can write for you, Monsieur Bladesworth," Gerald said. He stood up and cleared his throat, opening and closing his mouth several times until he could speak. "There is a way that you can repay me, sir," he said.

"Speak up then," Malcolm said.

Gerald held out his hand for Phoebe. She rose gracefully and stood by his side. "I wish to marry your daughter when we finish this first week's run," Gerald said. "We ask your approval." His voice was firm; only his more pronounced accent betrayed his nervousness.

Kate held her breath, and Hal winced at the look on Malcolm's face. He puffed out his cheeks until his face turned red, and then slowly let out the air. Gerald, his expression less sanguine, tightened his grip on Phoebe, who was quite pale by now.

"Papa… please don't—" she began, but Malcolm cut her off with a chop of his hand.

"Gerald, this is out of the question! Phoebe is only sixteen, and you haven't two farthings to rub together." He gestured around the room. "None of us have! What can you be thinking of? My answer is no."

Phoebe ran from the stage in tears. Gerald hesitated, wishing to follow, but held there by Malcolm's indignation. He came closer. "Sir, am I not good enough for your daughter?"

Malcolm passed a hand in front of his eyes. "Gerald, I have such high hopes for Phoebe. With continued training and the right luck, she might be performing at Covent Garden someday." He looked to Ivy, who had averted her gaze, and gestured broadly, performing for some unseen audience. "She might even attract the attention of a duke or a marquess."

His face set, Gerald jumped off the stage and started up the center aisle. When he was halfway to the entrance, he turned back and shouted. "She is too good for an actor, is that it, Malcolm?"

He was gone then, the heavy lobby door slamming behind him. The others looked at each other. "Oh, Papa," was all Maria could say. She hurried after her sister.

His eyes sad, Malcolm turned to the marquess. "All I want is for my children to live better than I have lived," he pleaded. "Is that so wrong?"

"No," Hal said. "It's not wrong to wish the best for your children. But maybe they don't want to take the easy way." He strolled off the stage, his head down.

Without a word Kate retreated from the stage with the youngest daughters, leaving Ivy and Malcolm together. She tucked the little girls into bed and sang to them until they slept tumbled together, their arms about each other. Such peaceful sleep, she thought, as she kissed them. I cannot recall when I last slept so peacefully.

She lay awake well into the morning, pretending sleep when the older Bladesworth daughters crept to bed, Phoebe to sob into her pillow, and Maria to sigh and toss herself about. Kate listened to them both, wondering to herself, why do we get into such a pelter over men? You would think that between the three of us, there might be one functioning brain.

Breakfast was a dreadful ordeal, full of sniffles, food pushed away, and proud silence when Malcolm tried to pass on some conversational tidbit. He gave up finally and ate all the oatmeal that his elder daughters scorned, muttering something about "how sharper than a serpent's tooth was a thankless child." No one applauded his quotation; quite the contrary. With a sob Phoebe leaped up, knocking over her chair, and fled the room, one hand clutched to her heaving bosom, and the other pointed ethereally upward.

Pausing from his contemplation of the oatmeal before him, Hal watched in real admiration. "My God," he breathed, "what a trial it must be for you at times, Malcolm! Think on it, Katie my love, such histrionics! Our children will not be so dramatic, my dear. I hope you do not mind."

Kate glared at Hal. "If you do not quit talking about our children …" she began.

He smiled beatifically and addressed the oatmeal again. "But I love to talk about our children. It is a subject that interests me greatly."

Kate rose with some dignity, grateful that Will was not there yet. "I am having a hard time resisting the urge to throw this bowl at you," she snapped.

Hal twinkled his eyes at her. "Our second quarrel. I forgive you, my love."

Speechless with indignation, Kate fled the room. "Men are so aggravating!" she said to Ivy as she hurried past her in the hallway and ran out the door.

It was still early, and the river was foggy. Her heart filled with mutiny and a marked distaste for anything in breeches, she leaned on the stone rail and watched the women washing clothes below her. The rhythm of hands on washboards, mingled with the slap of the clothes in the river was soothing to her jangled nerves.

One of the washerwomen, her skirt turned up and tucked into her waistband and sturdy knees showing, waved to her.

"Hello, love," she called. "Are yer ready to open in two days?"

Kate forced herself to smile and wave. "That we are," she called down.

"Ooh, love, we'll be in line for tickets!" the woman shouted back. The other washerwomen nodded.

"Oh, my word," Kate said quietly as the women turned back to their timeless work. "Half of us are not speaking to the other half, the lobby carpet has not been delivered yet, and I am sure I saw bats in the theatre this morning."

"And you are now talking to yourself in the hopes of sensible conversation?"

Hal stood beside her. She had not seen him approach. He leaned his elbows on the stone railing, looking down into the water. "I am sorry, Kate, truly I am. Forgive me for being a tease." He nudged her shoulder. "That's one of those faults you will have to overlook."

"There you go again!" she exclaimed. "No wonder I am driven to distraction!"

Before she could move away from him, Hal reached his arm around her and pulled her close. He touched his cheek to hers briefly and then released her. "I fully intend to marry you, Kate," he said as he strolled back toward the theatre.

"Even if I will not?" she called after him, wishing he would keep his arm around her, even as she kicked herself for being so traitorous to her sex.

"Oh, you will," he said and then was gone.

They began their last run-through before the final dress rehearsal in the afternoon so they would not require any candles. Hal arrived late and breathless with a quiet little man named Meacheam, who would play the vicar. Meacheam appeared to be somewhat hard of hearing, but he performed his small role with a little coaching from Malcolm. Kate signed the marriage lines without a bobble this time, turning her fuddled gaze upon the nearsighted Squire Pinchbeck and lisping, " 'I trust I spelled it right this time. I can never be too sure with names, especially my own.' "

The littlest Bladesworths burst into delighted laughter, and for once, Malcolm did not glare at them for stepping out of character. He threw back his head and laughed, too, and soon everyone was laughing, even Gerald.

Finally Malcolm wiped his eyes and blew a kiss to Kate. "I defy even Dorothy Jordan to deliver that line any better," he declared. Meacheam, the vicar, his black eyes darting about, tugged at Squire Pinchbeck's sleeve to remind him to sign his name, and the play continued.

"Magnificent!" Malcolm chortled when the curtain closed. "Come, my dears, and gather around."

Phoebe, her face still a tragic mask, arranged herself with great dignity into a chair, while Maria and Will stood by, close to each other but not touching. Malcolm eyed them fondly.

"My dears, we have such a wonderful play. Let us all study

our lines tonight and get plenty of rest. Tomorrow is the final dress rehearsal." He beckoned his little daughters to come to him. "And then, my beauties, we will walk through town to announce our play, and you two can carry the drum."

"Drum?" asked Kate. "I do not understand."

Ivy tucked her arm through Kate's. "An old theatre tradition, my dear. We will show you tomorrow."

"So we shall," declared Malcolm at his expansive best. "And now I suggest we adjourn to the green room for something to eat. Mr. Meacheam, you may join us, too. Mr. Meacheam?"

The little vicar had vanished. Hal pulled out his watch and snapped it open. "He hates to miss Evensong at his church," the marquess explained. "Come, dear wife, and let us see if there is something besides oatmeal …"

He stopped. A man stood at the back of the theatre, outlined in the late afternoon sun of the open door. As they watched, he strode toward the front of the stage, waving a piece of paper in his hand. "I say, who owns this theatre?" he called out.

Kate stepped forward, shading her eyes with her hand in the hopes of seeing the man better. "I do, sir. What do you want with me?"

"Merely this." The man reached up to the stage and slapped the piece of paper in her hand. "You must have a license to open this theatre."

Kate stared at the writ in her hand. "What?" she exclaimed. Her eyes went down the closely scripted lines, then she paused and sucked in her breath. The others gathered around her. With a shaking hand she pointed to the document and looked down at the man who stood so complacently before them.

"Three hundred pounds?" she asked, her voice quavering. "I must pay the city of Leeds three hundred pounds before I can even open this door?"

Malcolm grabbed the paper from her nerveless fingers. He read it quickly, Hal and Gerald looking over his shoulder.

"What do you mean by this?" he asked, the shock evident in his voice, even as he tried to hide it.

"I mean that you cannot open this theatre!" said the man, emphasizing each word with a jab of his finger. "Three years ago when the Banner Street Theatre closed, those rascally, thieving actors left town without paying their tradesmen's bills. After the drubbing our merchants took, we in Leeds decided that we needed writ of guarantee." He pointed to the document with a flourish. "There it is."

Kate stared at him, her eyes wide. "Sir, at this juncture I have scarcely three pounds remaining!"

"Then you will not open, will you?" said the man. As they stood in silence, he marched up the aisle and closed the door behind him, leaving the Bladesworth Company to stare at each other in disbelief.

16

~

KATE STARED DOWN AT the writ in her hands, her face bleak. Hal put his arm around her waist, and she did not push him away. "Hal, what am I to do? We have three pounds! He might as well have asked for the Crown Jewels."

By his expression daring Malcolm to say anything, Gerald took Phoebe by the hand, helped her off the front of the stage, and sat with her in the audience chairs. One by one, the others joined them and sat staring at the stage, with its elegant set furnished as a country home drawing room of the last century. The chipped paint on the chairs did not show from the audience, and the well-turned corduroy curtains that had seen a thousand other uses glowed like velvet at the imaginary windows. Even the bookcase, filled with fake books with tattered covers that the runner insisted would fool nobody, looked elegant and solid from their audience vantage point. It was all so beautiful, and to no purpose. They could not open Gerald's wonderful play.

With a gulp Kate turned her face into Hal's shoulder and sobbed. "I wanted this play to happen," she whispered finally from the protection of his encircling arm. "I … I didn't really care at first, but I wanted it to happen!"

"Hush, dear wife," he said mildly, the disappointment evident in his voice, but without her discouragement. "I am trusting you to think of something." He kissed her on the cheek. "M'mmm, salty," he said.

"But I can't think of anything!" she whispered back. "We have pinched and contrived to get us this far. I do not know what to do!"

He drew her back within his embrace again, his lips close to her ear. "Don't tell them that. You're supposed to be the leader. Now, lead."

"But. Hal!"

"No buts," he whispered firmly. "You bought this theatre. Now, stand up there and tell them what you're going to do!"

He took his arm off her shoulder and gave her a little push in the small of her back. She was on her feet in front of the cast, propelled there by Hal's loving boost. Kate looked at the Bladesworths, more solemn than she had ever seen them, and the runner, whose concern was etched on his face in the way he gazed past her to the stage. He had built most of the set himself, she recalled with a pang as she stood shaking before them and attempted to draw her shattered wits about her. And there was Gerald, head down, inconsolable, author of this bewitching confection that no one would see, if she did not think of something.

Kate took a deep breath and cleared her throat. The others looked up, discouragement written on their expressive faces. She faltered, then glanced at Hal. His lips set firmly together, he nodded to her. She took another deep breath.

"We are going to open," she managed, her voice scarcely audible.

The cast only looked at her.

"I didn't hear you."

It was Hal, his face implacable, his arms folded. She had

never seen him so serious. Somehow it gave her the courage to reach down deeper inside herself.

"We are going to open," she said, her voice firm. It carried to the back wall.

"How?"

Malcolm spoke the one word that they were all thinking, the word that she feared the most. His face was drawn and pale and his arms hung at his side. "I think we must see reality this time, Kate. We have been diddled by a damnable ordinance, and we cannot open."

"I refuse to accept that," she replied quietly. She hiked herself onto the stage and sat there in front of them. "Now, if one of us were hurt and unable to perform, that would be different. This is merely money, and I will find it somehow."

No one said anything; no one moved. Kate looked at Ivy, who was leaning against her husband. "Ivy, go next door to the baker's and buy a cake. We're all tired of oatmeal, and it's time we had a sweet." She looked at Maria. "Friend, see if there is any Madeira left. If there is not, send Will for a bottle or two." She got to her feet on the stage. "When you are through, I want everyone to get a good night's sleep. We will begin our final rehearsal—in costume—at 10 of the clock tomorrow morning."

Kate stood there. If Ivy does not move, I will die, she thought. Please, please, Ivy.

After a moment's reflection Ivy Bladesworth stood up and squared her shoulders. She held out her hands for her youngest daughters. "Come, my dears," she said, her voice calm. "Let us go next door and find the best cake. Maria, you heard Kate. She is in charge; do what she asked."

Kate let her breath out slowly, turned on her heel, and left the stage. Her stomach was churning, and she didn't know if she could make it to the stage door, but she did. On her hands and knees in the back alley she vomited until her stomach hurt. She heard the stage door open, and she sat back, exhausted.

Without a word Hal took out his handkerchief and wiped

her mouth. He took her by the shoulders as she crouched there in the alley. "Bravo!" he whispered, his voice fierce. "By God, we could have used you at Salamanca, or Busaco! You're a great gun, Kate, did you know?"

Still shaking, she let him pull her to her feet. "I am nothing of the sort, Hal, and you know that better than anyone. And now I think I'll go find my favorite tree and think a bit."

"Good. I know you'll come up with something."

The door banged open again, and the runner slammed it behind him. Before Hal could move, Will shoved him up against the wall.

"I can't believe you!" he hissed. "You have the capacity to end this farce right now, and you will not!"

Hal only looked at him. "I don't know what you mean," he said, his face perfectly blank.

Will pushed harder, as if to force Hal into the bricks themselves. "Why do you not just admit who you are? I know you are the marquess. You know you are the marquess. This borders on the insane! You could save this little lady from enormous worry, if only you would exert yourself."

"Please, Will, let him go," Kate urged, tugging on his arm.

To her relief Will released the marquess. "I'm not sure you are worth the trouble," the runner said. "I really thought you cared about Kate."

"I do," Hal replied.

"Well, you have a damned strange way of showing it."

He turned to go, then whirled around suddenly and cracked the marquess hard across the face with the back of his hand. Hal reeled from the surprised blow, crashed against the wall, and slid to the ground, his hand to his face. As Kate watched, her face white, he struggled to his feet. Will stood his ground, his breath loud in the alley.

"I should call you out for that," Hal said.

Will thrust his face closer. "I wish you would," he declared, spitting out the words. "But I am sure it would be too much exertion! Stay away from him, Kate."

He left then, hurrying away from the theatre, heading toward his lodgings at the Scylla and Charybdis.

Hal leaned against the wall and dabbed at his lip, which was bleeding freely. "Remind me to make sure those foils are buttoned tomorrow during dress rehearsal," was all he said. Without another word he went back into the theatre.

Kate stared after him. She listened to the runner's rapid footsteps receding down the empty street. She covered her eyes with her hands, but no tears came. She was beyond that. Her whole body numb, she walked to the tree, sat on the lower limb, and wrapped her arms around the trunk. She closed her eyes, wishing with all her heart that Will had not said those things. He had expressed the doubts she was feeling, but was afraid to voice.

"You could help me, Hal, I know you could," she whispered into the bark. "You could probably snap your fingers and three hundred pounds would appear, but you will not."

The tears came then, but she forced them back. Surely Hal could reveal himself as Lord Grayson. Algernon would not dare do him harm, especially after that botched kidnapping. Hal could demand protection from the magistrate, and if the runner had been sent by Algernon, as she feared, he could do no harm. Then Lord Grayson could easily arrange a bank draft for the money and her worries would be over.

"But you will not," she said. As she sat in the tree and watched the stars come out, the thought occurred to her that Hal expected her to solve her own problems. She looked up at the night sky, watching the stars through the slowly moving leaves. "Why are you so determined that I should stand on my own two feet? What does it matter to you?"

Her questions remained unanswered. She watched the sky until she was too tired to hold onto the tree, then went back into the theatre. It was dark, and she was grateful that everyone had taken her at her word to go to bed. She tiptoed onto the stage, which was still set for the fifth act, with its play within a play and wonderful conclusion. She stood in the front of the stage and held her hands out.

"How nice it would be if everything could be so tidily wrapped up by the fifth act," she said out loud, pressing against her stomach and remembering all of Malcolm Bladesworth's patient lessons on projection to the back wall.

To her amazement someone in the dark began to applaud. She stood there, her hand to her stomach, and then she smiled and tossed a kiss into the darkness. "Hal, go to bed," she said. "I'm perfectly all right."

"Oh, I know that, Mrs. Hampton. I know that."

KATE WOKE IN THE morning, feeling better than she had any right to, considering that she was no closer to three hundred pounds than when she fell so solidly asleep. She stretched and lay there with her hands over her head, staring up at the ceiling, wiggling her fingers.

The gleam of gold on her third finger caught her eye. She wiggled her hand, watching the light catch the precious metal. I wonder what this is worth, she thought idly, and then sucked in her breath. She leaped out of bed and threw herself beside her trunk. She rummaged in the bottom of it and drew out a small velvet bag. In another moment she was in her clothes. "Bother this long hair," she exclaimed in irritation as she swept it over her shoulders, looked around for her shoes, and hurried into the hallway, still buttoning the last button.

As she had suspected, the company was assembled in the green room, that refuge from reality that actors always turned to. She went to the packing crate cupboard where they kept their dishes and pulled out a soup bowl, setting it on the table. The others watched her with interest, but no one said anything.

Without a word she pulled apart the drawstring bag that she held and dumped the contents into the bowl. She steeled herself for the effort, but discovered to her pleasure that she didn't even feel a pang as her father's wedding ring and her mother's pearl necklace tumbled into the soup bowl.

"It's all I have, and I am going to pawn it." Her voice was deadly calm, even as her insides quivered, and she feared another run into the back alley to retch up an already empty stomach. "If you have any faith in this venture …" She paused and winked back tears. "No. If you have any faith in me, please give me everything you have."

The others sat staring at her, and her heart sank into her sorely tried stomach. Lord Grayson was the first to move. He drew out his heavy gold pocket watch and clicked it open. He inclined it toward Kate and pointed to a dent on the lid. "Badajoz, my heart," he said, and his voice was unsteady. "A little closer and I would have had more than a bruise." He snapped it shut and added it to the meager pile. "No reason why it won't bring you good luck, too."

"Thank you," she said, smiling for the first time. She looked into his eyes and liked the reflection she saw there.

Phoebe darted out of the room and returned bearing a ring triumphantly overhead. "It's only garnet," she apologized, tossing it in the bowl.

Maria burst into tears. "I don't have anything!" she cried. "Oh, I wish I did! You could have it all!"

Kate dabbed at her own eyes. Will, sitting on the side of the room far away from the marquess, pulled out his wallet and threw in a handful of sovereigns. "See here, Kate," he admonished, his voice gruff, "I expect a return on that, or else I will owe my soul to the Scylla and Charybdis."

"Silly! Papa can show you how to shinny down a rope, and with your baggage, too," exclaimed Maria. "It's called an actor's fire escape."

The Bladesworths burst into laughter. "You're not supposed to confess things like that to a runner," Will protested, but his eyes were merry.

Malcolm was next. He made his ponderous way to the room next door and returned with a silver-tipped cane. He flourished it from the doorway, and his daughters and son gasped.

"Papa, not Shakespeare's cane!" Davy said, speaking in hushed tones.

"Well, as to that, I do not know that it really belonged to Willie the Bard, though it has made a prodigious fine story all these years," Malcolm said as he twisted off the head. "But I do know this is silver." He plunked it on top of the pile. "And here's my watch, too."

Gerald had been sitting silent throughout the growing excitement. He got up quietly and left the room. Phoebe looked at Maria. "Sister, you don't think he will …"

Maria took Phoebe's hand. "It's all he has. Oh, Mama, don't let him!"

Ivy shook her head as Gerald returned. In his hand was a porcelain music box, exquisitely gilded and painted with a delicate hand over its entire surface. He wound it and opened the lid, smiling faintly as the gentle tones of a French lullaby filled the room.

Maria took Kate by the arm. "It is all he has of his mother. Oh, Kate, don't take it!" she whispered.

The tune finished, and they were all silent for a moment more as Gerald closed the lid and handed the music box to Kate. "I know the tune," he said as her fingers closed over the precious box. "The memory will hold me."

"That does it!" said Ivy. She leaped to her feet and hurried to the next room. The girls looked at each other, frowning. "Mama pawned her last bauble years ago," Phoebe said. "What can she be doing?"

Ivy returned, moving slower than she had left. She did not look at her husband, but continued resolutely forward and handed a small bag to Kate. She pressed it into Kate's hand and tightened her fingers over it. With a sigh she let go and patted Kate's cheek. "I have every confidence in you, my dear," she said, and there was only the slightest quaver in her voice. "You have become very much like a daughter to me."

With fingers that trembled, Kate opened the bag and gasped. The others gathered closer around the table as she pulled out a magnificent ruby brooch, emerald-cut with diamonds winking around it. It glowed in her palm, the deepest red imaginable, the color of a magical beating heart.

Malcolm took Ivy's hand. "My dear wife, I thought that was gone years ago," he said, his voice hushed for a change.

Ivy shook her head. "No. I have hung onto it through thin times and thinner." She smiled at Kate. "Perhaps I was saving it for just such an emergency."

"I … I couldn't possibly …" Kate began, holding out the jewel to its owner.

"Of course you can! We have a magnificent play that deserves to be seen." Ivy raised her chin and swallowed. "I refuse to be defeated by small-minded merchants."

Malcolm brought Ivy's hand to his lips and kissed it. "You are a wonder. Just when I think I know you and nothing you do can ever surprise me—" He stopped, unable to continue. He coughed and cleared his throat while his children admired other parts of the room.

Ivy only sighed "Well, Kate, now we have to give until it hurts." As the others looked on in further amazement, she removed her wedding band and set it gently in the full soup bowl.

"I can't," Kate whispered. She looked down at her hand and the band Hal had tossed so carelessly in her lap a month before. It is all I will ever have of him, she thought, that and the paltriest memories. She stared down at the ruby in her hand and considered all that it meant to Ivy. Her face set, she put the brooch on the pile and stripped off her ring, too.

She clasped her hands together so they would not shake. "Very well, then," she said. "Does anyone have the time?"

Hal burst out laughing and pointed to the soup bowl. "You'll have to dig for the time, my darling," he said.

The others joined in the laughter as Hal pulled out his watch by the chain. "It is eight o'clock."

"Very well, then," Kate said. "Ivy, I submit that you and I should go to the pawn shop. Perhaps if we cry for them, we will get more money."

"It's certainly worth the attempt," Ivy agreed. "Malcolm, find a bag for this. Maria, you and Phoebe look over the costumes one more time while we are gone. Kate, do you have the writ of guarantee? We will go directly to the magistrate from the pawn shop." She reached for her bonnet on the hook by the door. "Hal, don't stand there like Squire Pinchbeck! I know I saw a bat circling in the fly loft this morning." She tied the ribbons firmly under her chin. "Kate, I will wait while you create some order out of your hair and find a hat."

Kate hurried to do as she was bid, grateful for Ivy's brisk commands. She quickly braided her hair and wound it around her head, and stuffed on her bonnet. Hal met her in the hall as she swirled her shawl about her shoulders.

"Suppose it is not enough?" he asked, his voice serious.

She kissed his cheek and darted away from him as he reached for her. "Then I will find a medical college and sell my body to the anatomists," she called over her shoulder.

"I would call that a shocking waste!"

She laughed and closed the door behind her. Ivy waited for her on the stage, a small basket over her arm. Holding tight to each other's hands, they ventured into the street, walking with brisk steps and eyes straight ahead, each afraid to speak to the other for fear of bursting into tears.

Their steps slowed as they reached the street of the money lenders. "Courage," Ivy whispered under her breath and tugged Kate after her into the first promising shop.

To Kate's relief it wasn't necessary to cry more than a few tears for the pawnbroker. He remained noncommittal as each item was proffered to him, until Ivy's brooch was laid in his outstretched palm. Kate noted with secret delight that his eyes opened wider and his nostrils flared before he remembered his audience and resumed his frosty, offhand demeanor.

"A pretty good piece," he allowed at last.

"A magnificent brooch," Ivy corrected.

He folded his hands in front of him and eyed his customers across the counter. "I can give you two hundred and seventy pounds for the lot."

"We need three hundred," Ivy said quietly.

"I can go no higher."

Kate burst into tears with no difficulty and slid to the floor in as graceful a faint as Steinberg and Sons had ever seen in their establishment before. Her eyes rolled back in her head as the broker hurried around the end of the counter and began to fan her. Perched on the brink of laughter, she heaved her bosom as he leaned closer.

"Well, perhaps two hundred and eighty," he said, his face close to her breast.

Her eyes fluttered open and filled with tears again.

When he could see that she was well on her way to complete and total recovery, the broker helped her to her feet, holding her rather nearer than she would have liked. She thought of how much fun it would be to tell this adventure to Hal and leaned against the broker.

"Two hundred and ninety," he amended as he gazed at her bosom. "That is my top offer," he stated as the shop door opened and another customer entered. "And do not think you will get better on this street."

"Very well, we accept," Ivy said, her arm around Kate.

In a few moments they were on the street again, the money tucked discreetly in the basket, along with a notarized list of the pawned items. When they were out of sight of the building, Ivy permitted herself a smile.

"Kate, you were positively shameless," she said. "That was a sterling performance. I defy even Sarah Siddons to duplicate it."

"I cannot wait to tell Hal," Kate said, and then she sobered. "But look you, we are yet ten pounds shy of the mark!" She tucked her arm in Ivy's. "I told Hal I would find a medical school and sell my body."

Ivy stood still and grabbed Kate by both arms. "I have an even better idea! Oh, come with me!"

17

THE DEED WAS DONE in a matter of minutes. Kate kept her eyes tightly shut during the entire ordeal. She took the money and hurried into the street again, her head high.

Ivy didn't give her a chance to mourn. "On to the magistrate's, my brave one," she said. "Chin up, Kate. We have a theatre now, and it will grow back."

They hurried back to the theatre a few minutes after ten, the magistrate's license clutched in Kate's hand. The green room was empty, and they could hear voices from the stage.

"Goodness, I must hurry," Ivy declared after listening to the dialogue. She tossed her bonnet toward the green room door. "My costume must wait. I am on in only a few minutes!" She hugged Kate and darted for the stage.

Kate rummaged in the green room, found a tack, and fixed the license to the doorsill, where everyone could see it. She listened to the dialogue and hurried for the changing room.

Her dress was laid out and already unbuttoned down the back, and her wig waited close by on its stand. "Bless you, Maria and Phoebe," she murmured as she took off her bonnet, gulped as she fingered what remained of her hair, and hurried out of her walking dress. I won't think about it, she said to herself as she struggled into the narrow hoops of the Georgian era. Truly, the hair did curl prettily around her face, but she would miss it.

As she stood there in hoops and chemise, wondering how to get the costume on, there was a light tap on the door. She hurried across the room, exclaiming, "Maria, I hope that is you," as she opened the door.

Hal stood before her in his elegant tapestry coat. His eyes opened wide and his jaw dropped, and he leaned back against the doorframe as if someone had shot him. Before the tears had time to well up in her eyes, he grabbed her, hoops and all, and whirled her around the room.

She pushed against his chest. "Hal, this is so improper!"

"I don't give a hang," he said when he set her down. He touched her curls, a grin on his face that only grew wider as he walked around and looked at her shorn hair from the back. "You are so à la mode, my dear wife, and simply the most magnificent fighter I have ever known."

Kate grabbed for her dress and held it in front of her. "I obtained ten pounds for all that hair." Tears started down her cheeks. "And it will grow," she wailed.

Without a word Hal took the dress from her, set it aside, and held her close. She clung to him and sobbed into his coat. Finally he tipped her chin up and looked deep into her eyes.

"Silly, I don't love you for your hair," he said, his voice soft. "You know I love you for your bosom."

"Wretch!" He ducked as Kate swung at him and then dissolved in laughter. Her face flaming even as she laughed, she scooped up the dress, pulled it over her head and turned around for him to button it. "Button it fast, and don't look!" she commanded.

"You mean I cannot stare in absolute admiration at your more-than-perfect shoulders?"

"Hal, you try me," she said. "Just button it."

"I have to keep my eyes open," he protested, "else how can I button? And these are deucedly small buttons."

When he finished, she set the wig on her head, pulling it down firmly, and noting with grudging satisfaction that it rode much better on her head without all that hair tucked underneath. There wasn't time for makeup, except to snatch up a star patch from the dressing-room table and fix it by her mouth.

"Well? Shall we?" she asked and held out her arm.

He took it. She angled sideways through the narrow doorway and let him hurry her to the wings, just in time for him to put on his spectacles and enter together on their cue.

The rehearsal went without a bobble. Malcolm summoned the cast to sit in the audience chairs as he talked them through final suggestions. He smiled kindly upon Mr. Meacheam. "Sir, you are an excellent vicar!"

The little man nodded and smiled, all the while cupping his hand to his ear. "My pleasure, sir. Who of us hasn't wanted, at some time, to tread the boards?"

Gerald stood up and bowed to the old man. "He reminds me, sir. We must have something written on that marriage paper that Kate and Hal sign, else when Phoebe capers about with it, the audience will see it is only a blank page."

"I have some paper," Hal spoke up. "I'll scribble a few lines on it, and none will be the wiser."

Malcolm continued a discussion of the small touches still lacking, then stopped suddenly at the sound of a drum. Kate looked at the stage in surprise as the youngest Bladesworth daughter entered from the wings carrying the drum on her head, while her sister pounded upon it. Malcolm rose in applause for his daughters and then turned back to the rest of his cast, holding his arms open wide to them.

"Come, my dears and fellow thespians, let us march!"

Maria noted Kate's surprise. "It is such an old custom that I don't know when it began. The youngest member of the troupe always bears the drum on her head. We will walk behind in costume, and distribute handbills for tonight's performance."

Malcolm clapped his hand around his wife's shoulders and looked down at her fondly. "And it is the last time we will do it! Kate, thanks to you, this troupe of strolling players will remain here, firmly fixed, as long as we can draw breath, open the curtain, and remember our lines. If we do our best, Ivy will have a home where she can finally plant flowers and watch them come up, instead of leaving them for someone else to enjoy."

He kissed the top of her head as Ivy blew her nose and dabbed at her eyes. The girls continued to pound the drum as Malcolm helped them off the stage. In pairs the actors fell in behind, grabbing up handbills as they moved through the lobby and into Banner Street.

Her arm tucked firmly in Hal's grip, Kate strolled through the streets of Leeds, smiling, blowing kisses, and handing out playbills advertising the evening performance. Hal nodded and waved to the merchants, shoppers, and children who stopped their daily pursuits and looked with appreciation on the players. He leaned closer to Kate. "Did you ever think you would be walking down the middle of the street with a bunch of actors?"

She waved and tossed a kiss to one gaping farm boy who loped along beside them. "There are many things I never imagined would happen this summer," she said and looked back at Malcolm and Ivy. "I trust I have become sufficiently flexible to suit these dear ones."

"We shall see," was all Hal said in reply. "We shall see."

The rest of the afternoon dragged by, as though all time had stopped when the men pawned their watches. The others divested themselves of their costumes and laid down to rest, but Kate could not sleep. She pulled on her simplest muslin frock, fingered her hair, sighed, and let herself out of the theatre. She had a farthing in her pocket. It was the last one of all the money Socrates Cratch had paid her for the Giotto. She walked along the river, thinking to throw it in for good luck, when she noticed a small church beside the water.

It was old, so old, in the Romanesque style, and almost hidden by the buildings that crowded close on either side. There was only a postage stamp of a cemetery about it, and the stones were as weathered as the building, leaning at about the same angle. ST. PHILEMON was carved into the lintel over the door. She went inside, blinking in the cool darkness, breathing in the smell of incense lingering at least from the Crusades.

The wink of candles caught her eye, and she knew what she would do with her last farthing. She put it in the box, took up a candle, and lit it off one of those already burning. She knelt on the prayer bench and rested her arms on the railing, thinking of all the petitions, serious and trivial, that must have floated up beyond the low-ceilinged church. Her first thought was to pray for success in tonight's bold venture, but all she could see before her was Hal's face. "Bless him, dear God," she whispered, "and help me to forget him as soon as I can."

Her mind at peace with herself, she reflected on the events of the summer. I have made friends, and bought a theatre, and fallen in love, and discovered that I could stand up for myself.

I wonder which was most important? She rested her forehead against the dark wood, mellowed by centuries of smoke. I stood up by myself. When everything else was gone, the calm assurance would remain that nothing need ever frighten her again. She was equal to the tasks of life, no matter how onerous they were at times.

She rose and moved to a back pew, enjoying the quiet. Someone shifted to her left, and she noticed Mr. Meacheam, sitting only in front of her, a smile on his face. Every now and then he looked down at a prayer book and then back toward the altar, his lips moving. Hal had said something about his never missing Evensong, but it was still early for that.

She made her way back to the aisle, genuflected and left the church. The August sun was warm on her skin, and she raised her face to it, wondering why she should feel so good when her glorious hair was gone, Hal's ring that meant so much to her was pawned, and its owner was probably soon to return to London. I think it is because I know myself now, she thought. And I do have Hal to thank for that. He bullied me into bravery.

Her stomach began to growl as she hurried back to the Banner Street Theatre. Even oatmeal will taste excellent, she thought, and perhaps there is a touch of Madeira left. Oatmeal and Madeira! I have become quite as eccentric as the Bladesworths.

She went in through the front door. Davy nodded to her from the box office and waved a sheaf of tickets. "We have already sold a fair amount, Kate," he said.

"Excellent!"

She looked around her at the high ceiling, remembering Hal perched so precariously on the ladder, touching up the gilt, and then painting the walls. I shall write a letter to Abner Sheffield and tell him that he was entirely wrong about Lord Grayson, she told herself. He is neither lazy nor devoted to frivolity.

The oatmeal went down smoothly, even without sweetening. The touch of Madeira helped. Malcolm found some bonbons, which he offered to the cast members. "Tomorrow night, there will be a loin of beef and—"

"Oatmeal," Maria chimed in as she accepted a bonbon from her papa and wrinkled her nose at him.

"No!" Malcolm said, his good humor unruffled by his daughter's quizzing. "I was thinking more in terms of—"

"Oatmeal," Phoebe stated, in her finest tragedian's voice.

Everyone laughed. Phoebe tucked her hand in Gerald's and dared her father to say anything. He overlooked the gesture and continued around the circle until the bonbons were gone.

At five thirty they lit all the candles along the walls and positioned the footboard at stage front, with its double row of candles. The chandeliers over the stage were lit and raised into place. Kate sucked in her breath and held it, captivated by the warm light that bathed the curtain, turning it from a patched piece of green baize to something elegant and magic.

The theatre began to fill with patrons. Kate fought down the butterflies that flitted about in her stomach and hurried backstage. Hal waited for her in the wings, motioning to her to join him.

"Is my wig on straight?" he asked, crouching down so she could reach it more easily. "I must own to a certain sinking feeling that Malcolm assures me will depart when I speak my first line. He calls it stage fright; I call it abject terror."

"Your wig is fine. Lord Grayson," she whispered, making sure that the runner was nowhere in hearing. "Do you know, there is a hank of black hair, about so long and quite thick, I might add, floating about Leeds. You could probably have a wig made for your own head," she teased.

"You are a bit of a baggage," he replied, straightening up. "While some of us may not be as well-endowed in certain areas, we do compensate in others, my dear Mrs. Hampton." He grinned at her. "And if you blush at that, I will know you have a rascally mind."

She was spared the necessity of comment by Davy, who stood just offstage and beckoned to them.

"I almost think I'd rather be with Beresford at Badajoz again," said the marquess under his breath. "Tally-ho, Miss Rowbottom."

Malcolm was right about that first line, Kate discovered. Once it was out, once she forgot about the upturned faces just beyond the footlights, once she devoted herself to the missish antics of Agatha Rowbottom, fear left her. In fact so heartily did she enter into the twists and turns of Gerald's marvelous play, when the first act ended, the applause that roared across the stage startled her. Only Phoebe's tugging at her arm reminded her to curtsy to the other cast members and then curtsy to the audience before the curtain closed.

"Oh, well done, well done!" Malcolm whispered when the curtain closed and they gathered close together, arms about each other, on the stage. "No time to marvel; get the props in place for act two."

And so it went, each act more triumphant than the one before, the applause now mingled with cheers. When the third act ended and the long intermission began, they hurried into the green room to sit staring at each other in delighted stupefaction. Gerald leaped to his feet, grabbed up Phoebe, hoops and all, for a mad waltz about the crowded room. Malcolm mopped his forehead and looked on in paternal delight, clutching Ivy close to him.

"Well, my dear, I think we are in Leeds to stay," he chortled.

Davy stepped into the room, grinned at his capering sister, and handed his father a folded note.

"A gentleman told me to give this to you," Davy said.

Kate watched Malcolm as he opened the note, read it, paled, and handed it to Ivy, who gasped and fanned herself with it. She came closer.

"It is not trouble, is it?" she asked, keeping her voice low so the cavorting cast members could not hear.

His smile crooked, Malcolm retrieved the note, folded it small, and tucked it in his waistcoat, out of her sight. "No, my dear."

"I hope you are not keeping anything from me," she said.

With an expression on his face that she could not divine, Malcolm shook his head. "Rather let us say, it can keep until the play is over. Now, don't tease me about this, Kate!"

Before she could protest, Davy was calling for act four. She followed the others back toward the stage again. From the wings she watched the sword fight scene, the audience shrieking with laughter as Hal, his spectacles gone, stumbled about the stage and still managed to best Gerald and the runner.

Malcolm stood beside her, his hand on her shoulder. "The lad has a future," he murmured, his eyes on the action.

"Who, Hal?" Kate asked, her voice merry. "Perhaps in the House of Lords."

"No, my super-dainty Kate. I am thinking of Gerald. He may be the next Goldsmith or Sheridan. And to think he wrote this little wonder in three days in a stuffy balcony, dodging bats."

"I have always been amazed what desperation will make a person do," Kate whispered back, thinking of Mr. Cratch and the Giotto, and Hal fleeing from his wicked nephew. It makes us do things we would never attempt, she considered, watching the marquess lumber about the stage.

As much as she still dreaded her own journey before the footlights, act five was almost fun for her, as Mr. Meacheam, smiling as beatifically as ever, "married" her to Antonionus Pinchbeck in the play within a play, right before the final scene. She boldly scratched Katherine Billings on the marriage document and presented the quill to Squire Pinchbeck.

" 'Bless me,' " she said, her eyes a-goggle. " 'I trust I spelled it right this time. I can never be too sure with names, especially my own.' "

With a skill borne from four preceding acts, Hal waited for the laughter to quiet down before speaking his next line in all amazement. " 'Egad, Miss Rowbottom, do you have that same problem? I cannot believe how well-suited we are! Who would have thought it?' " He dipped the quill in the inkwell, dropped his spectacles several times, and then signed the document as she swooned into "Father" Malcolm's arms and the laughter rolled on.

It took him rather long to sign the document, she thought, as she waited, swooning in Malcolm's arms, for the next cue. He signed with a flourish, sanded and blotted it, and handed it to Phoebe, who waved the paper about and danced around the stage. Gerald and Will winked at the audience and congratulated themselves on the subterfuge of actually marrying off the spinster. Maria and Phoebe fell into their arms, and the curtain closed for the final time to thunderous applause.

Hal was ginning as he helped her up. "It's done, my dear, it's done." He grabbed her, kissed her, and then released her as the curtain opened.

Everyone in the audience was standing as the actors stepped forward for their bows. Incredulous, Kate stared out at the playgoers, all on their feet, all applauding, some stamping their feet. The sound hurt her ears, and she looked at the Bladesworths, wondering if it bothered them, too. They appeared oblivious to the volume, but bowed and curtsied over and over, their faces lit from within, relishing the applause, nourished somehow in a way that she would never understand, even if she stayed with them for years and years.

She tugged Hal's arm, and he leaned down. "Look at them, Hal," she urged, her lips next to his ear. "This is food and drink to them, isn't it?"

He nodded. "Much better than oatmeal and Madeira, I vow. It makes them happy." He bowed, too, and she curtsied to the audience, and then he whispered, "What makes you happy, my darling?"

You do, she thought. Only you. "I think, my own smallholding in Kent, a cow, and chickens. The magnitude of this reception makes me think that could actually become a reality. Perhaps I will not starve, after all, and may still avoid Leavitt Hall," she teased, hoping that she sounded more cheerful than she felt.

They bowed again as the applause rolled on. "Fancy, Mrs. Hampton, my principal seat is in Kent," he commented, his voice offhand, his eyes on the audience.

"Then I shall sell your steward butter and eggs," she said, keeping her voice light.

"Perhaps," he said noncommittally as he tugged her down for another bow, and then another, as the ovation refused to die.

Finally Malcolm stepped forward, his arms upraised, and the

audience quieted. He bowed. “We will perform *Well Married* four more nights and encourage you to return.”

The applause began again. Their heads together, Malcolm and Phoebe consulted, and then she stepped forward toward the flickering candles and with a simple gesture quieted the house. “Lady Macbeth,” she said, and began the sleepwalking soliloquy.

The others withdrew quietly from the stage as Phoebe put the audience under her spell and led them from *Macbeth* to *King Lear* to *Hamlet*, and finally to *The Merchant of Venice*. Kate watched from the wings, her eyes on Malcolm, who stood next her, mouthing the words, tears shining on his cheeks.

“She is magnificent,” Kate whispered.

He only nodded as the tears slid, unabashed, down his face. “It is the moment I have waited for.” Without another word he handed her the note.

She unfolded it slowly, praying for good news. I have no more hair to give, she thought. It will have to be the anatomists. She read the note once, sucked in her breath and held it, and read the note again.

“ ‘Bladesworth—may I speak to you backstage when the play is finished? We have a great deal to talk about. Edmund Kean.’ ”

“Good God!” she exclaimed, and then clapped her hand over her mouth when the others hissed at her to be silent. She stared at Malcolm, who was smiling at her now through his tears. “Not *the* Edmund Kean?” she whispered. “I mean, even I have heard of him.”

“Who has not?” Malcolm took back the note. “Pray God he is paying close attention to my darling daughter now.”

They watched in silence until Phoebe finished. The applause poured over her, as rhythmic as waves cresting on the shore. Her face a picture of joy, Phoebe extended her hands gracefully to her audience and curtsied as deeply as a debutante at court. After basking another moment in the acclaim, she quieted the audience with another simple gesture and left the stage.

She fell into Malcolm's arms, laughing and crying at the same time. Kate watched in complete admiration. I feel as if they are my family, she thought, and I am so proud to be counted with them.They progressed backstage slowly, moving against a current of well-wishers, smiling, shaking hands, bowing. The greenroom door looked so far away, but eventually the crowds thinned, and they made it inside that haven.

A little man was seated on a packing crate. There was nothing that distinguished him from the other playgoers, and yet there was everything. He radiated a certain air that Kate could feel from the doorway. He seemed like a coiled spring, his eyes intense, a slight smile on his rather dour face. Malcolm came forward quickly, his hands extended. "Mr. Kean," he said. "This is indeed a pleasure."

"I rather think the good fortune is mine," Kean replied, standing and shaking hands. "Here I had thought to spend a boring evening in the inn, when what should arrive with my dinner but a playbill? The landlord claims that he serves them up with every tray."

Malcolm grinned at Ivy, who hurried to his side. "My wife has been indoctrinating the entire town, sir. Even diners are not safe."

Kean bowed to Ivy. "An excellent idea, madam!" He turned back to Malcolm. "I am returning from a summer's engagement in Edinburgh."

"I had heard that you were there," Malcolm murmured.

Hand in hand, and flushed from the crowd of admirers that continued to mill about, Phoebe and Gerald entered the green room. Malcolm gestured to them to come closer. "Sir, let me present my daughter Phoebe and Gerald Broussard, the author of this play."

Kean bowed again and took Gerald by the arm. "Lad, you have a rare talent. And you, too, my dear." Without releasing Gerald, he looked to Malcolm again. "That, sir, is what I wish to speak of."

"Speak on," Malcolm said his voice suddenly breathless.

"When I return to the inn, I will write a note to John Kemble, telling him that he must take a post chaise to Leeds at once. When will you perform *Well Married* again? He must see it."

Maria gasped. Kate tugged at her. "Who is John Kemble?" she asked.

"Only the manager of Covent Garden Theatre," Maria explained when she caught her breath. "Our fortunes are made!"

Long after the last well-wisher left, and Edmund Kean finally broke away from reminiscence to return to the inn, the Bladesworths sat in the green room. Davy and Will brought in the night's receipts to count in front of the others. As the sky began to lighten, everyone retired to bed, assured that there would be bacon and eggs for breakfast.

"But I was beginning to like Madeira with my oatmeal," Will protested and then tried to defend himself when Maria pummeled him.

Kate did not sleep. Her mind was in a turmoil of activity, reliving the play, savoring the delicious triumph, enjoying the comforting sight of the box office receipts, even with her eyes closed. When Steinberg and Sons reopened, she would redeem Ivy's brooch and Gerald's music box. Everyone had agreed that the other items could wait until another night's success. "No sense in tempting the gods," was Malcolm's way of putting it.

She was there in the morning before any of the others were up, impatient for Steinberg to turn the key in the lock. In a matter of moments the brooch and music box were safely in her hands. Instead of leaving the shop, she went from case to case, looking for Hal's wedding ring. It was gone, the little ring with flowers carved in the gold that he had tossed in her lap so casually, and which fit her finger as if it belonged there.

It is a sign, and I shall be philosophical about this, she told herself as she gave up finally and started back to the theatre. It will be easier to forget the marquess if I do not have any visible reminders. The sooner I get over my little infatuation, the better. I should begin getting him out of my system right now.

It was an easy matter to avoid him the rest of the day. She was the only one awake until the middle of the afternoon, and then they were all too busy preparing for that night's performance for any private conversation. They acted *Well Married* for an overflowing audience that night. Patrons stood along the walls and laughed and cheered to the antics of the Rowbottom sisters and their quest for suitors. Phoebe spent more time in front of the curtain afterward, speaking Shakespeare's lines, and delving into the sonnets, too.

"How delightful to have an audience that wants more and more," Malcolm whispered from the wings, his eyes on his daughter. "Tomorrow we will send you out to sing!"

Kate only smiled and shook her head. "My dear sir, since I own this theatre, I can tell you no!"

"She has vowed only to sing lullabies to our children from now on," Hal whispered to Malcolm as he stood behind her.

"Hal, stop that!" she said, her voice weary. To her complete misery, he did just as she said.

Exhausted, she went immediately to bed after the play, making a point not to catch Hal's eye. She slept late the next day, and even after she woke, she busied herself about the room, straightening things already tidy, until she ran out of excuses and her stomach began to rumble. I wish he would go away, she thought, and then felt tears start in her eyes as she looked about the theatre and he was not there.

"Where is everyone?" she asked Maria finally when she found her brushing costumes in the wardrobe room.

"Oh, do you mean where is the marquess?" Maria replied, a smile playing about her face.

"Maria! Am I so transparent?" she asked, and picked up a clothes brush.

"You are," Maria teased. "And he told me he is feeling ill-used because you will not speak to him."

Kate brushed her costume with a vengeance. "All he does is tease and flirt, and it is driving me to distraction." She sank onto a chair and looked up at Maria. "And I wish he would hurry up and leave so I could forget him."

Maria took the brush from her hand and kissed the top of her head. "Perhaps you will have your wish. Papa and Hal have gone to meet the mail coach. It seems that our fame is spreading. We are being rejoined by our actors! We won't really need Hal now," she said and then sobered. "Or Will, either."

To her relief there was again no time for conversation, not with former Bladesworth company members reassembled and priming themselves to resume old roles and learn the new and clever *Well Married* that everyone was talking about. As she fidgeted and stewed, Hal sat quietly, smiling to himself and listening to their improbable stories of summertime successes as though he actually believed them.

She made a disquieting discovery during that third performance which should have pleased her, but only increased her dissatisfaction. Hal was avoiding her, too. He did not stand by her, his hand on her shoulder in that proprietary way, or catch her eye and wink while they waited backstage and listened for cues. He was quieter, and when she did feel his gaze on her, it was a measured look, as though he were sizing her up for bad news. He seemed several times on the verge of speaking, but he always thought better of it.

She waited, head down, on her side of the stage, chilly with the knowledge that it was only a matter of time before Hal ended his charade, threw himself on the mercy of the magistrate, and left her life. He must be trying to get the courage to tell me that it was only a summer flirtation, she thought. I should really spare him the trouble.

She couldn't bring herself to do it. Just leave, Hal, she told herself as she hurried from the stage when the applause died down and fled to her room. Don't explain why, or that you knew we wouldn't suit, or turn red and stammer your apologies.

Let me remember the pleasure of that one night when we almost made love, and you did propose. Leave me that. It is a frustrating memory, because we did not go far enough, but it is better than nothing at all.

When the end came, she was not prepared for the pain.

Costumed, wigged, and made up, she sat in the green room the night of the last performance, waiting for the others to join her, hoping that Hal would not come in first. Her luck failed her. She looked up to see him standing, costumed, in the doorway, watching her, hesitating, on the verge of speaking.

"Kate, my dear," he began before she could leap in with some distraction, "I really need to talk to you."

Her heart plummeted into her stomach and stayed there.

"You don't need to say anything, Hal," she began quietly. "I knew there was nothing permanent in your attachment." There. She had come out with it. She waited for the knife to twist and braced herself against it.

"You don't understand," he said, coming closer, his face red. "I have done something that you need to know about." He chuckled, in spite of his obvious discomfort. "I mean, you really need to know." He took her hand and kept her close as she rose to leave.

"Surely, it's nothing that you can't forget, once you have returned to London," she said, wishing he would not hold her that way, so close that she could smell his cologne.

"Actually it is not that simple, my dear wife." He picked his words carefully, as though on some diplomatic mission.

"I wish you would not say that!" she exclaimed, tears in her eyes. "Will is not here, and I am not your wife."

"Well, as to that…"

"Here he is, Pinky! Uncle, surprise, surprise!"

Hal went suddenly pale. He dropped her hand as though it scalded him and whirled around to face the open door.

Two men stood there, one tall and thin and dressed in the latest London mode, complete with fobs and seals and a collar so high that he could not look around. The other man was older, Hal's age perhaps, with pale complexion and almost-white hair.

Hal groaned as the thin man in the tight pantaloons minced into the room and took the marquess's hand. "Uncle Henry, we have come to rescue you from low company!"

Kate gasped and threw herself between the two men, pushing Hal back. "You cannot have him! I shall scream!" she shouted. "Run, Hal! I'll stop them!"

The thin man—it could only be Algernon—gaped at her in amazement and then began to giggle, while the man in the doorway raised a quizzing glass. He surveyed her and smiled indulgently at the marquess, who stood transfixed, holding his breath and making no attempt to flee.

"Oh, Henry, Henry," he scolded, his tone indulgent, "what frivolity have you been engaging in this summer?"

Hal said nothing. Kate looked from him to the other men, both hands to her mouth. She swallowed several times and took a deep breath, wondering if any words would come out if she tried to speak.

"You… you… Hal, why didn't you run? Isn't Algernon trying to kill you?"

Algernon laughed. "Oh, my, no! Did he tell you that?" He rolled his eyes. "Uncle, Henry, you are positively wicked! What a famous joke this is! I cannot wait to circulate it about!"

18

NO ONE SPOKE FOR the longest minute. Hal, his face pale, his expression unreadable, seemed incapable of words. The man Algernon called Pinky resorted to his quizzing glass again, turning it on Kate.

"Ah, well, friend, I cannot blame you. She is a pretty piece." Kate gasped. Algernon laughed and nudged his uncle. "She is quite an actress. That sounded almost genuine. Really, Uncle Henry, it is better to call her a piece than an aunt!" He bowed mockingly to her. "Do introduce us."

Kate's eyes filled with tears of humiliation as Algernon bowed before her. She stared at Hal, who still seemed bereft of sense. "How could you?"

Her words, wrenched from her heart, seemed to rouse him from his shock. He looked from his nephew to Pinky, and back to his nephew.

"Algernon, as always, your timing is impeccable," he said, his voice dry. "May I introduce Katherine Billings? Kate, this is my nephew, Algernon, and my former best friend, Pinky D'Urst."

"Algernon? Did you say Algernon?"

Davy and Will burst into the room, knocking Pinky aside,

and tackled Algernon, throwing him to the floor, where Muggeridge pinned his arms behind him as he shrieked and begged for mercy. The runner, all business, called for Gerald, who ran into the room, with his fencing foil and flicked it at Pinky.

"I call that wondrous brazen," the runner said as he jerked Algernon to his feet. "How dare you come in here like that to kidnap the marquess? You must think he has no friends."

Hal put his hand on Will's arm. "Let him go, sir," he said, "and call the others. I have something to say." He smiled wryly at Kate, but there was no humor in his eyes. "I fear when I finish, I will have no friends."

Will frowned. "Are you sure you will be safe from these ugly customers?"

"Will, I have never been safer," Hal insisted. "Algernon, I fear you have a hole in your pantaloons. It will match the hole in your head."

The nephew stared in horror at the little rip below his knee. "This is the thanks we get for only following your instructions? I like that!"

"My instructions?" Hal repeated, his face a blank.

Moving slowly, Pinky edged toward Hal, and out of the reach of Gerald's foil. "I distinctly remember that you told us to give you a week, and that then you would have things arranged to your satisfaction. Well, it has been a week. Here we are, and obviously not a moment too soon."

Unable to stand steadily, Kate plopped onto a packing crate as she tried to sort out what he said. "One week? Then these are your kidnappers, aren't they, Lord Grayson?" she asked, her voice formal.

"That, and the two biggest bunglers I have ever known," he replied. "Kate, I have to talk to you when this is over. I really must."

She gazed at him, measured him, and found him wanting. "I think that there cannot be too little said, my lord."

"Kate, please!"

She turned away as Malcolm entered the room, looking about him in dismay. "I do not know why you have to call us together now, Hal! We go on in fifteen minutes." He stared at Algernon. "And who is this man milliner?"

"That is Algernon, the wicked nephew," Kate explained. "Do enlighten us, Hal. I believe it is about the least you can do."

"Kate, don't …"

They waited in tense, thick silence until all the Bladesworths had crowded into the green room. Algernon continued to mourn the injury to his pantaloons, looking about him for sympathy, and finding none on anyone's face. "Riffraff," he muttered under his breath.

When everyone was silent, watching him, Hal cleared his throat. "I have played you all a deceitful game," he began, his eyes looking straight ahead at some spot on the wall. "While it is true that Algernon was involved in that shooting on the Great North Road, it was more in the nature of a rather misguided prank." He looked at Kate, and then looked away, visibly shaken. "I was never in any danger from him, or anyone else, for that matter."

None of the Bladesworths were slowtops, so the news, and its implications, sank in swiftly. "Then you have been deliberately lying to us, boy?" Malcolm asked, his voice too calm. Ivy and her daughters looked at each other and moved closer together.

"Well, yes," Hal said after a pause, mistaking Malcolm's calmness for complacency. "I thought at first that it would be great fun, and you all were so concerned. Then it seemed that I could be useful. I did not think there would be any harm done …" His voice trailed away.

"Harm?" asked Malcolm, his voice suddenly too jovial. "Will, here, nearly gets his head kicked in by one of these friends of yours." His voice rose several notches. "We spend anxious hours wondering about your safety, and even before the kidnapping, wondering how we could protect you better. And Kate, Kate—"

"No, stop, Malcolm," Kate interrupted and rose to her feet. "I was a fool all by myself. You see, I thought …" she gulped. "I thought he loved me." Ivy, her face full of pain, reached out for her, but she backed away, shaking her head. She could not bring herself to look at Hal. "I was an idiot, to be sure, but at least that is all I need repent of. I can thank you for being a gentleman that one time, my lord. I am grateful that your frivolous nature has some checks to it. But everything considered, perhaps Abner Sheffield was right about you, after all."

She turned to Hal then, her heart bounding from her shoes to her throat at his stricken expression. "We will perform this play tonight because we have to. When it is over, I do not wish to see you ever again. Now, I think we should take our places."

Malcolm nodded. "Lord Grayson, if you are out of here by the time we come off the stage after act five, that would be best."

"By God, it will be fine with me, too," Pinky burst out. "Who do you people think you are to sit in judgment of a marquess?"

Malcolm stared down any more comment. "Well, for one thing, Lord D'Urst, we are honest folk. Good-bye, Hal. It was pleasant there, for a while, but it's time we parted company." They took their places on the stage for act one.

Considering the general devastation felt by all the cast, it was a remarkable performance, Kate admitted as they began the last act. The audience, unmindful of backstage trouble, cheered them on, inspiring them by their applause to reach deep inside, overlook the hurt and shock, and perform like the troupers they were.

He is only Squire Pinchbeck, Kate kept telling herself as she flirted and goggled at Hal. I will not think about his fine hands, his elegant profile, his wonderful lips, and the way I feel—felt—all giddy when he came close to me, she thought as she smiled and simpered about the stage, to the delight of the audience. I won't even think about the courage that he loaned me when

I was the one wanting, and not he. She signed the marriage document, grateful down to her shoes that it was only a piece of paper, and swooned into Malcolm's arms as Phoebe danced about with it and the curtain closed.

When the curtain reopened, the audience was standing and stomping, and yelling for more. The actors bowed to each other, and then Hal grasped her hand as they headed forward for a bow to the audience.

"I wish you would hear me out, Kate," he whispered as they bowed. "You really need to hear what I have to say."

She forced herself to look at him. "I think it is too late for any arrangement that you had hoped to make with me, my lord. I am not the arranging type."

He let go of her hand and grabbed her shoulders in front of the footlights as the audience gaped. "Hold on, now, Kate! Do you think for even one moment that I would make an improper offer?" he roared, oblivious to the sudden silence that fell over the entire theatre. "By God, you are a stubborn female! I wonder why on earth I can't live without you!"

She jerked herself away from him and slapped him so hard that she stumbled backward and would have fallen into the footlights if Will hadn't grabbed her and held onto her when she struggled to take another swing at him.

"Kate, do behave yourself," Will murmured as he set her upright.

With a sob she ran from the stage and locked herself in the bedroom, indulging in a hearty bout of tears that everyone had the good sense not to interrupt. When she emerged an hour later, pale and still shaking, Hal was gone. Will met her in the hallway.

She wiped a hand across her eyes. "I am sorry for that outburst, Will," she managed. "I don't know what got into me." He shook his head, put his arm around her, and gave her a little shake. "I think everyone in the cast wanted to land that punch,

Kate." He chuckled. "I don't think Lord Grayson will see out of that eye for at least a week."

She gasped. "Oh, I didn't mean to do him an injury!"

"Well, the rest of us did," he said frankly, then handed her a folded paper. "He left this note for you in the green room."

She ripped it into tiny pieces, scattering them about the floor. "I doubt he has anything I need to hear."

His arm about her, they went into the green room, where everyone was still assembled. She looked from dear face to dear face and finally felt her heart climbing up out of her stomach and back where it belonged. "Forgive me," she said simply. "I intend to put this episode behind as soon as possible." She turned to Malcolm. "Sir, what have you planned for next week?"

Everyone seemed to relax visibly. Malcolm regarded her fondly and patted the seat beside him. "My dear, we have been discussing that very subject. Now that we have augmented our numbers, we feel ready for anything. What would you say to *Othello* and *She Stoops to Conquer*, on alternating nights?""I think it would be a wonderful bill," she said. "Will, can you and Maria concoct another playbill tomorrow? Your other one was so fine."

Will grinned. "I'm sure we can. Maria already has some drawings."

"Excellent. Ivy, perhaps you and I can talk about costumes in the morning. Malcolm, I leave it to you to conduct rehearsals. I trust they will not include me this time." She paused then and looked down at her hands. "I would like to help in any way possible, but give me another week."

"As you wish, my dear." Malcolm stood and clapped his hands together. "You heard Kate, everyone. I suggest that we retire and prepare for hard work tomorrow."

The plays were received with the same enthusiasm as *Well Married*, to the Bladesworths' complete delight. Each night the audience wanted more and more. After the final curtain call

Phoebe, dressed in her nightgown as Desdemona, would come in front of the curtains, and a hush would fall as the patrons settled back for her private performances, delivered with such artistry and truth that Malcolm never failed to cry.

"Kate, 'tis a funny thing. I have heard these scenes over and over, but each night I want to leap out and say, 'That is my daughter,' " he told her as they stood in the wings and watched.

Gerald, his face filled with love, watched from the other side, mouthing the words along with Phoebe. Kate could not fail to notice how, at the end of each soliloquy, she looked in his direction for his nod of approval, and not toward her father.

A letter came every day from Lord Grayson at D'Urst Hall, but every day she returned it unopened. Finally a letter arrived from Bow Street, and she carried it to Will, on his hands and knees with Maria in the empty front lobby, sketching another playbill for the following week's presentation of *As You Like It* and *The Saracen*. He opened the letter with a hairpin snatched from Maria's head and sat cross-legged to read it. He frowned.

"Well, it seems I am to return to Bow Street to collect my pay," he said, folding the document. "Precious little good I did, anyway." He glanced at Maria, who waited in silence beside him, her eyes on his face. "And they will give me a new assignment."

"Will, do you really not have any idea who hired you in the first place?"

"No, Kate. They do not tell us that. I was merely to locate Lord Grayson and keep an eye on him." He shrugged. "That was all, and I didn't even do that very well. Now I must return to Bow Street." He glanced at Maria and touched her cheek. "Excuse me, you two."

Maria watched him go. "Kate, I will die if he leaves," she whispered.

Kate gathered her close in her arms. "No, you will not! I can tell you that you will get through it." I did, she thought, as she patted Maria's back. Maybe in ten years or so, I won't even think about Hal Hampton above three or four times a day.

Maria had returned to her sketch of the playbill when Malcolm, his face wreathed in smiles, came into the lobby, his arm clapped about Will's shoulders.

"Kate, may I present the newest member of our company? Will has decided to abandon Bow Street and tread the boards with the Bladesworths."

With a shriek Maria jumped up and threw herself into Will's arms. He glanced at her father, who nodded and smiled, and then kissed her. She clung to him in a fierce embrace that made Kate close her eyes in misery and turn away to brush the dust from Ivy's potted plant.

"And he has also asked for permission to marry you, Maria," Malcolm continued. "I asked him if he thought he would relish a life of teasing and disgusting good humor, and he allowed as he would manage. Congratulations, you two. I couldn't be more pleased to gain a son-in-law *and* another actor." He laughed. "And a policeman! I call that economy in numbers."

The afternoon mail brought the usual letter from D'Urst Hall, and a special delivery from London, addressed to Katherine Billings, owner and proprietor of Banner Street Theatre. Kate handed the first letter back to the postman and walked slowly inside the theatre with the other. She found Malcolm on the stage, rehearsing his actors. He called a break when she waved the letter at him.

"I am almost afraid to open it," she said as she broke the seal. " 'My dear Miss Billings,' " she read out loud. " 'Mr. Edmund Kean has been pestering me these two weeks about a play which he declares I must see. Now, as I value the continued services of Mr. Kean, I have agreed to journey to Leeds in his company for a command performance of *Well Married, or Love in Many Guises*. We will arrive September 5.' "

She looked at Malcolm, who was motioning Ivy to join him. "Well, here is your chance for Phoebe," she said, her voice breathless. "Oh, Malcolm, that is tomorrow!"

"Please go on," Malcolm said, his eyes on the letter. "I want to savor every word."

She turned back to the letter. " 'I must insist upon one stipulation. Rumor has reached me—I do not know how reliable it is, but theatre folk have a network that is vast, indeed—that one of the principal roles was performed by Lord Grayson, Henry Tewksbury-Hampton, of Grayson, Kent.' "

Kate stopped. "Will he plague us forever?" she murmured.

"Go on, go on," Ivy insisted.

"Let's see, 'Tewksbury-Hampton, of Grayson, Kent. I insist that he perform the role. I may try to have him condescend to reprise it in London, and I would defy Drury Lane to come up with a scheme half so guaranteed of audience in any of their paltry plays. What a hook this will be! Yours, John Philip Kemble.' "

Her fingers numb, Kate handed the letter to Malcolm, who read it again, and then once more, as if willing the message to change. He looked at Kate. "It appears that one of us must approach Lord Grayson."

Kate turned away. "He will not consent, not after the way he left."

"I believe that he will," Ivy declared. She touched Kate on the shoulder. "And I think perhaps you ought to hear him out."

"I have heard enough," she replied quickly. "But I will go to D'Urst Hall."

"Surely I could do it," Malcolm said.

She nodded. "I am sure that you could, Malcolm, but Hal did teach me to stand on my own, no matter how difficult the situation. I would hate him to think that I have not learned something from this whole wretched business. Perhaps I can convince Will to accompany me."

By the time Kate had changed from her day dress into a traveling outfit, Will returned with a hired gig. "It's no more than five miles," he said, "and the day is fair."

Kate nodded. "I might even enjoy the drive in the country."

She looked back at the theatre, where Davy was replacing the As *You Like It* marquee with BY SPECIAL COMMAND, *WELL MARRIED* TOMORROW NIGHT ONLY. "It seems as though I have been in this theatre for months and months! I can hardly believe it is September."

The sun was warm, but there was a cool breeze blowing. Soon the leaves would fall, and the year would make is stately progress into another season. I hope I am wiser, she thought, as Will whistled tunelessly under his breath and kept his eyes open for signposts.

"Have you and Maria decided on a day yet?" she asked as he slowed to make a turn down a long lane.

"We are thinking the middle of October. Malcolm says he will take a two-week break so we can mount a new curtain and make other repairs. I would like to take Maria to meet my parents in Norfolk."

She nodded. "Good for you. I think I will journey to Kent and contact a land agent."

He glanced at her and then back at the road, as if troubled by the expression on her face. "I wish you would stay with us, Kate."

"No, it's not for me, Will," she replied and drew her shawl closer about her as the wind increased. "I have trod the boards, but I have no illusions about my talents."

"That's a humbug, Kate," he said, not mincing words. "You just don't care for the memories, no matter how much you say you're over Lord Grayson. You still love him."

He was so right that she could not scold him for impertinence. She nodded, unable to speak, and they continued in silence to D'Urst Hall.

It was a huge, sprawling manor, intimidating and tall, with crockets, spires, ogives, and battlements, all mingled into one vast monument to bad taste. "Goodness," Kate said as they slowed to a stop at the graveled entrance. "I don't know whether to be impressed or horrified."

Will laughed. "Perhaps Lord Grayson should learn to pick his friends more wisely." He regretted his words the moment they were uttered. "You know what I mean, Kate." He leaped down and hesitated. "You don't have to go in. I am sure I can deliver the message."

She held out her arms and he helped her down. "I refuse to be a coward about this. I only hope we do not run into Lord D'Urst or that odious Algernon." Goodness knows it will be difficult enough with Lord Grayson, she thought, but did not say.

Will lifted the knocker, and it boomed deep within the bowels of D'Urst Hall. Kate shivered and drew her shawl tighter about her. This side of the building was plunged into deep shadow, and the wind teased sharply at her ankles. "We could loan them some bats for atmosphere," she suggested as he knocked again.

The butler who finally made his way to the entrance looked over them to the modest gig and single horse. "Tradespeople to the back," he intoned, and started to close the door.

Will put his foot firmly in the way. "We are not in trade," he said with that edge of command from his runner days that had so irritated her earlier, but which only brought a feeling of security now. "Please tell Lord Grayson that Katherine Billings and Will Muggeridge would like a moment of his time."

"I do not believe that he is receiving visitors."

"He will see us."

Will removed his foot and the door opened scarcely wide enough for them to squeeze through.

"Wait here, and do not touch anything."

Kate looked about the front hallway, done in the Egyptian style popular during the earlier days of Napoleon's tenure in France, and twinkled her eyes at Will. "I do not think there is a thing here I would care to examine at closer quarters, much less touch!"

Will put his hand on her arm as they heard someone

descending the staircase. The skinny legs appeared first in their vision and then a waistcoat of vulgar proportions.

Kate sighed in disappointment. "Oh, it is Algernon! Why can we not have a pinch of good luck?" she whispered.

He pranced toward them as they waited by the front door, twirling his monocle on its riband as he came.

"Who do you suppose died and made him God?" Will whispered.

"Hush, Will!" she whispered back.

Algernon's expression told her everything she needed to know. It was even colder than the front hallway, but the most disturbing part was the utter contempt on his face, as though they smelled bad and should only be shooed from the manor like puppies leaving puddles.

"I have a message for Lord Grayson and wish to speak to him," Kate said when Algernon made no effort to show them into another room.

"He is not receiving callers," Algernon replied, his tone bored, his eyes raking her over in that disgusting fashion that rendered her naked.

"Then would you give him a message for us?" Will asked, his voice dangerously polite. "Would that be too much trouble?"

Algernon considered the question, as the air hummed with his blatant disapproval. "I can do that," he allowed reluctantly.

Kate took the letter from John Philip Kemble out of her reticule. "Please see that he gets this," she said. "He will understand how important the matter is for Phoebe and Gerald. I am asking nothing for myself. Make sure that he understands that."

Algernon took the letter between thumb and forefinger. He looked over his shoulder at the butler, who hovered about like a large insect. "Show them out."

Will took her by the hand and pulled her out of the hall, the muscles working in his face, his eyes alive with anger. The door slammed shut behind them as he silently helped her into the gig, climbed in, and called to the horse.

They traveled the lane in awful silence and then Will reined in. "How much would you care to wager that Hal does not receive that letter?"

Kate sighed. "Never wager on a sure thing, Will. You know that. What are we to do?"

Will considered the question. "I could go back tonight with a grappling hook and rope and climb in a window. Or pick the lock. With any luck at all Algernon would offer resistance, and I could pitch him over one of those impossible battlements."

Kate laughed because he expected it. "Oh, Will, this is a muddle! Perhaps if I had just answered one of his letters. Oh, but it is too late. He wouldn't receive it in time."

They sat close together, partners in distress, as the horse wandered from the lane to graze beside the road. Will took her hand. "I suppose we had better leave. Perhaps one of the new actors can study Squire Pinchbeck's role tonight."

He released her hand and gathered up the reins again, urging the horse back onto the road. Kate gazed at the field beyond, idly watching two men on horseback as they took a fence and headed at a lazy canter toward D'Urst Hall. She tugged at Will's sleeve.

"I am sure that is Hal!" she exclaimed. "Will, call to him!"

He handed her the reins and stood up in the gig, hallooing and waving his arms and shouting Hal's name. The riders stopped, looked at each other, and watched Will a moment. To Kate's vast relief, one of them started at a trot toward the fence by the lane. Will sat down, took Kate's hand, and kissed it as Hal's horse leaped the fence and stopped before them.

He was dressed in riding clothes that were obviously too large for him. He smiled rather shyly at Kate as he patted his horse's neck. "Nothing fits anymore, Kate," he said, his head down. "All those clothes I sent ahead to D'Urst Hall in June make me look as though I have suffered a major illness and am only now recovering. My tailor will be ecstatic when he presents me with a bill for another wardrobe."

"Lord Grayson, we need your help!" Will burst in. He released Kate's hand. "Kate left a message with Algernon, but pardon us if we doubt that you will receive it."

He nodded. "What can I do?" he asked simply, looking at her now. The eye she had blacked two weeks ago was an interesting shade of pale yellow and green, a decided contrast to his deep blue riding coat. Kate blushed and looked away, mortified.

"Kemble of Covent Garden will be in Leeds tomorrow night for a command performance of *Well Married*," she said, when she could organize her thoughts into well-chosen words. "He has specifically requested your presence in the role of Squire Pinchbeck."

"I hardly think that will please anyone at the Banner Street Theatre," he commented dryly.

"Well, no, it does not," Will broke in. "But this could be a big opportunity for Phoebe and Gerald, if Mr. Kemble likes what he sees."

Hal threw his leg across the saddle, his fingers light on the reins, considering them. Tears rose to Kate's eyes. The humiliation of Algernon's rude reception, coupled with this measuring regard from Lord Grayson was more than she could bear. She swallowed her tears and her dignity.

"Please, Hal," she pleaded, "Oh, please! If you want me to get down on my knees, I will do it. Only ask."

And then it was Hal's turn to look down, his own face red. It was a long moment before he could speak. "You remind me that I just did something I said I would never do, Kate," he murmured.

"Wh … what?" she asked, wiping her face with her hand and wishing for a handkerchief.

He reached inside his coat, leaned down, and handed her his handkerchief. "I once promised you I would never trade on your dignity, and here I have done just that. I will be there tomorrow night. Six as usual for the performance?"

She nodded and blew her nose. "I'll have it washed for you tomorrow night."

He smiled then. "I know you will. Probably with starch." He looked back over his shoulder at the other rider, who was heading toward the fence now. "You must excuse me. I would hate for Pinky to be as rude to you as I fear Algernon has been. And I." He put his leg back in the stirrups. "Besides that, I have to go write my daily letter to a proud little chit who keeps sending them back. I wonder when she will read one."

He watched her a moment for some reaction and finding none, turned to go.

"Wait!" Will called. "Kate, you forgot his watch."

He turned back, coming close to the gig again. Her head down to hide her confusion, Kate rummaged in her reticule and pulled out his watch. "Here, my lord," she said, holding it up to him as his horse nuzzled her shoulder.

He took it from her and snapped it open.

"I… I kept it wound," she whispered. "Thank you for the loan of it. We could not find the ring…" Her voice failed her and she winked back tears.

"I thank you for the watch, my dear. I'll hand it down to a son, someday. Maybe it will give him good luck in battle. It certainly helped us in ours, eh, Kate?"

Before she could make any comment, the marquess wheeled his horse about and trotted along the lane toward the gate. Will smiled as he watched him go. "He sits a horse pretty well, Kate."

"I don't want to discuss it!" she said and buried her face in Hal's handkerchief again. It smelled of bay rum, and her cup ran over. She had time only to wipe her eyes and steal a peek at Hal, elegant of posture, his hands sure on the reins, as he trotted down the lane. She blew her nose again and managed a watery smile at Will. "Let's not sit here any longer and give Lord D'Urst a reason to turn his hunting dogs on us scurvy actors."

THE MARQUESS WAS THERE at five o'clock the next evening for his costume and makeup. He greeted everyone affably and nodded to Kate as they passed in the hallway before the green room. "Hello, my dear Kate," he said, bowing. "Have you sent back the daily letter?"

She nodded. "Of course I have."

He appeared unruffled by her words and more like the Hal she remembered. "Ah, well, there will be another one tomorrow. And the day after, and the day after, until you tire of returning them. The message is the same, by the way, and will probably make you even more angry than you are now." He chuckled, shook his head, and continued toward the makeup room. "But I will take my chances, dear wife," he called over her shoulder.

She stared after him. "You are the most aggravating man who ever stuck his legs into breeches," she said softly.

"Yes, I am," he agreed, his voice serene. "And you are positively certifiable."

She laughed in spite of herself, covering her mouth with her hand too late.

She waited by herself in the wings for the curtain to rise on act one. Hal joined her, putting on his spectacles.

"Did Messrs. Kemble and Kean arrive?" he whispered.

She nodded. "Oh, Hal, this could mean everything to Phoebe."

Davy was approaching the ropes to pull open the curtains. Hal touched her arm. "You and Will should know one thing. When I arrived at the Hall, and asked Algie if he had any messages for me, he said he did not."

"We feared as much," she whispered back.

"There was a rather incriminating mound of hot ashes in an otherwise empty grate in the sitting room." The curtain opened, and he put his lips closer to her ear. "I sent him packing and cut him off without a sou. I probably will need a runner now. He was wondrous pissed."

She turned to look at him, and he quickly kissed her on the lips, then strolled on stage for the opening line. She could only follow, her face red, and perfectly in tune with her following line, " 'La, Squire, you distract me beyond all that is allowable. I am nearly undone.' "

To her distress he looked back at her and winked before he stumbled on cue into a coat rack and an end table and into Malcolm's arms. The audience roared its approval. Offstage, and out of the corner of her eye, Kate saw Gerald clasp both hands high over his head in triumph.

Each act only got better as the Rowbottom daughters traveled the rocky road of courtship. When she dared, Kate glanced into the audience, searching for any sign of approbation from John Philip Kemble, who sat, arms folded, his expression unreadable, halfway up the house in an aisle seat. I wish he would smile, she thought, and redoubled her own efforts to perform Gerald's wonderful lines.

Finally it was over. The crowds left reluctantly, as usual, and Malcolm, his face serious, called them all down into the front row seats. Hal sat apart from them, looking at the floor, until Ivy motioned him closer. With a smile he joined her, taking the youngest daughter onto his lap. She settled back against him with a sigh of pleasure.

John Philip Kemble, elegant in black, stood before them. "First, may I congratulate you on a fine performance. It was everything Mr. Kean had suggested, and more."

The actors looked at each other and smiled. Gerald grasped both Phoebe's hands, his face pale. He edged up on his seat and leaned closer, as if willing the words from Kemble's mouth.

With a nod to Malcolm the great manager of Covent Garden turned to Gerald and Phoebe. "Malcolm, I fear I will displease you here. I would like to make Gerald Broussard an offer to join us in London."

Kate blinked. She waited for him to say something about Phoebe, but he did not. The others looked at each other in surprise. But Kemble was still speaking.

"Gerald, we would like to commission you to write us several original plays and to help us mount a production of *Well Married*. What say you, sir?"

"Well, I … I …" He looked at Phoebe, whose face was white with disappointment.

"Kemble, you have all the finesse of an elephant in a drawing room," came Edmund Kean's carrying voice from the middle of the house. "Kindly put this young lady out of her misery, who is clutching our Frenchman as though she would never let him go!"

He left his seat and strolled to the front, hoisting himself onto the stage with the ease of someone in complete command. "My dear Phoebe," he began, "how old are you?"

"Sixteen, sir," she said, struggling with tears and losing.

"Sixteen," he repeated, his eyes dreamy. "Sixteen." The word rolled off his tongue and carried all the hopes and dreams of sixteen with it. "My dear Phoebe, I think that two more years in Leeds will find you amply prepared for the rigor that is the London stage."

"Two years!" she exclaimed, the words wrung out of her.

"Yes, my dear," Kemble said, his voice gentle. "It is a hard life you would choose, if you attempt theatre. Best be completely prepared for it." He inclined his head toward Kean.

"I could not agree more. You'll be there, my dear, but give yourself time."

The cast was silent, some of them nodding. Malcolm held out his hand to the manager. "Very well, sir, I will continue her training."

They shook hands. "And I will observe her progress each year, Bladesworth," Kemble promised. "Do excuse me for snatching your playwright, but I cannot resist."

"And I, for one, would not stand in his way. Gerald, you leave with my best wishes."

Broussard smiled. "Thank you, Malcolm. And you, Ivy.

We … I will miss you more than I can say."

Kemble clapped his hands together. "Then it is done! We will see you in a week at Covent Garden?"

"You have my word on it," Gerald replied quietly while Phoebe sobbed beside him.

Kemble turned to Lord Grayson. "And you, my lord? When will we see you there?"

"Never." It was quietly but firmly delivered. "I expect to be otherwise occupied in the near future."

"Not even one performance?" Kemble wheedled. "I hope to open *Well Married* in February. Do consider it, my lord. How I would love to push that in Balfour's face at Drury Lane!"

Hal laughed. "You are completely unscrupulous! This, I understand! Perhaps we will talk, but not now."

The men took their leave. The others quietly left the auditorium while Phoebe sobbed and Gerald, his arm around her, spoke softly.

"IT BREAKS MY HEART, too," Maria said as they prepared for bed. "I know how terrible I felt when I thought Will was leaving." She sighed. "Two years!"

Kate blew out the lamp and lay down to sleep. It is better than never, she thought. I wish Hal had said something to me before he left. Perhaps I ought to read his letter tomorrow when it comes. She closed her eyes and slept.

It seemed only minutes before someone was shaking her awake. Maria, her eyes wild and her hair tumbled around her face, had raised her off the pillow as she shook her. Kate was awake in an instant, all sleep gone.

"Gracious, Maria, what is the matter?" She squinted at the window where early dawn was breaking. "Is the building on fire?"

Maria groaned and thrust a note into her hands. "It is worse, Kate! Phoebe and Gerald have eloped!"

19

KATE DIDN'T BOTHER TO dress, but dashed after Maria into the green room, where Malcolm sat, his head in his hands. Ivy was fanning him, her face as white as her nightgown and cap. Wordlessly she pointed to the paper on the table.

Her fingers shaking, Kate picked it up, noting with some irony that Phoebe had scrawled her tidings on the back of the latest marriage lines signed by Agatha Rowbottom and Squire Pinchbeck. "'Dear Mama and Papa,' " she began, but Ivy held up her hand.

"Oh, please, not aloud. I cannot bear it again," Ivy pleaded. Will, still in his nightshirt, hurried into the room with a glass of water for Ivy, who dumped in some powders, swirled them around, and commanded Malcolm to drink. He did as she said, his eyes already glassy with hurt and disappointment.

"Phoebe and Gerald have eloped to the border," Will whispered, his eyes on Malcolm. "If they caught the midnight mail coach to Gretna Green, they have five hours on us."

"Oh, my Lord," Kate murmured. "Why would she do such a thing? I mean, I know she loves Gerald, but …"

"She is too like her father," Ivy said, resting her head against

Malcolm's broad back. "She is proud, and a little hurt that Mr. Kemble did not choose to make her fortune right now in Covent Garden." She looked at Maria and Will, who stood with their arms around each other's waists. "My dears, please go after them. Gerald will see reason right away, I am sure, and I trust you to bring her back."

Will detached himself from his fiancée. "I can engage a post chaise, and if we change horses at every posting house, perhaps we can get there in time to stop a marriage across the anvil."

Ivy shuddered at his words. "It is so irregular! Oh, please try!"

He left the room immediately. They heard him in the next room, and then he came out, stuffing his nightshirt into his breeches. "There is cash in the drawer," Ivy called to him. She looked at her daughter and Kate. "Help me with Papa. He will be asleep soon enough, I think."

They half-walked, half-carried him back to bed, where he sank with a great sigh, rolled over, and was soon snoring. Ivy sank down beside him on the bed, the tears rolling down her face. "I pray you will be in time!" She looked at Kate, her eyes desperate for understanding. "I know what people think of theatre folk, my dear, but this is not anything we condone."

"I know it is not," Kate said quietly. "Maria and I will accompany Will." She held up her hand to ward off any objections. "Maria has always had a good influence on Phoebe, and between the two of us, she'll do what's right."

Ivy took her hand. "Thank you," she said simply, then let Kate fold her in a strong embrace. "You are like a daughter to me, my dear."

When her tears stopped, Kate released her. "Maria and I will go get dressed now, Ivy."

They hurried into their clothes. Maria found a bandbox in the corner and threw in their nightgowns, brushes, and a change of clothing. "Oh, I could willingly wring her neck," Maria muttered as she strapped down the bandbox.

Kate shook her head and tied on her bonnet firmly. "I know how she feels, and so do you, Maria. Imagine if Will were to leave you for two years." Or Hal forever, she thought. I know what drives people to desperation. Phoebe, drat her proud little hide, has my complete sympathy.

Maria managed a wry smile. "Well, put in those terms, I think I understand. But I can't say I like it!"

Will was back with the post chaise as the market town came to life. He hurried inside to dress more carefully, and then joined the two of them in the carriage. The coachman closed the door, climbed to the box, and cracked his whip. The Banner Street Theatre was soon behind them.

To say that the day was long did not begin to describe the situation for Kate. To compound the misery, it began to rain, a heavy, pounding rain that turned the roads to glue and slowed them to a turtle's tread. Kate found herself pushing against the floorboards, urging the coachman faster.

"Kate, it won't help," Will said, eyeing her feet. "Look at it this way: from the condition of the roads, I suspect it has been raining even longer here. Phoebe and Gerald are crawling along, too, I vow." He turned to Maria, who sat close with her hand resting proprietarily on his knee. "Well, beloved, what do you say we get out those playbooks? Malcolm seems to think I will make a good Tybalt to Davy's Romeo. I have several years of plays to catch up on, it appears."

As Kate listened and dozed, Will and Maria traded lines, going over and over cues until he could snap out the lines from *Romeo and Juliet* and then *Twelfth Night*. They handed her another book, and she read along, laughing in all the right places, as the time passed and the rain drummed down, noisier than a house full of applause and cheers.

The darkness settled in sooner because of the rain, and then the post chaise moved even slower. It was too dark to read, so they quoted from memory, switching from one play to another, until Muggeridge ran out of memory. "Maria, that's my best," he declared finally, throwing up his hands. He relaxed against the squabs and then tensed as the coach moved even slower and then stopped. The chaise jiggled as John Coachman climbed down and tapped on the door.

Will opened it, and the rain blew in.

"Sir, we'll have to stop at the next town."

"Where are we, then?"

"Outside of Postlethwaite."

"Damn! We're yet fifty miles short of the border."

"I'm sorry, sir, sorry indeed, but we can't do any better."

"Very well. Go on a little farther, and we shall stop at the first promising inn."

They were silent then, watching the rain, occupied with their own thoughts. Ivy and Malcolm will be devastated, Kate thought as she rested her chin on her hands and stared out the window. As she watched, her eyes burning from lack of sleep and unshed tears, she saw flickers of light ahead. The post chaise slowed to a crawl as they drove abreast of a coach turned on its side.

Will whistled. "Look at that!" he exclaimed to Maria, who was dozing against his shoulder.

The chaise stopped, and the coachman got down again, this time to talk to the other coachman, who stood beside his yellow-painted vehicle.

"I believe it is a mail coach," Kate said. "Oh, do you think …"

After a lengthy confabulation with the other driver, their coachman sloshed through deepening puddles to the chaise. Will opened the door again. "Tell us, sir," he demanded.

The rain dripped off the coachman's hat and down his coat. "A nasty business. It seems the mail coach broke both axles more than four hours ago."

"Oh, God," Kate breathed. "Maria, say a prayer."

"No one hurt," said John Coachman, "and everybody finally started out walking to the next village." He shook his head and dripped rainwater on them. "I except to see some angry people at the next stop, don't you know!"

It was approaching midnight when they finally pulled into Postlethwaite. "We can find an inn less crowded than the one on the main road," the coachman called down from his perch.

"No," Will called back. "We want to go to the one where the mail coach usually stops."

"Suit yourselves."

The inn yard was deserted when they drove in, and the inn nearly dark, except for the lights in the taproom.

"It appears that everyone has already bedded down for the night," Will commented as he opened the door.

"Don't say that!" Maria exclaimed.

They hurried inside and shook the rain off their cloaks in the entryway. The landlord, looking midnight-tired, met them at the taproom's entrance. "Come in and warm yourselves. Is that mail coach still in the ditch?"

Maria shrieked and dodged under the tavern keep's arm, throwing herself down beside a small, muddy figure sitting fiercely upright on a settle.

"Oh, thank God!" Kate murmured. She looked around. Gerald sat by himself at a table, his eyes weary, his fingers tight around a pint. He nodded to her and took another sip.

Kate hurried to Gerald as the sisters hugged each other, and Phoebe began to cry. He pulled out a chair and motioned Will into another one.

"We have both had second and third thoughts," he said, his eyes on Phoebe. "You would be amazed what revelations of character a four-mile walk through knee-deep mud will bring out in a person." He sighed, but there was the ghost of the old glimmer in his tired eyes. "I think Phoebe can be convinced to return to Papa and another year or two of instruction."

"Gerald," was all she said.

He gave a Gallic shrug and touched her hand. "She loves me, Kate, but you should have seen her face grow longer and longer the closer we came to the border!"

"Cold feet in muddy boots?" Will teased.

"Something like that." Gerald motioned toward the bar. "I am sure the tavern keep will find some more ale, Muggeridge. You need only tap the bell and …"

The outer door banged open, and the keep in question hurried to the entrance, calling out his welcome in a weary voice. Kate idly glanced toward the door as someone shook out a many-capped riding coat and slapped it onto a peg. Her eyes widened as Lord Grayson strode into the room, stripping off his gloves, and then stopped in astonishment at the sight of the two sisters consoling each other on the settle.

Will swallowed his amazement and put his hand to his mouth, his eyes merry. "He looks like the last rose of summer," he whispered to Kate, who still stared, her mouth open. "Go do something appropriate, Kate. For the life of me, I can't think of anything."

When he had his fill of Maria and Phoebe, who had stopped her sobbing to stare at him in wide-eyed wonder, he turned slowly around, his eyes narrowing as he spotted Will Muggeridge.

"Oh, wait a minute, now," Will said as he scrambled to his feet and backed toward the door. "Whatever you are thinking, it's not what you're thinking!"

"Will, that is so stupid," Kate said. "Now, see here, Lord Grayson."

With scarcely a glance in her direction, the marquess grabbed Will and raised him off his feet, forcing him against the wall. "So you thought to elope with Kate, did you? My good man, that won't do!"

"Do something, Gerald!" Kate implored.

Gerald set down his pint with a bang, leaned back in his chair, and laughed until he fell out of his chair and lay on the floor, still laughing. "*Mon dieu*, it hurts!" he groaned and then laughed some more.

Startled by the helpless laughter behind him, Lord Grayson set Will on his feet. With an oath he went to the bar, banged on it until the glasses jumped, and demanded rum. The tavern keep obliged him. Hal took a mighty swallow and then looked at Kate finally.

He was mud from head to foot. Only the whites of his eyes gleamed bright in his face. He was not smiling. Not taking his eyes from her, he took another swallow of the rum. When he spoke, his tone was almost conversational, but not quite.

"Kate, I rode over to Leeds this morning—no, yesterday morning now—to deliver my daily letter in person this time. Who should approach me but Ivy all a-twitter, lathering something about Gerald and Phoebe eloping to the border with you and Will."

"Oh, but—" she began and stopped when he held up his hand.

"We simply can't have that, my dearest wife," he murmured, lulled finally by the rum. "You would be committing bigamy. Well, almost. I couldn't have my wife in jail. How would it look, Kate? I ask you."

It was her turn to stare. "What on earth are you talking about?"

Wearily he motioned to her to join him at a table. She sat and clasped her hands in her lap, scarcely daring to breathe.

"I could pull out my daily letter, except that it is probably as muddy as I am." He took her hand, mud and all, running his long fingers over the delicate bones in her fingers. "Kate, I've been trying to tell you …"

He hesitated, then plunged ahead. "I'm trying to tell you that we've been leg-shackled—at least partly—ever since that first performance of *Well Married*."

It was so quiet that even the rain seemed to have stopped to eavesdrop. Kate stared at the marquess. Without a word she pulled the rum from his grasp and took a deep swallow. It burned a trail down her throat that would probably be there for days, but when it glowed in her stomach, she took another swig before pushing it back.

"I think you had better explain yourself, Lord Grayson."

He sighed and swiped a muddy hand across his face. "Call me Hal, for heaven's sake!" He reached in his pocket and pulled out an oilskin packet. "I had every intention of giving this to you in person this morning—or is it yesterday morning now?—along with the daily letter, when I went back to Leeds." He pushed it across the table toward her and went back to the rum.

Mystified, Kate opened the pouch and took out a close-worded document. Her mouth opened as she read quickly through it and then stared at the two signatures at the bottom. "Heavens, Hal, is this what I think it is?"

He nodded. "I am afraid so." He looked at the others who had gathered close to the table, their own trials abandoned for the moment. "I know you were all wondering why it took me so long to sign my name to the marriage document during that first performance of *Well Married*."

Kate nodded, remembering. "There I was, swooning in Malcolm's arms, waiting for that next cue."

"My dear, have you ever tried to write 'Henry William Augustus Edward George Tewksbury-Hampton, Fifth Marquess of Grayson' in a hurry?" He touched her shoulder and gave her a little shake. "Kate, that document you signed on stage was a special license, a real one."

She shut her mouth and looked deep into his eyes, which glowed with something besides irritation now. "And Mr. Meacheam is a vicar, isn't he?" she asked, her voice filled with wonder as she remembered that afternoon when she wandered into St. Philemon to light a candle and found the little man there.

"He thought it would be fun to tread the boards. I am sure he had no idea what I was up to."

She looked at the document again. "My lord, it is not dated, and there are no witness signatures, so it cannot possibly be legal."

He took it back from her. "Yes, well, so much for my brilliant idea." He took her hand then, edging his chair closer. "I had planned, after the final curtain, to show it to you and ask Mr. Meacheam to read the lines all over again, speaking our real names out loud, so they could be witnessed properly. Then I would have registered this document in the parish of St. Philemon, and everything would have been right and tight. Don't ask me what made me think this would be just the trick to push you over the edge into matrimony."

He released her hand, sat back, and just looked at her. She waited for him to speak, and when he did not, it was her turn to lean forward. "Why didn't you show it to me then, Hal?"

"Once I had done it, I was struck with the stupidity of such a stunt, and how angry you would be at me for pulling your strings like that. How on earth could I ever explain this much audacity?" He shook his head. "And then it was too late." He handed the document back to her. "Keep it, or bum it, or rip it up and throw it at me. I don't mean to stand in the way of any marriage you may wish to contract with Will. Personally I had thought Maria partial to you, Will, but Lord knows I've made such a muddle of this summer. I could easily be wrong."

"Kate, I suggest that we put this man out of his misery at once. Maria and I are engaged, not Kate and I, although I certainly am fond of her," Will said quietly. "Hal, I think Ivy committed serious prevarication to get you to pursue us to the border."

Hal smiled then for the first time. "And she looked so innocent!"

"She is, after all, an actress," Maria chimed in, her hand in Will's.

"So she is," Hal murmured. He rose. "Well, I wanted you to know, Kate. Keep it for a souvenir of this summer." He squared his shoulders and turned toward the tavern keep, who had remained transfixed during this entire recital. "I'd like a room, keep. I'm too tired to go back tonight. And have them put a bath in it."

"Yes, and make sure the bed is not too narrow," Kate said quietly, rising to stand beside the marquess. "And I like a fluffy pillow." She took hold of the marquess's hand. "When the others leave in the morning, we would rather not be disturbed."Hal looked at her, and a smile spread slowly across his face. Without another word he gathered her in his muddy arms and kissed her. She clung to him as the others applauded.

"Is that your answer?" he asked, breathless.

"Yes, of course," she replied, reaching up to flick some of the mud out of his hair. "Obviously you are so deranged that I daren't send you home unmarried." She glanced around Hal to the innkeep. "Sir, is there a church in this town? Can you give us direction? Darling, do you think this special license is still valid?"

"Yes. We should have the lines read again, with our proper names this time, and then dated. Once it is witnessed—Gerald? Will?—we can register it here in the Postlethwaite parish. Are you sure, Katherine?"

"Oh, Katherine, is it now?" she asked. "I have never been so sure of anything. I love you most amazingly."

Unable to hide his grin, the tavern keep directed them to St. Stephen the Martyr and begged to accompany the midnight wedding party. "I disremember when anything this entertaining has ever happened in Postlethwaite," he said as he threw on his cloak and held open the door.

It was no easy matter to wake up the vicar, but required any number of pebbles thrown at his window on the second story of the vicarage. And when Hal explained the nature of the visit and showed him the special license, it took that worthy a moment to rub the sleep from his eyes and determine that it was truly a marquess requesting his services.

He examined the special license. "It's already signed," he protested.

"Ah, but not dated and not witnessed," Hal replied, holding Kate's hand tight.

"Monsieur, you are dealing with one of England's greatest eccentrics," Gerald stated when the vicar appeared to hesitate.

"And he will make a generous donation to your parish poorhouse when you've done the deed," Will added.

"You are so free with my resources," Hal murmured to the runner.

"Just payment for a summer's aggravation, Hal," Will said.

"How generous?" the vicar asked, his voice warming considerably.

"Five hundred pounds," the marquess said, tugging at his riding cape as the rain started down his back.

"Then step inside, my lord!"

It was a quick wedding inside the dim church, with no more light than a candle or two that the vicar lit. They murmured their responses, Hal slid a ring on her finger, and they were married. After they signed again at the vicar's insistence, writing over their names written on stage in act five of *Well Married,* the document was duly registered.

"I love weddings," Maria sighed. "If only Mama could have been here."

"You'll have one of your own soon enough," Kate said, her hand firmly clasped by her lord. "And you, Phoebe."

"In a few years, Kate. We can wait."

They sloshed back to the inn, where the tavern keep, who had hurried ahead, presented mulled wine for a toast to the happy couple.

Will raised his cup. "Long life and many children, and may none of them have aspirations for the stage."

"Especially that!" said Hal. "From now on, the Tewksbury-Hamptons will confine their thespian agility to aisle seats, halfway up the house." He set down his cup and took Kate's hand again. "And that is the end of our public performance," he said. "Phoebe, you and Maria find a room together. I'll pay everyone's shot, but you had better all be out of here tomorrow morning and on your virtuous way back to Leeds."

"Yes, my lord," Phoebe said meekly.

"Tell Malcolm we will name our firstborn after him."

"Pray God it is a boy!" Will exclaimed.

Hal laughed and kissed Kate again. "I don't know about that. I suspect that the daughters in our family will be smarter than the sons."

"Oh, one moment!" Will exclaimed.

"Sir, we have delayed our wedding night three and a half weeks already, and neither of us, I might add, is getting any younger. Ow! Kate, you are a dreadful minx."

Will approached the stairwell. "It is merely this, Hal. Have you any idea who hired me to watch you?"

With a twinkle in his eyes Hal motioned for Kate to sit on the stairs. "Rest yourself, my dear; it's going to be a long night." He turned back to Will. "You will never believe it. My wretched valet, the one who shot me in the first place, felt so remorseful that he spent his entire severance fee to make sure that I was located and in good hands."

"Your valet?" Will repeated.

"The very same. About a week ago I received quite a contrite letter from him, apologizing yet again and begging his pardon for creasing my already thinning hair." He helped Kate to her feet. "He wrote me the letter from the safety of a Russian spa, so I do not think I need fear another attempt, as long as I stay safely in Kent and avoid actors, valets, and bats. If he does molest me again, I will set Kate on him. Now good night, sir."

Kate laughed and allowed Hal to tug her toward the stairs. "You really have a place in Kent?" she asked, her voice surprisingly alert for one o'clock in the morning.

"Yes, a lovely one. And I am richer than you can imagine. What a catch I am, Lady Grayson!"

"Rich enough for me to deed over the Banner Street Theatre to Malcolm?" she asked.

"What a capital idea, wife. Kate, I love you."

The room was low ceilinged and snug, with the invitation of bed covers turned back and the pillows fluffed. The maid was pouring the last bucket of hot water into a tin tub by the fire. She giggled and hurried from the room.

"Maria has my nightgown in her bandbox," Kate exclaimed.

"You won't need it," Hal assured her and grinned at her embarrassment. "I'll even let you bathe first. Once I get in, the water will look like the last eighty miles of road. It will look better in the tub than on you."

"Really, Hal," she murmured, "my blushes."

He winked at her and took off his jacket, sighing with pleasure as she undid his neckcloth, threw it down, and started on his buttons.

She stopped then, her hands pressed on his chest. "I need to know something," she said.

"Say on, lovely one," he replied, gathering her close, "but make it brief."

"It is only this, my love. You could have solved my money woes at any time, couldn't you? Surely it was quite possible for you to arrange a draft on a Leeds banking firm. I mean, all those contortions I went through to raise money for that writ of guarantee, including hair loss …"

His hands went to her hair, and he kissed the top of her head. "Why should I be the only one suffering hair loss?"

"Do be serious! I mean it. Why were you so determined that I should struggle through this by myself?"

"That's easy. You may outlive me. I'd like to know that if something ever happened to me, you would not fold with the first blast of cold air. I've seen it happen, and I never wanted that in a wife. You're a strong woman, Lady Grayson, and I will never fear for my children or their inheritance."

She stood on tiptoe to kiss him, and he stooped obligingly.

"That compliment fair takes my breath away," she whispered, her arms tight about his neck. "Now, set me down so I can get on with your buttons."

He did as she said, pulling out his shirttails as she redoubled her efforts on the buttons. It was then that she noticed the ring she had received in the dim church and stopped, her eyes lighting up with even more pleasure.

It was the wedding band from the pawn shop, the one with flowers etched in the gold. She turned it around on her finger, and then rested her forehead against Hal's bare chest. "You wonderful man. I thought it was gone. I looked and looked when I went to redeem Ivy's brooch."

"Well, I beat you to it," he said. "Turn around now and let me see how small your pesky buttons are." He unbuttoned her dress, pausing every button to kiss her along the spine. "Mercy," he breathed. "What a lot of buttons." He undid the last button and turned her around as she pulled down her dress. His sigh of appreciation went all the way down to his boots. With an effort he tore his gaze back to her eyes. "You know, I could get you a finer ring, at least one that didn't come from a pawn shop, but something tells me you have formed an unnatural attachment to this paltry little thing."

"You know me so well," she marveled.

"I wager I will know you much better by breakfast time, wife."

CAMEL PRESS

Other Camel Press Books by Carla Kelly

Two Regency Romances

Carla's very first novel ←

AND

→ Book 1 in the all-new Spanish Brand Series

Coming Soon

With This Ring
Miss Milton Speaks Her Mind
Mrs. McVinnie's London Season

Bryner Photography

A well-known veteran of the romance writing field, **Carla Kelly** is the author of twenty-six novels and three non-fiction works, as well as numerous short stories and articles for various publications. She is the recipient of two RITA Awards from Romance Writers of America for Best Regency of the Year; two Spur Awards from Western Writers of America; a Whitney Award for Best Romance Fiction, 2011; and a Lifetime Achievement Award from Romantic Times.

Carla's interest in historical fiction is a byproduct of her lifelong interest in history. She has a BA in Latin American

History from Brigham Young University and an MA in Indian Wars History from University of Louisiana-Monroe. She's held a variety of jobs, including public relations work for major hospitals and hospices, feature writer and columnist for a North Dakota daily newspaper, and ranger in the National Park Service (her favorite job) at Fort Laramie National Historic Site and Fort Union Trading Post National Historic Site. She has worked for the North Dakota Historical Society as a contract researcher. Interest in the Napoleonic Wars at sea led to a recent series of novels about the British Channel Fleet during that conflict.

Of late, Carla has written two novels set in southeast Wyoming in 1910 that focus on her Mormon background and her interest in ranching.

You can find Carla on the Web at:
www.carlakellyauthor.com.

Made in the USA
Lexington, KY
19 April 2015